"I've never struck a woman in my life,"

he retorted, offended. Then his brow lowered. "But you tempt me. You tempt mightily."

"Ha!" Her chin jutted. *"Amerikanski promyshlenik!"*

Josh had no idea what he'd just been called, but he didn't much like the sound of it.

"Listen to me, Countess. A man has but one use for a female in the mountains this time of year, and that's to keep his backside warm during cold nights. If you think you're up to that task, I might reconsider taking you with me."

She stared up at him, her eyes widening as she grasped his meaning. They reminded Josh of the sky over the New Mexico territory just before sunset, all deep, purply dark and endless. They also, he realized belatedly, showed no signs of retreat.

What in blazes did it take to put this female in her place?

Dear Reader,

We are very pleased that *USA Today* and Waldenbook bestselling author Merline Lovelace has taken time from her busy schedule of writing everything from fun-filled romances to action-packed thrillers to bring us a new Western, *Countess in Buckskin*. This passionate story of a Russian countess who falls in love with a rough-hewn American lieutenant as they make a dangerous journey over the snow-clad mountains of northern California proves once again Lovelace's extraordinary talent for storytelling. Don't miss this wonderful tale.

Cassandra Austin also returns with *Hero of the Flint Hills*, a ranch story about a woman who is engaged to an aspiring politician, but finds herself drawn to his rugged half brother. And in *A Wish for Nicholas* by Jackie Manning, a young woman who has been draining the income from her profitable land to improve the lives of the crofters must protect her secret, and her heart, from the dashing naval war hero who has been given her estate as a prize.

Margaret Moore's popular WARRIOR SERIES is still going strong, as you will discover with this month's *A Warrior's Bride*. Don't miss this wonderful tale of a peace-loving knight and a fiery noblewoman who make an unlikely match in a stormy marriage of convenience.

Whatever your tastes in reading, we hope you enjoy all four books.

Sincerely,

Tracy Farrell
Senior Editor

Merline LoveLace

Countess in Buckskin

Harlequin Books

TORONTO • NEW YORK • LONDON
AMSTERDAM • PARIS • SYDNEY • HAMBURG
STOCKHOLM • ATHENS • TOKYO • MILAN
MADRID • WARSAW • BUDAPEST • AUCKLAND

ISBN 0-373-28996-0

COUNTESS IN BUCKSKIN

Books by Merline Lovelace

Harlequin Historicals

* *Alena* #220
* *Sweet Song of Love* #230
* *Siren's Call* #236
His Lady's Ransom #275
Lady of the Upper Kingdom #320
Countess in Buckskin #396

* Destiny's Women series

Harlequin Books

Renegades
"The Rogue Knight"

MERLINE LOVELACE

Since she hung up her air force uniform and turned to writing romances, Merline Lovelace has discovered a passion for passion. When she's not out chasing golf balls or antiques with her husband Al, she's at her computer. She thoroughly enjoys getting lost in an ancient culture or caught up in the turbulent lives of her star-crossed lovers.

Be sure to watch for Merline's next Harlequin Historical, *The Tiger's Bride,* coming out in August 1998.

Merline enjoys hearing from readers and can be reached at P.O. Box 892717, Oklahoma City, OK 73189.

To my one and only Al,
my friend and partner in life's great adventures.
Here's hoping we discover many, many more
Fort Rosses.

Prologue

Somewhere off the Northern Pacific Coast
December 1839

"Countess! You must go below!"

Tatiana Grigoria, Countess Karanova, barely heard the captain's shout over the scream of the wind and rattle of sleet on the deck. As much as she wanted to obey his frantic command, she couldn't! God help her, she couldn't! Not until she knew the precious cargo entrusted to her care was safe.

Her numb hands slid along the ice-encrusted lifeline the sailors had strung just moments before the storm hit. Heart pounding with fear, she placed one foot before the other on the treacherous, tilting deck. Spray drenched her. Sleet stung her face, her eyes, her hands. She gave a scream of terror as a huge, black wave crashed out of the inky darkness and slammed against the schooner's wooden hull. The vessel turned almost on its side. Tatiana's feet went out from under her, and only the rope she'd wrapped around her arm at the last second kept her from being swept overboard.

By the mercy of God, the ship righted itself. Her stomach heaving, Tatiana choked seawater out of her nose and mouth and scrabbled for purchase on the wet deck. She dragged herself to her knees and fought to find footing amid the sodden layers of petticoats, velvet traveling dress and sable-lined cloak.

She no longer heard the captain's shouts, didn't know if he'd survived the avalanche of water that had swept the decks. Hanging on to the lifeline with both hands, she inched forward against the screeching wind that buffeted her face and tore the breath from her lungs.

She spotted the huge wooden chest that held the tsar's treasure just as another towering swell of black water came rushing out of the night. With a sob of terror, she flung herself forward. Her hands clutched frantically at the ropes securing the chest to the decks. To her horror, she discovered that the ropes had slackened in the violent pitch and yaw of the ship. The wooden box began to slide across the tilting, slippery planks, taking Tatiana with it. Her last thoughts before the wall of water thundered down on her were of the tsar.

Nikolas had warned that her life would be forfeit if this cargo was lost, and now it appeared he was right.

Damn, and thrice damn him!

Chapter One

In the Valley of the Hupa
February 1840

Cho-gam, headman of the Green Snake clan of the Hupa tribe, folded his arms across his massive chest. The movement caused his elaborately worked collar of toothlike shells to clink and clatter.

"A new woman came into my household two moons ago," he announced to the visitor seated cross-legged beside him. "I will give her to you as wife."

Murmurs of approval rose among the elders gathered around the fire, punctuated by a sharp exclamation of protest from one of the younger warriors. Cho-gam silenced the lone dissenter with a stern look.

Josiah Jones hid a grimace behind the bushy whiskers that had protected his cheeks and chin from frostbite during the long journey to this isolated valley high in the northern Sierra Nevadas. He knew all too well that any gift the tightfisted Cho-gam offered would cost the recipient dearly, one way or another.

Josiah had wintered with the Hupa three years ago, during a previous expedition to Mexico's vast, unexplored northern California territory. He'd repaid the tribe's hospitality with frequent forays into the jagged mountains for elk and deer to supplement their staple diet of smoked salmon. He'd also spent endless hours in the sweat house that formed the center of all male activity during the winter months, deftly dodging Cho-gam's determined efforts to sell him a wife at an astonishingly exorbitant price. Josh had even less time or use for a wife now than he had three years ago.

"I thank you," he replied as solemnly as the broad-faced, dark-eyed headman. The Hupa phrases he'd learned during his previous stay with the tribe came easily to his tongue. "But I must travel fast and hard this trip. I cannot take a woman with me."

"You do not travel fast, nor do you travel far if I do not sell you a horse to replace that which is lamed," Cho-gam pointed out with irrefutable logic. "You will take this wife I offer with the horse."

His pronouncement prompted another protest from the younger Hupa at the edge of the circle. The warrior pushed himself to his feet, his layers of shell necklaces clattering.

"The fringe person doesn't want the woman," he said angrily, employing the term the peoples of the West used to describe the whites who adopted their utilitarian buckskin clothing. "I will buy her."

"You can't afford her price," Cho-gam replied with unruffled calm. "This one can."

The younger man cast a furious glare at the outsider,

then spun on his moccasin-covered heel and stomped out of the low-roofed lodge.

Biting back a sigh, Josh dug into his possibles bag for the pouch that held the last of his Virginia tobacco. He'd hoped to stretch the precious blend until he reached Fort Vancouver, but Cho-gam was proving surprisingly intractable. The headman had resisted Josh's every offer for a pony to replace his sore-footed packhorse. Now he'd started in on this blasted wife business again. Obviously Cho-gam thought he had a prize and was determined to get top dollar for her. It looked as if Josh were in for some long, temper-testing bargaining.

Hoping that a pull of prime tobacco would soften the headman up, he tamped a wad into the bowl of a carved bone pipe, fired up with a glowing ember and passed the pipe to Cho-gam. The headman's many necklaces rattled once more as he lifted the pipe to his lips and took a deep, satisfying pull. When he breathed out, the rich aroma drifted up to mingle with the smoke of the pine-fed fire. Sighing in pleasure, Cho-gam passed the pipe to the man on his other side.

Schooling himself to patience, Josh sat easy while the bone pipe made the rounds of the elders. He knew better than to rush this prelude to serious negotiations. Finally Cho-gam named his price.

"For the horse, I will take four strings of shells. For the woman, not less than six woodpecker scalps."

Josh huffed in derision at the outrageous demand. Four strings of the rare shells for a mountain pony! Not if he had anything to say about it.

"I have no need of a wife," he insisted again.

"Only a horse. Nor do I bring with me shells, only beads from the East and slabs of obsidian from the plains. I will pay three strings of beads and two pieces of obsidian the size of your palm for a sturdy, sure-footed pony."

Cho-gam considered the counteroffer with the seriousness it demanded. The Hupa used chunks of obsidian from the plains and the thin, tubelike dentalium shells from the coast as money. Even more than money, they prized the brilliant woodpecker scalps that decorated their elaborated headdresses. Like most of the Northwest tribes Josh had encountered in his years of travels, the Hupa defined their social status in terms of personal wealth. The more wealth a man acquired and displayed, the higher his place in the tribe. Their main means of acquiring this wealth was through trade...and, Josh had learned two winters ago, through the bride-prices they demanded for their sisters and daughters.

While he waited patiently for his host to respond, his gaze slid to the group of women at the far end of the cedar-plank lodge. They sat a respectable distance away, as was proper, but not too far for him to miss the lively, laughing glances they sent the men clustered at the fire. Their hands flew as they shaped a pastelike dough made from ground acorns into flat loaves for baking atop the oven stones. After almost two months of solitary trekking through the Rockies and then the Sierra Nevadas, the idea of fresh-baked bread made Josh's mouth water.

Second to the thought of bread came the realization that he might find himself wedded to and bedded with one of these whispering, giggling females if he wasn't careful. Not that he'd object to the bedding part of the business. The Hupa women were among the more beautiful and talented he'd encountered in wanderings. He'd shared a blanket with several willing women during his previous stay, paying generously from his trade goods for their enthusiastic services.

Wedding one of these dark-eyed beauties constituted a different basket of berries, however. Aside from the fact that Josh's orders required him to travel to the northwest territory as swiftly as possible, no woman could ever replace Catherine in his heart or his life.

To his surprise, Cho-gam didn't appear willing to negotiate. "You will take the woman I offer you," the headman repeated with impenetrable calm. "She has great beauty and a strong will. She will trek beside you through the snows."

Josh felt the first stirrings of suspicion. He knew darn well that the headman had a notorious eye for a shapely figure and bright smile. Cho-gam's collection of wives was another mark of his wealth and the envy of the rest of the tribe. That he was willing to sell a female he considered comely set off warning bells in Josh's mind.

"If she's so beauteous," he asked bluntly, "why do you wish to sell her?"

When the headman didn't answer right away, one of the elders leaned around his bulk to peer at Josh with cloudy, watery eyes. "She comes from beyond the mountains," he put in. "She knows not the ways of the Hupa, nor does she wish to learn."

Cho-gam's majestic calm slipped for the first time. He scowled, and an aggrieved note entered his voice. "My uncle speaks the truth. I've had to pay many fines already for the offense she gives to other members of the tribe without meaning to."

Ah, now they'd got to the heart of it! She was costing the headman fines!

As Josh had discovered during his stay, the peace-loving Hupa lived by a complicated social code that required monetary compensation for injuries done. An impartial mediator negotiated with the parties involved and levied fines for each infraction of the social code. Everything from murder to public insult was settled this way. As tightfisted as Cho-gam was, it would surely stick in his craw to hand over a portion of his hoard of treasure as recompense for an outsider's infractions.

"She is of your kind," the headman added, as if that clinched the deal.

Josh threw him a startled look. "My kind?"

"She is not of the people," the elder confirmed in his wavery voice.

Swiftly Josh ran through the possibilities in his mind. She could be a Californio, he reasoned, a Mexican up from Monterey or the presidio at San Francisco, several hundred or so miles to the south. Or possibly a French trapper's wife. He'd heard that Pierre Levesque had brought his Canadian-born bride with him into the mountains. He'd also heard rumors that a white woman had joined her husband at the British Fur Company's outpost at Fort Vancouver.

Had one of these women somehow ended up in this remote, isolated village?

However she'd arrived at the village, Josh determined grimly, here she'd have to stay. Until the spring thaws made travel through the high passes less hazardous, she was far safer among the peaceful Hupa than trekking through the mountains. Josh himself had barely survived the journey that had brought him and his lamed packhorse through the jagged, snow-covered peaks.

"I will speak with her," he told Cho-gam, "and take messages to her people with me when I go. They will buy her back at a far richer price than I can pay. If you will summon her, I'll—"

He broke off as a chorus of deep, full-throated barks and excited yips arose outside the lodge. A child shouted. A woman's voice commanded something Josh couldn't catch. The barking rose to a furious crescendo, then ended with a high-pitched yelp.

Cho-gam's face folded into a resigned expression. "I don't need to summon her. She comes...without invitation or permission." He heaved a long, heavy sigh. "Such is her way."

Sure enough, the deerskin door covering was thrown back a few moments later and a woman stood silhouetted against the blinding sunlight. Josh formed a fleeting impression of a tangle of dark hair and a female form clad in a shapeless buckskin tunic, then the flap dropped and the newcomer marched into the lodge.

As she stepped out of the shadows into the circle of light cast by the fire, Josh realized that Cho-gam hadn't said the half of it. This woman was more than beauteous. With her mane of sable hair, winged brows and high cheekbones, she looked somehow exotic and aristocratic at one and the same time. Even in the loose tunic, she displayed a set of slender curves that caused a man to sit up and take notice. Full breasted and round hipped, she strode across the lodge with a loose, long-legged grace. Instantly, instinctively, the muscles in Josh's lower belly went rawhide tight.

He'd been on the trail for too many weeks, he decided wryly. Spent too many nights with only his long-toothed packhorse for company. He couldn't remember the last time he'd felt such a randy, polecat kind of reaction to the sight of a female. He might not have any use for a wife, but his body was sending unmistakable signals that he could sure use a woman. Uncurling his legs, he rose.

She stopped abruptly a few feet away. Even through the smoke of the fire he could make out her magnificent eyes. Thick lashed and slightly tilted at the outer corners, they formed pools of deep purple in her pale, oval face. They also, Josh noted, regarded him with something less than approval.

Her dark brows slashed down in a frown as her gaze traveled from the tip of the turkey feather decorating his broad-brimmed, flat-crowned beaver hat. Over his bushy beard, bleached to a mixture of dun and muddy gold by the sun. Down his stained, well-worn buckskin shirt. Past his wolf-fur leggings to his tough, rawhide moccasins. When her gaze returned to his face, it held a mixture of disappointment and poorly disguised disgust.

A tinge of heat crept up Josh's neck. Granted, he wasn't exactly the feminine ideal, even when clean shaved and turned out in trousers and starched shirtfronts. Catherine had always teased him about his lean, rangy height and heavily muscled shoulders, saying he looked more mountain lion than man. Still he didn't remember causing such a revulsion of feeling in a female before.

Controlling her reaction with an obvious effort, the woman addressed him in a clear, ringing voice. *"Vyi gavariti parruski?"*

Ruski? Josh had picked up a word or two of Russian in his travels, but not enough to communicate. He shook his head. Frowning, she took a step forward, then stopped abruptly. Her aristocratic nose wrinkled.

The heat rose from Josh's neck to his jaw. He'd walked and slept in his clothes for the past three weeks. As a consequence, he'd been looking forward to several long hours in the sweat house after his smoke with the elders. Now, he realized, a good sweat wasn't just an agreeable luxury, but a necessity.

She overcame her momentary pause. *"Parlez-vous Française?"*

Like most of the men who made the mountains their home, Josh could switch easily between a singsong mixture of Spanish, French, backwoods American, and any one of a number of Indian dialects. His vocabulary in all but his native tongue was limited, however.

"Oui," he drawled. "I *parlez* a little French, but not the kind a man rightly uses in conversation with a lady."

"You are of the English!" she exclaimed, throwing

up her hands. "Why did you not say so most immediately?"

Her heavily accented phrases came out in an irregular, up-and-down pattern, but Josh had no trouble understanding them.

"You didn't ask. And I'm not of the English. I'm American." He tipped two fingers to his hat brim. "Josiah Jones, ma'am. Out of Kentucky, by way of Missouri."

"Ahh. You are Amer-i-kan."

The slow, drawn-out syllables carried a wealth of unspoken meaning. Her gaze flicked over him once more, as if she now understood the reason for his disreputable appearance. Evidently she didn't hold Americans in high esteem and Josh only confirmed her low opinion.

No wonder Cho-gam was so anxious to rid himself of this woman, he thought sardonically. She dished out insults with every other look and word. She must have cost the headman a passel of fines.

"I am Tatiana Grigoria, Countess Karanova," she announced grandly. "I am of Russia."

A republican to his bones, Josh didn't set much store by titles. The fact that his father had taken a British ball through the throat at the Battle of New Orleans when Josh was no higher than a bean sprout only added to his antiroyalist sentiments.

"I figured out where you hail from, Countess. What I can't figure is what you're doing here, in the Valley of the Hupa."

"I was on the ship," she explained, her eyes darkening to a deep, shadowed purple. "From New Archangel. There was the great storm. Rain and sleet rained down, and waves, they washed me from the deck.'' An involuntary shiver racked her frame and set the tiny shells decorating her dress to tinkling. "I clung atop a wooden chest for many hours. Someone pulled me and this chest from the sea. Fishermen, I think, in great, fantastical boats.''

Chinooks, Josh guessed, or possibly Yuroks. The seagoing tribes roamed the waters of the Pacific in huge canoes carved from a single, towering redwood.

"I do not remember much of these men," she continued. "I had the fever from the time in the sea, you understand. These fishermen, they passed me to another tribe, who brought me here, to the Hupa.''

She interrupted her tale to scowl at Cho-gam. The headman blinked at her fierce look.

"This chieftain bought me," she said in a voice of deep disdain. "He thought to take me to his bed, but I, I was not of the willingness.''

This tousle-haired female was damned fortunate she'd ended up with the Hupa instead of one of the coastal tribes. Josh had spent enough time with these peace-loving people to know it went against their way to force an unwilling woman.

Cho-gam might not have forced his reluctant bride into his bed, but he certainly wasn't above trying to recoup his losses by selling her off. Frowning, Josh realized he'd have to make sure the headman didn't get rid of the Russian woman until her people could come for her. Which meant, he supposed, that he'd have to buy her himself...and pay the exorbitant fee Cho-gam would no doubt charge for her keep. This countess in buckskin was going to cost him dearly, he realized resignedly.

She interrupted his thoughts with a long, gusting sigh. "Then the snows came, and I could not leave this valley. It is most inconvenient, you understand."

Inconvenient? Josh would have termed the killer storms that swept through the mountains as something more than inconvenient, but then he'd spent a good part of the past six years dodging them.

A determined smile charted its way across the woman's face. Dismissing shipwreck, sickness and snow-clad peaks, she turned the full force of that smile on the man before her. "Now you have come, Jo…Jo…"

"Josiah. Josiah Jones."

"*Da!* Josiah Jones. You have come, and you will take me to the Russian settlement at Fort Ross."

For a moment…one fleeting moment…Josh considered acceding to her request. She had pluck, this countess, and she needed his help. No mountain man worth his salt ever turned his back on someone in need, whether friend or foe. Given the harsh, unforgiving land he traveled, chances were that he would need aid sooner or later himself.

Almost as quickly as the idea of taking her with him occurred, Josh dismissed it. Even if he hadn't been under orders from the president of the United States, he couldn't risk exposing a woman to the mountains at this time of year. As tough as Josh was, the snows had nearly bested him this time. No, she'd best stay with the Hupa until her people could come for her.

"I'd like to oblige you, Countess," he began, "but I'm heading north, not south."

She dismissed that minor point with an imperious wave of one hand. "You will go south first, then you may go north. I will pay you—" she gave him another, rapid once-over "—fifty rubles for your escort."

"It's not a matter of money," Josh replied patiently. "The snows are still deep in the passes. It's no trek for a woman. You're far better off here, with the Hupa. I'll send word to your people when I reach the coast, and they'll come for you as soon as the snows melt."

Her smile took on a brittle edge. "You do not understand. It is of the greatest importance that I travel to Fort Ross most immediately."

"So important that you can't wait a few weeks?"

Despite his orders, Josh lived by the unwritten code of the mountains. He'd alter his plans in the blink of an eye to save a life or prevent harm.

"No, no, I cannot wait! I must arrive at Fort Ross before the trees begin to bud!"

"What trees?"

"The apple trees, and the pear. I must...I must..." She sketched circles in the air with both hands, searching for words. "I must tend to them."

So much for a matter of life and death. Scratching his beard, Josh searched for a tactful way to tell her he had more important things to concern him than apple trees—like the future of a nation. He couldn't find one.

"Sorry, Countess," he replied bluntly. "I'm heading north. You'll have to remain with the Hupa until your people can come for you."

Angry disbelief chased across her face. "You will not take me?"

"I will not take you."

Her eyes narrowed, and she released a slow, hissing breath.

Since Catherine's death, Josh had lost his fear of all things mortal. In recent years, he'd heard himself described as a lone wolf. A reckless, restless wanderer. A westering man, gone tougher than the boiled rawhide he sewed into moccasins and boots. The stab of this woman's amethyst eyes gave him pause, however. With one fierce look, she could raise a man's fleece and send shivers all the way down his spine.

She let loose with a spate of furious Russian that Josh guessed didn't flatter him or his parentage. Hastily, Cho-gam intervened. Although the Hupa headman didn't understand the woman's words, he and every other male in the lodge could hear the disrespect in her voice. He took her arm in a firm grip and hustled her toward the door.

"Do not offend our guest and cost me more fines," he scolded in his own tongue. "Do as women do. Be circumspect in all things."

"I am always most circumspect!" She tugged at her arm. "But I must..."

"This is a matter for men to decide," the headman admonished sternly. Then he lowered his voice and hissed something Josh couldn't catch.

Scowling fiercely, the Russian allowed Cho-gam to draw her to the door and usher her outside. When the flap dropped behind her, a small silence gripped the lodge. The women at the far end remained still, their eyes huge and their hands buried in dough. The elders sat stiff and disapproving in their circle around the fire. Josh stared at the deerskin flap for long moments, wondering why the outsider's abrupt departure left a queer sort of emptiness behind.

It wasn't so hard to figure, he told himself. Despite her tendency to throw out orders and exclamations, this Russian was a first-class, genuine belle. Not in Catherine's exquisite style, of course, but then few women could compare to Catherine Van Buren's serene, spun-gold beauty. As always, the memory of his betrothed caused a twinge of hurt just under Josh's breastbone. Determinedly he pushed it aside.

Cho-gam returned to his seat, muttering under his breath. Folding his legs under him, Josh joined him on the bearskin mat. Slowly, reluctantly, the American reopened negotiations.

"I have reconsidered your offer. I will buy the woman...but not at the price you quote," he added hastily as the headman's face lit up.

Chapter Two

Tatiana strode toward the lodge that housed the spill-over of Cho-gam's extensive family. Her borrowed, fur-lined moccasins punched an angry beat on the snow-packed path. Frigid air frosted her breath and nipped at her cheeks, but she barely noticed its bite.

Holy Father above! How was it possible, that which had just occurred? After all these weeks of waiting and worrying, a traveler had finally made it through the snow-clogged passes surrounding this quiet valley. The moment she'd heard the news, she'd rushed to the headman's main lodge, relief and excitement pounding through her veins. Despite her most urgent request, however, the broad-shouldered, scraggly bearded American had refused to escort her to Fort Ross.

The oaf! Her clenched fist swiped her thigh in frustration. The peasant!

Had her circumstances been less desperate, Tatiana would never have considered traveling anywhere with such a rough-looking individual. The women of the Hupa tribe knew him, however, and had assured her that he could be trusted. Still, she certainly wouldn't have put herself in such a one's hands for the trip through the high peaks, had she a choice.

The frightening truth was that she had no choice. No choice at all. If she didn't arrive at Fort Ross with what was left of the tsar's treasure before the sap began to rise in the fruit trees, when she returned to Russia, her life would be forfeit, as would her father's. What little remained of her husband's estates would revert to the crown, and the tsar's vengeance would be complete.

Damn and thrice damn Nikolas!

Her breath puffing on the cold air, Tatiana paused outside a long, earthen-roofed lodge. Her fingers curled around the pole supporting the door covering. How in God's name had she come to this? she wondered bleakly. A petitioner in a borrowed dress begging aid from an unkempt, uncouth American? She, who was once the spoiled darling of the Russian Imperial Court. Wife to a dashing captain of the guards. Daughter to a gentle, most learned scholar.

She leaned her forehead against the pole, fighting a wave of despair. Was it only three years ago that she'd plied her painted fan and tossed her curls and laughed like any silly, carefree fifteen-year-old? Only two since she'd gained a husband and lost the tsar's favor? Only one since she'd been forced to watch in horror as the Imperial executioner placed a garrote around the neck of the handsome, irresponsible man she'd wed?

It seemed longer. So much longer. A lifetime of tears and tragedy.

She closed her eyes, refusing to give way to the hot, prickly rush behind her lids. Tears resolved nothing, she'd learned these past years, and only left her angry with herself for displaying such weakness.

She managed to stop her tears, but she couldn't stop the memories that chased after them. Like the fluttering skirts of the ballerinas at St. Petersburg's famed Bolshoi Theater, images danced across the landscape of her mind. Fragments of pictures formed, then reformed. She saw the Italian rococo magnificence of the tsar's Winter Palace. Swayed to the music of the court orchestra. Felt again the heady, breathless joy of first love.

And the sleigh bells. Heavenly Father above, the sleigh bells! They tinkled merrily in her mind as a brightly painted troika carried her through the snowy night to her impatient groom.

How young and foolish she'd been then, Tatiana thought bitterly. How naive to believe in such an empty, meaningless emotion as love! Aleksei's passionate devotion hadn't lasted beyond the next smiling face that caught his eye. Eventually, Tatiana supposed, she might have learned to live with her husband's weak character and perhaps even forgive his escapades. But she would never forgive him for bringing the tsar's relentless fury down upon her and her father. She shuddered, remembering once more her horror when she'd learned of Aleksei's involvement in an insane plot to curb Nikolas's absolute power.

When the plot was exposed, only the tsarina's personal intervention had saved Tatiana from execution alongside her husband. Still young, but no longer naive, the frightened widow had been stripped of all but the poorest of her husband's estates. In desperation, her father had tried to redeem the family honor by sinking every ruble he had into the tsar's Russian American Fur Company. Now, with the fur trade almost dead and the Russian settlement at Fort Ross in dire financial straits, Tatiana's father stood to lose everything he'd invested.

She had brought them both to the point of ruin, Tatiana acknowledged, her ragged nails digging into the pole. She and her silly, girlish dreams of love. Now only she could pull them back from the brink.

She...and this rude, uncouth American. This Josiah Jones.

Tatiana raised her head, despair giving way to the implacable determination that had brought her across a vast continent and a winter-dark ocean. She had to convince the American to provide her escort to Fort Ross. She *would* convince him, one way or another.

Her jaw squaring, she lifted the doeskin flap and stepped into the lodge. The warmth of many bodies and a bright, leaping fire welcomed her. Blinking to clear her eyes of the acrid smoke from the cooking fire, Tatiana made her way to a young, very pregnant woman seated on a rug of thick beaver pelts.

Cho-gam's fourth wife glanced up from the basket she was weaving and smiled a welcome. The cheerful, lively woman had taken Tatiana under her wing when the Russian had first arrived in the Valley of the Hupa, weak and confused from the fevers that still racked her on occasion. The countess would always be grateful for Re-Re-An's skilled care...and for the way the beauteous Hupa had coaxed a sullen Cho-gam into her furs the first time Tatiana turned him away. She would miss Re-Re-An when she left the valley, which she must do most immediately!

"Did you see him?" the young wife asked eagerly. "The fringe person?"

"I saw him."

Re-Re-An patted the furs beside her. "Sit! Tell me what occurred!"

Tatiana sank down into the nest of silky beaver pelts. Of necessity, she'd picked up a working knowledge of Hupa phrases these past weeks. Luckily she'd always possessed a facility for languages. She'd learned English during her father's appointment as the old tsar's ambassador to the Court of St. James. French had been the preferred means of address of the Russian aristocrats until that demon Napoleon had marched his armies into the heart of the Motherland. Tatiana spoke both tongues with commendable fluency, as well as several dialects of Russian. By comparison, she thought the Hupa language simple in construction, but more difficult to speak in that a single sound could have so many different meanings.

"Is he not as I described him to you?" Re-Re-An demanded in her soft, musical voice. "Tall and straight and pale of face?"

"No. He is a great, ugly, hairy bear."

The young woman stared in surprise. "Perhaps it was not the one called Jo-Sigh-Ah."

"It is he."

"And you think him ugly?"

Tatiana picked at her braid, shooting a frown at the woman beside her. "Don't you?"

"He is not handsome as are the men of the Green

Snake clan, it is true. Yet when he wintered here three years ago, he lured many women to his blanket with his smile and his generous gifts.''

The Russian gave a little huff of disbelief. She couldn't imagine any woman voluntarily bedding with such a man. He might be tall and straight and, yes, he was certainly broad of shoulder. His bushy whiskers would rasp a woman's skin painfully, however. And he stank. There was no other word for it.

''It was not his smile that lured me,'' one of the other women put in dryly. ''The fringe person carries a veritable lodgepole between his legs. What's more,'' she added with a smirk, ''he knows well how to use it to pleasure a woman.''

Sputters of laughter rose from the other women, followed by astonishingly frank observations about the outsider's manly attributes. Tatiana sat in silence during the ribald commentary. She had gone beyond being shocked by the ways of the Hupa, who considered sexual congress between men and women as natural as breathing. No, the Hupa could not disgust her, but this American did. Evidently he was much like Aleksei had been, she thought contemptuously. Eager to find his way under the skirts of any woman who would lift them.

Re-Re-An caught her friend's expression and sighed. Tatiana's adamant refusal to lie with the wealthy, handsome Cho-gam had stirred a great deal of curiosity among the women of the tribe. The outsider had said little to satisfy that curiosity, only that she'd already had one husband and was of no mind to take another.

"Someday you'll want again the pleasure only a man can give you," the young Hupa predicted softly. "You have too much of the eagle in you not to wish to soar."

"When I do," Tatiana muttered, "you can be sure I'll choose most particularly who I soar with. Now let us speak of other things...such as how I shall persuade the outsider to take me with him when he leaves."

"Cho-gam will attend to that matter," Re-Re-An predicted, her dark eyes dancing. "With your strange ways and sharp tongue, you are a very costly wife. He wishes heartily to be rid of you."

When Tatiana huffed again, the Hupa smiled and picked up the half-finished basket. Her fingers flew as she twisted two weft strands of dried grass around stiffer warp stems of willow. After every dozen or so twists, she wove a downy white feather into the pattern. When she finished with the basket, Tatiana knew, its surface would feel as soft as a bird's breast.

She watched in silence for a few moments, marveling at the woman's skill. She'd never seen basketry as fine as that produced by the Hupa. The people of the valley used their exquisitely crafted products for every imaginable purpose, from gambling trays and burial containers to the more mundane tasks of cooking and storage.

Her gaze drifted to the far end of the lodge, where the oblong, lidded basket Re-Re-An had given her was propped against one wall. The straw container held all that remained of the tsar's treasure...all that Tatiana had been able to salvage from the ocean's depths.

The seafaring men who'd snatched her from the

huge chest she'd clung to through those endless, ter-rifying hours had tried to capture the chest, as well. Attaching long ropes, they'd tugged the wooden box through the crashing waves, only to have it break apart on the rocks lining the shore.

Delirious and half out of her mind with fear, Tatiana had broken away from the men who held her and gath-ered what she could of the precious cargo. Through the weeks that followed, she'd guarded the remnants as ferociously as a mother would a child. The men who'd brought her to the Hupa didn't recognize the value of the treasure she carried with her. No one did, except Tatiana, and her father, and the tsar.

Unless she got the treasure to Fort Ross most im-mediately, however, it would lose all value. Chewing on her lower lip in worry, Tatiana could only pray that Cho-gam was as determined to be rid of her as she was to leave the Valley of the Hupa.

The minutes passed slowly. The hours even more slowly. The men would talk for some time, Re-Re-An advised, sharing news of the mountains and negotiat-ing trades. Then they would repair to the sweat house to relax and gamble and attempt to win back that which they'd just sold. Only later, when the moon tipped the mountain peaks, would they emerge from their male domain and settle down to the feast pre-pared in the visitor's honor.

The women went about their tasks with a compla-cency that comes from ruling absolutely in their own domain. Hands slapped and shaped loaves from pounded acorn flour. Fingers sorted through dried on-ions to pick out weevils before soaking the flavorful roots in a tightly woven basket. Mothers spitted smoked salmon steaks and chided children to have a care of the fire.

Only Tatiana could not lose herself in the busy routine. She paced the length of the lodge, the shells decorating her borrowed dress jangling with each agitated turn. Her impatience mounted with every passing hour, as did her nervousness. When the door flap lifted and Cho-gam's senior wife finally entered, Tatiana almost tripped over a cache of storage baskets in her eagerness to reach the older woman's side.

"It is done," the senior wife announced calmly in answer to her anxious question. "The fringe person agreed to your purchase price."

Tatiana murmured a fervent prayer of thanksgiving. She would see that the American was repaid. Whatever he'd given for her, she'd see that he was repaid the minute they reached Fort Ross. She was so excited by the prospect of reaching her journey's end at last that she almost missed the other woman's next comment.

"...generously for your lodging until he sends for you."

Her chin jerked up. "What do you say?"

"Do you not listen, Ta-Ti-An? You will remain with the Hupa until the fringe person sends one of your own tribe to collect you."

Disappointment and disbelief crashed over her in great waves. "I cannot stay here! I will not!"

The senior wife drew herself up in offended dignity.

Tatiana stuttered an apology. "I'm...I'm sorry. You've been most kind. I thank you from my heart for your generosity. But I must, I will, go to Fort Ross most immediately.''

The older woman clucked in reproof. ''That is for your man to say.''

''My man?''

''The one who has purchased you. You belong to him now, and he will decide where you are or are not to go.''

''We will see about that,'' Tatiana muttered through clenched teeth. ''Most immediately.''

She stalked to the door, determination in every line of her taut body. Re-Re-An pushed herself up awkwardly and snatched at her friend's arm in alarm.

''Ta-Ti-An! The men have gone to the sweat house! You must not disturb them!''

''You say not? Watch me.''

She marched through the camp, trailing a retinue of shocked, disapproving women, openmouthed children and yipping dogs.

The small, flat-roofed lodge that served as sweat house for the tribe stood at the edge of the village, close by the ice-encrusted stream that fed it. Although not strictly forbidden to females except during that time of the month when evil spirits flowed from their bodies, few Hupa women had the time to waste in the sweat house. The men, on the other hand, lazed away many hours casting painted bones and gossiping like magpies while a cleansing steam sizzled with each drip of water onto heated stones.

Consequently, a ring of astonished male faces turned to Tatiana when she threw back the flap and stalked inside. One by one, jaws dropped. Dozens of dark eyes rounded. Cho-gam started up in dismay, only to remember that he was no longer accountable for her actions. A wide grin splitting his sweat-streaked face, he sank back to his woven mat.

Ignoring the headman, Tatiana stalked to the flab-bergasted outsider. He scrambled to his feet, snatching at the closest object to cover himself. Skin already flushed a bright pink from the damp heat turned a furious shade of red as he slapped a flat gambling bas-ket across his midsection.

The sight of his powerful body glistening with sweat stopped Tatiana in her tracks. By the saints, he was most—she swallowed—most impressive.

Another long-forgotten memory flitted through her mind. Once, when her father was yet the tsar's am-bassador to the English court, he had taken her to see the famous marble statues Lord Elgin had brought from Greece. The statuary had scandalized Tatiana's governess and left an indelible impression on her gog-gle-eyed young charge. Yet none of the magnificent, sculpted male forms Tatiana had glimpsed that day could compare to this one.

Unclothed, the American appeared anything but rough and unrefined. Freed of the ugly beaver hat, his golden brown hair curled with the dampness and molded a strong, proud forehead. Even his beard looked less scraggly, curling likewise in the wet heat. The sun had burned his face and neck and lower arms to leather toughness. In contrast, the corded muscles of his chest and shoulders gleamed like the purest al-abaster. More honey brown hair traced lightly across his chest and tapered to an arrow just above the basket's rim. Lean, muscular flanks quivered in what Tatiana guessed was outrage. She caught a glimpse of a tight, white buttock before he noticed the direction of her interested gaze and shifted the basket.

"Are you snow-bit?" he demanded in a low, furious voice.

"I do not think so."

"You can't mean to tell me it's the Russian way to come busting into a roomful of naked men?"

"We are not in Russia," Tatiana observed tartly. "We are in the Valley of the Hupa, where I do not wish to remain any longer."

"You'd best resign yourself to it, Countess, because here is just where you're going to stay until your people come for you."

Her hands went to her hips. "No, I tell you, I will not stay longer."

Josh stared at the woman in disbelief. Hellfire and damnation, had she no shame? No sense of decorum? Sweet, refined Catherine would have been mortified at the very idea of catching a roomful of men in their altogether! Yet this Russian female stood toe-to-toe with him, arguing like a fishwife, with only a dad-blamed basket between her and his unfeathered hide.

Sniggers of male laughter stiffened Josh's spine. He didn't need to catch Cho-gam's eye to know that the Hupa men were enjoying this scene mightily...and that this display of poor manners by the woman Josh now owned would cost him. His jaw tight, he realized that he'd have to exert his mastery over the Russian or lose all standing with the men of the tribe.

"It appears to me you don't rightly have much say

in what you will or will not do," he growled. "Just count yourself lucky that you're safe, and haul your behind out of here."

"Be-hind?" Her winged brows lifted. "What is this be-hind?"

Juggling his basket and his dignity, Josh took her arm and swished her around. He put the flat of his palm to the body part in question and propelled her toward the lodge's door.

"That is your be-hind, and this is the end of our discussion."

He expected a screech of outrage. At the very least, a yelp or two of feminine indignation. What he didn't expect was the swiftness with which she whirled back to him...or the feral snarl that curled her lips.

"In Russia," she hissed, "you would lose your hand for daring to lay it on the Countess Karanova."

"We are not in Russia," he retorted, throwing her own words back at her. "We are in the Valley of the Hupa, and the Countess Karanova is making a dang-blasted spectacle of us both."

"I? I make the spectacle?" Her purple eyes flashed as they raked Josh from nose to toe. "I am not the one who hides his nakedness behind a basket."

Maybe it was the scorn dripping like rainwater from her voice. Or her display of disdain for his manly physique. Or the cussed Kentucky stubbornness that Catherine had often chided Josh about in her gentle way. When it came right down to it, he didn't much care what put up his hackles. He bent until his nose was scant inches from the tip-tilted one in front of him.

"Now you look here, Countess. I'm not taking you

with me through the mountains and that's that. So I suggest you hightail it right out of here, before—''

"Before you strike me again?" she challenged, her face as flushed and angry as his.

"I've never struck a woman in my life," he answered, offended. Then his brow lowered. "But you tempt me. You tempt mightily."

"Ha!" Her chin jutted. *"Amerikanski promyshlenik!"*

Josh had no idea what he'd just been called, but he didn't much like the sound of it. Another snigger from the watching Hupa told him he had to end this farce. Reaching out, he took her chin in a hard, relentless hold.

"Listen to me, Countess. A man has only one use for a female in the mountains this time of year, and that's to keep his backside warm during the cold nights. If you think you're up to that task, I might reconsider taking you with me."

She stared up at him, her eyes widening as she grasped his meaning. They reminded Josh of the sky over the New Mexico Territory just before sunset, all deep, purply dark and endless. They also, he realized belatedly, showed no signs of retreat.

What in blazes did it take to put this female in her place? Tightening his grip on her chin, he tilted her head back.

"Maybe I should take a sample of what you're offering. Before I decide whether or not I want you to warm my backside...or any other side."

Her mouth opened in a sputter of protest at the same moment Josh bent and covered it with his. He meant

to frighten her. He intended to make her realize the
folly of attempting the mountains with a stranger. Yet
the touch of her butter-soft lips under his sent his righ-
teous intentions winging. What remained was the urge
to plumb the depths of the hot, moist mouth. He angled her head and did just that.

The taste of her carried the kick of Taos lightning.
Like that fiery, potent brew, she sent heat streaking
through his body straight to his gut. His muscles stiffened in response. All of them.

Josh had barely registered his own reaction when
he felt the ripple of shock that coursed through her.
He'd made his point, he knew. He'd put the fear of
God and man into her. He should pull back. Should
release his hard hold on her chin. He might have, had
she not jerked it out of his hand first.

They faced each other, their breath rasping in the
sudden stillness that gripped the lodge. Josh saw the
thunderclouds billowing in her eyes and braced himself. Whatever she threw at him, he deserved. Even
Catherine, demure, dainty Catherine, might have
rocked back, wound up, and planted her fist alongside
his jaw for such rough, backwoods behavior.

Once more the Russian woman surprised him. Her
eyes stormy, she stared at him for several moments.
Then she lifted her chin and gave him an in-your-eye
countess kind of look.

"You have dropped your basket," she announced
with a curl of her lip.

Josh had been in some uncomfortable predicaments
in his life. Once, he'd wrestled a grizzly to the ground.
Another time, he'd stretched out under a crust of ice

in a frozen stream for nigh on to an eternity to escape detection by an unfriendly band of Crow. But it took more pure, cussed nerve not to snatch up the damned basket at that moment than he remembered exercising in either of those other memorable events. Squaring his shoulders, he pasted a mocking grin on his face.

"If I took you with me on the trail, there'd be no baskets or anything else between us come nightfall. I'd want you bare-skinned and buck-ass naked when you shared my blankets. Think about that before you pester me again, Countess."

That shook her tail feathers a bit. She reared back, shock wiping the haughtiness from her face.

Josh ignored a sharp prick of conscience at speaking so coarsely to a woman. He'd been raised by a mother who pounded Bible passages, respect for others and a modicum of manners into her son with the end of a broomstick. Colonel Sylvanus Thayer, superintendent of the gray fortress perched high above the Hudson River, had taken up the task where Elizabeth Jones had left off.

Four years at West Point had sanded down a good many of Josh's rough, fiercely independent Kentucky edges. After that, Catherine Van Buren had done her best to polish those edges to a fine shine. She would have been horrified to hear him speak so crudely.

The countess didn't exactly appear horrified, but she made no effort to hide her contempt. She gave Josh another, scorching once-over. Then, to his infinite relief, she surrendered the field. Shell ornaments clinking, she spun around and headed for the door.

He was just letting out a sigh of relief when she

halted. She turned slowly, her face a pale blur in the shadows. Involuntarily his muscles tensed.

"I shall think about that, Josiah Jones," she informed him in a low, flat voice. "Most assuredly, I shall think about that."

Chapter Three

Tatiana hugged her knees and stared into a darkness broken only by the faint glow of the banked cook fire. The distant sounds of revelry drifted to her from Chogam's main lodge. The feasting in honor of the unexpected guest had gone on for hours now, and sounded as though it would continue for hours yet.

Tatiana had taken no part in the lively activity. She'd retreated to the lodge she shared with Chogam's lesser wives to do as she'd told the wanderer she would do...think. Unfortunately, several hours of that laborious activity had only added to her turmoil.

Her gaze slid to the sleeping woman a few feet away. Re-Re-An had left the feast some time ago, driven by her advanced state of pregnancy to seek her bed. Tatiana studied her back for a moment, then called softly so as not to disturb the small children hunched under furs all around them.

"Re-Re-An."

When no sound emerged from the bundled woman, she called again.

"Re-Re-An."

The wolfskin blanket shifted. "What?"

"Tell me again what you know of the one called Josiah."

The young Hupa muttered a sleepy protest. "It's late, Ta-Ti-An."

"Please."

"What more is there to tell? He is much a man." She gave a low gurgle of laughter. "As you have discovered for yourself."

"Do not speak to me again of lodgepoles!"

Muffled chuckles rose from Re-Re-An's form, causing Tatiana's face to heat. The Hupa women had teased her unmercifully about the happenings in the sweat house. They'd also shared every intimate detail with those who'd not been present. With each telling, the fringe person's masculine attributes became more exaggerated, until Tatiana could not listen without turning as red as one of the Hupas' prized woodpecker scalps.

She, a habitué of the tsar's worldly, sophisticated court! A woman truly wed and cruelly widowed! Blushing in the dark like an untried girl at the memory of the American's outrageous response to their kiss. He'd hidden it behind the basket tray, or tried to. When the tray dropped, however, half of the Green Snake clan had seen evidence of his randiness.

Such were the ways of men, Tatiana thought with a lash of contempt. Men like Aleksei and this American, at any rate. They'd rise like an overeager wolf pup at the mere scent of a female, and lie with any woman who would lift her skirts.

And yet...

Grudgingly Tatiana admitted that perhaps the American was not quite like Aleksei. For all his surprisingly skilled kiss and blatant male arousal, he still balked at taking her with him into the mountains. If this Josiah Jones were truly of the same nature as her reckless, feckless husband, he'd experience no such qualms. He'd pull her headlong into danger with him, heedless of all consequences.

Resting her chin on her knees, Tatiana frowned into the shadows. He was a puzzlement, this American. One she could not decipher, any more than she could decipher her own reaction to his kiss. Even now the memory of his mouth on hers added to the heat in her cheeks and the tumult in her mind.

She shook her head in disgust at her so foolish reaction. By Saint Igor! It was only a kiss! Bestowed upon her by a rough, hairy peasant, no less. Of a certainty, she'd been kissed before. Many times. By her husband…and by one or two of the courtiers who'd danced to her merry tune before she'd run off with Aleksei. She had no reason to remember the press of the American's lips every time she closed her eyes, or taste him on her tongue at odd moments, as she had for the past few hours. Kisses weren't worth a copper kopeck. Had she not learned that lesson all too well from her husband?

The memory of Aleksei's perfidy sent a lance of regret and pain shafting through her. He was dead, she reminded herself stonily. Strangled before her eyes at the orders of a vengeful tsar…as she might be, if she did not fulfill her mission. Shuddering, she forced her thoughts back to the American.

"Tell me about him," she demanded again of Re-Re-An.

Sighing, the tired woman rolled over to face Tatiana. "I don't know more than I have told you. He lived with us three winters ago and contributed much meat to the cook fires with his long rifle. He took no wife, although he shared his blanket with several willing women." Re-Re-An slanted her a sideways look. "As he would share it with you, should you wish it."

Wishing had little to do with the matter, Tatiana thought starkly. Was she prepared to lie with the American to get to Fort Ross? That was more properly the question she must answer.

This Josiah Jones wanted her, in the way a man wants a woman. She'd tasted his want on his mouth. Felt the strength of it in his hard grip. Seen it in his physical arousal. As he'd made clear, if Tatiana truly desired to go with him, she must offer the use of her body in exchange for his escort.

Could she do that?

Holy Mother above, should she?

It would be only her body that she offered, she reasoned bleakly. Not her soul. No matter what occurred between her and this crude American, her soul remained hers and hers alone. It had survived Aleksei's perfidies and the tsar's unrelenting fury. It would surely survive the act of lying with a stranger.

That much she'd learned from her father. In his scholarly wisdom and simple faith, he had taught her well. The outer vessel mattered not if the inner core was pure and strong.

The thought of her father stripped Tatiana's dilemma to its most essential element. He'd looked so frail when last she'd seen him, his shoulders stooped as he watched her carriage drive off. He would not last a week in one of the tsar's dank prisons.

She must get to Fort Ross.

Tatiana's inner turmoil subsided. Her father was all she had left in the world. All she'd ever had, really. Whatever she must do to spare his life and hers, she would do.

Unlacing her fingers, she eased down onto the elk hide that served as her sleeping mat. She'd best get what sleep she could. Once she left the Valley of the Hupa with Josiah Jones, she would not rest easy again. Squeezing her eyes shut, she commanded herself to ignore the sounds of laughter and male voices drifting from Cho-gam's main lodge. She would not think more. She would only sleep, and do what she must.

Tatiana rose before the sun, as did the others in the lodge. She dressed quickly and snatched a hurried meal of boiled acorn mush. From all reports, the out- sider planned to leave the village early, and she in- tended to leave when he did.

With Re-Re-An's assistance, she rolled a few es- sentials into a small bundle and tied it with rawhide thongs. Then she pulled on several layers of borrowed outer garments, promising to send gifts in payment. Re-Re-An accepted her promises with a nod and pressed a cloak of thick fox pelts on her.

"No," Tatiana protested, pushing the silky fur back into her friend's hands. "It is too fine, and the air is not as chill as it was a few weeks ago."

"The mountains still hold their winter spirits," the young wife insisted. "You will need this cloak, and more, to keep warm at night."

Tatiana's throat went dry. She'd keep warm enough at night. The American would heat her, or she him. Swallowing, she tried to refuse Re-Re-An's gift.

The Hupa woman would not be denied. "Take this, Ta-Ti-An, in recognition of our friendship."

Moved to tears by the generosity of a woman whose standing in the tribe was measured by her possessions, Tatiana gave her a fierce hug. "I thank you from my heart. This gift and the gift of your friendship I shall repay most particularly."

Wrapping the warm cloak around her shoulders, Tatiana shoved her arms through the side slits. In her thick leggings and layers of clothing, she must look much like the burly barrel maker on her father's summer estate beside the Black Sea, as round as she was tall. She slung the strap of the small bundle over her shoulder and moved to the long, rectangular basket that held the tsar's treasure. Grunting with effort, she dragged the basket forward and laced it securely with hide thongs.

"It is to be hoped Cho-gam sold the fringe person a healthy pony," Re-Re-An commented worriedly, surveying the bulky woven container. "This will add greatly to its burdens."

Tatiana didn't reply. Whatever else the American packed on the pony's back, her basket must take precedence. Dragging the basket behind her by a thong handle, she headed for the door. Re-Re-An joined her as she stepped out into the cold, crisp morning.

Involuntarily Tatiana paused. Even after all these weeks in the Valley of the Hupa, the spectacular beauty of the dawn had the power to take her breath away. Purple mountains surrounded the valley and thrust up like jagged teeth into a dark sky feathered with blue. Although the sun hadn't yet shown its face, its rays painted the snow-covered peaks a molten gold.

Tatiana drank in the splendor like fine, sparkling wine. Then the enormity of what she was about to attempt struck her. Biting her lip, she eyed the snows covering the mountain slopes in a different manner altogether. For a moment, fear slithered down her back.

Resolutely she shook her doubts away. She'd come through those craggy, forbidding peaks once, she reminded herself. They'd worn snow only on the highest reaches at that time, and she didn't remember much of the journey, but she'd come through.

Re-Re-An's gaze turned from the bursting dawn to Tatiana's face. Worry shadowed her eyes, but she kept it from her voice.

"I shall pray to the spirit of the mountains for your safe passage," she said softly. "You and your man."

"He's not my man." Tatiana gripped the basket's leather thong once more. "Only the one I travel with."

Re-Re-An's mischievous smile tugged at her mouth. "In our tribe it is enough that he pays your bride-price and you go with him. He is yours for as long as you choose to claim him, just as you are his."

"Right now, I want only to find the man," Tatiana muttered. Her breath puffing, she peered through the still, hazy light.

The village stirred with its usual morning activity. Smoke from cook fires curled through the rooftop openings of lodges. Children trudged to and from the icy stream with bulging water skins. Some yards from the village, a pack of dogs barked wildly and chased a fleeting rabbit across the snow, causing the penned horses to stamp and snort.

To her surprise, Tatiana detected no signs of activity outside Cho-gam's main lodge. She had expected to find the outsider's packhorse tied next to the entrance, already bundled for travel. The heavy basket thumped her heels as she trudged forward, frowning more with each step. Did he not leave today, after all? Had the late-night revels so exhausted him that he'd decided to remain another day in the village?

She thought she had the answer to her unspoken questions when Cho-gam stepped outside. He squinted at the two women through bleary, red-rimmed eyes.

"You look like a moose with a nose full of porcupine quills," his young wife informed him with a merry laugh.

The headman grunted.

"Is the one called Josiah within?" Tatiana inquired, wondering how long it would take before the American was ready to leave. Now that the final leg of her long journey was upon her, she wished only to get on with it.

"No," Cho-gam replied. "He's gone."

"Gone!" Tatiana's exclamation cut through the morning air like the call of a raucous crow. "How can he be gone? The sun just now rises."

Grimacing, the headman motioned with both hands

for her to take the shrillness from her voice. "He left an hour ago, saying he could find his way across the valley well enough by the moon's light on the snow. He wishes to make the first pass before nightfall."

Tatiana felt as though a great hand had grabbed her heart and squeezed. She stared at the headman in dismay. Her mouth opened, but no words could pass through her tight, closed throat.

"Jo-Sigh-Ah paid well for your keep," Cho-gam advised calmly. "You will stay with us until the snows melt. Then he will send outsiders to fetch you."

Dismay gave way to a whip of anger. After all her worrying! All her soul-searching! Her troublesome decision to pay whatever price the American demanded for his escort! She'd hardly slept the night through, and now she was greeted with the news that he'd left her. He'd walked off and left her. A vile curse rose in Tatiana's heart. If she ever came within sight of the cur again, he would rue his actions. He'd rue them most heartily.

As swiftly as the thought occurred, another followed closely on its heels. The American would see her again, and soon! Chewing on her lower lip, she considered a dangerous alteration to her plans.

Cho-gam eyed the woman before him warily. After many weeks of responsibility for the volatile, outspoken female, he could read the signs of impending trouble on her face as clearly as fox tracks in the snow.

He'd set a stiff price to house this woman until the snows melted, but now the headman wondered if the price was worth the trouble she would cause in the weeks ahead. Without meaning to, she offended. With-

out trying to, she shocked. Her heart was good, but
her mouth too often gave vent to sharp words that she
would do better to hold within her. Even worse, her
troublesome ways seemed to be spreading to the other
women of the tribe. Merry, smiling Re-Re-An had
never before dared to send her husband such glower-
ing, disrespectful looks, as she now did!

So when the outsider threw back her shoulders and
announced that she would take a pony in exchange for
the price the fringe person had paid for her keep, the
headman made only a halfhearted protest.

"You cannot follow where he does not wish to take
you."

"I can. I must."

Re-Re-An's hair ornaments tinkled as she shook her
head in protest. "Ta-Ti-An, you know not the valley
or the mountains. You will lose your way."

The stubborn female ignored the caution. "The
fringe person walks, does he not?" she inquired of
Cho-gam. "Leading the packhorse you sold to him?"

At the headman's nod, determination etched fine
lines in her face. "You will give me a surefooted
pony. One that will bear my weight. I will follow the
tracks and be up with him within a hour."

As troublesome as this female had been, Cho-gam
would not hear of such foolishness.

"You shall not ride out of the village alone," he
stated with unshakable authority.

"But..."

"I will send an escort. He will stay with you until
you are within sight of the fringe person. Then," the

headman muttered with heartfelt relief, "you become the outsider's responsibility."

Josh moved easily through the thin crust of snow that covered the valley's floor, leading the shaggy little pony by a long leading rein. Despite the pounding in his temples from a long night of storytelling and too many gourds of bitterroot beer, contentment feathered at the edges of his mind.

This was his world. He felt at home in it. Almost at peace. The vast, profound quiet of tall trees and blue sky soothed his soul and made all else fade into insignificance.

If he'd stayed back East, he mused, he might have been a colonel by now. A major at least. Rank was hard to come by without a war to kill off the seasoned officers and open the door for lieutenants. But even in the peace that followed the British defeat more than twenty years ago at the Battle of New Orleans, Josh could have anticipated regular promotions. He'd proved himself at West Point, and had almost married into the family of the man who was now president.

But Catherine's death had stripped the glitter from the sophisticated political world she'd introduced him to. Aching, Josh had taken his hurt west. Assignments to the frontier forts in Iowa and Missouri territories had kindled an urge to travel even farther west. The uncharted mountains that rose like silent sentinels, guarding access to the fertile valleys of California and the northwest territories, called to him.

He'd resigned his army commission to answer that call...or tried to. Catherine's uncle, then a United

States senator from New York, had convinced President Jackson's secretary of war to keep Josh on the
rolls as a scout and surveyor. For more than six years
now the lieutenant had wandered where and when he
would, charting rivers with no name and passes that
only the fur traders and Indians knew of. A few weeks
ago his wanderings had taken on a more urgent direction.

Inaugurated as president three years ago, Martin
Van Buren was worried by rumors that the French, the
British and even the Russians were eyeing the vast,
unclaimed Oregon Territory for possible expanded settlement. If necessary, Van Buren was prepared to go
to war to enforce the Monroe Doctrine, which sought
to keep foreign powers from staking further claim to
the American continent. Before he took such drastic
measures, however, he'd ordered Josh to scout the territory for evidence of increased foreign activity. It was
a mission the wanderer was eminently qualified for.

Josh squinted from beneath the floppy brim of his
flat-crowned beaver hat at the high peaks ahead of
him. The bright sun would speed a melting process
that had already begun. Here and there he spied a granite outcrop poking through the blanket of white.
Spruce and pine stood darkly green at the lower elevations instead of showing only their tips. With luck
and some steady trekking, Josh would make it through
the mountains before another late season storm blew
up. Tugging his hat brim down to shield his eyes from
the sun's glare, he lengthened his stride.

Sunlight cut at sharp angles through the trees when
he first sensed that he was being followed. Josh turned

and swept the area he'd just passed through. Head cocked, he listened intently. The only sound that disturbed the stillness was the angry scold of a squirrel whose territory he'd invaded, but Josh had lived by his wits too long to shrug off the tingling sensation.

Sliding his Hawken rifle from the fringed sheath slung over his shoulder, he pulled the hammer back and gently seated a percussion cap. With the rifle at first cock, he performed the same procedure for the long-barrel flintlock pistol tucked into his belt. A twitch of his shoulders positioned the powder horn and bullet pouches slung around his neck within easy reach. His precautions complete, he trudged on, alert but not unduly alarmed. He'd had curious mountain cats and the occasional wolf trail him before.

When a muffled, indistinct sound carried on the thin air, Josh decided he'd best investigate. Tethering his packhorse to a low-hanging bough, he circled in a wide arc. His hide boots skimmed silently over the snow as he tracked through the shadows cast by the tall pines. With one hand, he pulled the hammer on his Hawken from first- to full-cock. Sturdy, reliable and simple to operate, the .50 caliber Long Tom could drop a buffalo in its tracks or knock a grizzly onto its hindquarters with a single long-range shot.

The sound of a long, shrill screech raised the hairs on the back of his neck. That cry wasn't made by any cat. Lengthening his stride to a lope, he dodged through the snow-laden trees. Some moments later he burst into a small clearing, his Hawken at the ready.

A burly individual bristling with red fur was bent over an oblong shape in the snow.

"You want to tell me why you've been following my tracks?" Josh drawled.

The figure spun around, relief and wariness written plainly on her face. Josh gaped at the woman.

Damn Cho-gam. They'd made a deal!

"What in thunderation are you doing so far from the village without escort?" he demanded furiously. "And where's your mount?"

"The so silly beast bolted," she replied in disgust. "The basket falls and I stop to fix it, you understand. Then the…" She gestured extravagantly, searching for a word with both hands. "The creature with the great, mossy antlers and the long face, it comes out of the trees. When I make the noise to shoo it away, the horse, it runs, too."

"A moose? You *shooed* away a bull moose?"

Beads of sweat popped out on Josh's brow. There weren't many wild critters he'd go out of his way to avoid, but that was one of them. He'd once crossed the path of a bull hot on the scent of a rut and almost didn't live to regret it. The idea of this female coming close enough to shoo off a thousand pounds of ornery, antlered male made Josh's fingers go slick on the Hawken's smooth stock.

"Where's Cho-gam?" he snapped.

"In the village."

"What the devil does he mean by letting you traipse off like this?"

"He does not allow me to do anything," she declared loftily. "I choose to do this traipsing you speak of."

She was using her countess tone again, the one that

rubbed Josh's fur exactly the wrong way. His own voice rumbled with anger as he closed the distance between them.

"And I thought I'd made it plainer than spit that I don't 'choose' to have you with me."

Her eyes locked with his. "I do not know this speet you speak of. I know only that you told me to think about what would happen between us when the night falls. I have thought, and I will come with you."

Josh stared at her, poleaxed. Had she just said what he thought she'd said? Was this woman offering to share his blankets while they were on the trail? The idea sent heat spearing from his chest to parts straight south.

Elizabeth Jones had whacked enough respect for the female of the species into her son to make him ashamed of his instant animal response...but not enough to make him refuse the Russian's astonishing proposition. Not immediately, at any rate.

"You sure you understand what you're offering me?" he asked cautiously.

Her chin lifted. "I understand."

For a few atavistic moments, Josh unleashed his thoughts. Raking the woman before him with a thoroughly male assessment, he considered the ways she could make the journey through the mountains a whole lot more enjoyable than he'd anticipated.

He savored the vivid mental image of the Russian lying naked in his arms for as long as he dared, then reluctantly surrendered it. He wasn't the kind of man to make a woman pay for his protection with her honor, even if she offered it to him on a pewter platter.

Just as reluctantly, he altered his opinion of the Countess Karanova.

She was one determined female. If Josh returned her to the Hupa village, he'd have to hog-tie her and stake her out in the snow like a buffalo hide ready for scraping to keep her there. He supposed he'd have to take the blasted female with him.

He didn't intend to make the going easy for her, though. Neither one of them would survive if he carried her load and his, too. Uncocking the Hawken, he settled it into the crook of his arm and jerked his chin toward the basket lying in the snow.

"Get your gear. We've got a long trek ahead of us before we make camp tonight."

Chapter Four

Josh led the way to the tethered packhorse, setting a deliberately brisk pace. If the Russian couldn't keep up with him, she'd best recognize that fact while she could still return to the village.

She didn't ask him to slow. Nor did she request his assistance with her awkward bundle. But her breath rasped as she trudged behind him, dragging her basket through the snow. Josh closed his ears to the harsh, uneven sound. He'd done his damnedest to discourage her. He had no cause to squirm like a speared pike at the sound of each painful, gasping breath.

The little packhorse waited patiently under the lodgepole pine. Greeting the creature with a pat on its shaggy, rough-haired neck, Josh turned to his traveling companion. She struggled the last few yards, huffing. Sweat ran down her cheeks in silvery rivulets and dripped into the bushy fox-tail ruff that framed her face. When she slogged to a stop, Josh indicated her heavy cloak with a sweep of one hand.

"Take that off."

Her head snapped up. "What is it you say?"

"Take off that fur blanket."

Her face went from red to a sickly shade of puce. "You wish to…to…?" She mumbled a Russian word. "Now? Here?"

It took a few moments for her interpretation of his curt order to sink in. When it did, Josh felt himself turning as red as the woman before him. She thought he meant for her to strip off, lay herself down and spread her legs! Right here. In the snow.

He hadn't given her any cause to think otherwise, Josh acknowledged with a spike of self-disgust. Instead of refusing her confounded offer outright, he'd turned his back and trudged off, deciding to let her stew about it for a while. She'd stewed all right, and he'd once again confirmed her low opinion of him.

"What I wish," he growled, no more happy with himself than with her, "is for you to shed a few layers before you sweat yourself into a chill. I won't play nursemaid to you on this trip."

"I do not ask you to play anything," she retorted. "I ask you only to take me through the mountains."

"Ask?" His lip curled. "As I recall, you did a sight more than ask, Countess."

Her frigid silence told him she was regretting her outrageous bargain as much as he'd intended her to. Josh might have ended the farce then and there if her tilted chin and haughty stare hadn't raised his hackles again. Damn, she could tear a two-inch strip off a man's hide with a single look.

"Take off the damned cloak."

Brushing past her, Josh reached for the ropes binding the basket to swing it between the crossed poles that held his packs in place. He grunted in surprise at the weight. Propping the bulky object up with one hand, he threw a question at her over his shoulder.

"What the devil is in this?"

"Only what I could save from the chest that washes me ashore."

"You mean to tell me you're hauling female foofaraws along with you? Not food, or trading goods?"

"I know not this foofaraws."

"Fripperies. Fancy things."

"No! Not fancy things. Only..."

"Only what?"

She chewed on her lower lip. "Only that which I must take with me on this journey."

Josh jiggled the basket, gauging the weight it added to his already burdened pony. He shook his head. "We can't take this. It's too heavy."

The flush faded from her face, leaving it suddenly pale. "We must!"

"No, Countess, we must not."

He wrapped a fist around the ropes, intending to slide the added load off the pack. Before he got a good grip, she laid a shaking hand atop his.

"Please!" Her plea was dry and hoarse, as if it choked her to beg. "This...this is all I have left from the ship."

Josh glanced down at her hand. It lay against his tanned paw like a small, shaking bird. Calling himself two dozen kinds of a fool, he gave in.

"We'll take it as far as we can. If the going gets too rough," he warned, "or the pony flounders in the snow, we leave your precious basket beside the trail."

That we will not, Tatiana swore silently. If she had to pull that long, evil-looking pistol from the American's belt and put the barrel to his head, she would see that he did not leave the tsar's treasure beside the trail.

Silently she watched while he settled the woven container securely and tied it in place. That done, he repeated his abrupt command.

"Take off your cloak."

While she shrugged out of the heavy fur, her unwilling guide picked at one of the laces fringing his shirtsleeve and pulled loose a long, tough rawhide thong. With a swift economy of movement, he rolled the cloak and used the thong to secure it atop the basket.

Tatiana had already discovered the amazing durability and utility of the clothing she now wore. Impervious to damage from water and too tough to tear, the hide garments were yet soft and smooth against the skin. The fringes that decorated the side seams and sleeves of her dress provided a convenient supply of useful laces. The fringes also acted as a sort of a drain, directing rain away from the stitched seams. Even better, the loose tunic and leggings gave one an incredible freedom of movement. She would regret abandoning the comfortable clothing of the Hupa for petticoats and tightly laced corsets…assuming, of course, she made it though the mountains and returned to the land of petticoats and corsets.

Resting a palm on the pony's flank, the American skimmed a final, critical eye over the long-sleeved jacket she wore with her dress.

"You could stand to shed another layer or two, but I expect you'll find that out for yourself after a few miles." His whiskey-colored eyes issued a challenge. "You ready to walk?"

"I am ready."

"We'll have to set a fast pace if we want to make it through the first pass before sundown."

"I understand."

"It's a steep climb for the last mile or so."

"I shall climb it."

"The air gets thin the higher we go. You might feel dizzy, or..."

"Do we walk, or talk?" Tatiana demanded.

He reached for the pony's lead. "We walk."

As she paced behind the packhorse, Tatiana felt a brief, heady euphoria at having won her battle of wills. At last, she headed for Fort Ross. With luck and God's favor, she might yet stay the ax that was poised above her head and that of her father.

Her resolve to reach the end of her long journey firmed with each step. She was young. Strong. Stronger even than before she'd left Mother Russia. Her stay with the Hupa had developed leg and arm muscles she'd never had to use before. She followed easily in the American's footsteps, her stride loose.

True to his word, he set a hard pace. He didn't stop to eat, nor did he pause to answer nature's call. Tatiana sought privacy behind a tree when necessary, then scrambled to catch up. Around noon, she dug in her small bundle of supplies for some smoked salmon to still the rumbling of her stomach.

As she chewed, she studied the snow-covered mountains ahead. Their white summits thrust into a cloudless sky dominated by a bright, blazing sun. Tatiana knew well that the dazzling sun could burn and blister her skin at the higher elevations. She knew also that clouds could billow up seemingly from nowhere to obscure the peaks. For this moment, though, she dwelt only on the beauty and closed her mind to danger.

It was only after the sun began its slow descent that both the path and her spirits grew labored. Leaving the valley floor, the small party began to climb. Although Tatiana could see no evidence of a path, the American found a way across twisting ravines and tree-studded slopes. Gradually the trees thinned, as did the air.

Gasping, Tatiana stumbled around granite outcroppings and floundered through snow. In places, it rose as high as her knees. In other spots, it formed only a thin crust. The uneven snowfall surprised her, until she came to understand that the direction of the slopes had much to do with the amount of snow that clung to them. She soon realized as well that the American kept to the west-facing slopes as much as possible. Although this required a more circuitous climb and some backtracking, the lighter snow cover allowed a far faster pace.

When at last they reached a notch in the first line of peaks, her breath came in great, wheezing gasps. The thin air cut through her lungs like a sword blade. Thankfully, the American paused to water and rest the pony before starting the downward trek. Tatiana collapsed in a boneless heap right where she stood. Dragging a sleeve across her heated face, she looked up to find her guide standing over her.

"Are you all right?"

It was the first concern he'd shown for her state since their march began, and then it came only after he'd tended to the horse. With brutal honesty, Tatiana accepted the fact that the pack animal was more necessary to his survival than was she.

"I shall be fine, once the breath comes back to me."

He nodded, then hunkered down on his heels and surveyed the steep descent that awaited them. His broad chest didn't rise and fall like a farrier's bellows, Tatiana noted with a touch of resentment, nor did sweat film his forehead. She glanced enviously at his buckskin shirt, a fantastically decorated garment with no buttons or laces. Quills and colored beads banded the collar and dangled from the fringes. The front pieces crossed one over the other, and were held at the waist by his belt. He'd loosened the front opening to allow the air to circulate and cool his skin during the climb.

Tatiana sighed, wishing most heartily that she could open the front of her dress to catch the air. She'd removed her jacket and tied it around her waist by its sleeves hours ago. Unfortunately, the Hupa wore no undergarments, and her tattered pantaloons and petticoats had long since disappeared. The best she could do was flap a hand to cool her heated face.

The movement drew the American's gaze. "You're getting burned. Don't you have a Susannah packed in that basket of yours?"

"I do not think so," she replied cautiously.

Grinning at her obvious confusion, he gestured to her wind-tossed hair. "A hat. A sunbonnet."

Tatiana shook her head, too surprised by his unexpected grin to speak. This was the first glimpse she'd had of the smile that reportedly had lured so many Hupa women to his bed...along with his other masculine attributes.

Perhaps she could understand, just a bit, their attraction to this rough, unrefined woodsman. When the tanned skin at the corners of his eyes crinkled just so, and his mouth tilted in that rakish way to show fine white teeth, one could almost ignore the too-long beard and too-brawny shoulders.

"Here." He tugged his flat-crowned hat from his head. "You'd better wear mine or you'll end up with a complexion the same color as a boiled beaver belly."

Faced with that daunting prospect, Tatiana made no demur when he plopped the dish-shaped object on her head. Far too large, the beaver hat settled low on her brow and obscured everything but her view of his bunched, corded thighs. She tilted her head to peer doubtfully at him from under the broad brim.

His grin deepened. "Hold on. We'll fix it."

He worked another thong from the fringe on his sleeve and used it to anchor the hat. The wide brim bowed at the sides and rose in front and back, providing Tatiana with both relief from the sun and an unobstructed view.

"There, that's better."

His hands worked the ties into a loose knot under her chin. At the brush of his knuckles against her throat, a ripple of sensation darted down Tatiana's spine. Startled, she jerked away from his touch.

She saw at once she'd made a mistake. The American's easy grin faded. In its place came a hardness that sheened his eyes and reminded Tatiana all too forcefully of the snow-clad granite peaks.

"I forgot about your aversion to having anyone lay hands on the Countess Karanova."

She took refuge from his mockery in a cool reply. "It is not done."

"Is that right?"

His biting drawl grated on her...as it was intended to.

"Yes, that is right."

With a male arrogance that set her teeth on edge, he let his gaze drift down her throat. His gold-flecked eyes lingered on her breasts, then rose again with maddening deliberation to her face.

"Just how do you figure you're going to live up to your end of our little bargain without some laying on of hands?"

He was taunting her, she knew. Baiting her, just as the peasants baited shaggy brown bears at the fair. She set her jaw.

"I shall contrive."

This time his smile held no trace of its earlier friendliness. It dragged down one corner of his mouth in a most unpleasant manner.

"You'll have to do better than contrive, Countess. We've got a long trek ahead of us."

"Then let us get on with it."

He rose without another word and strode toward the

pony. Tatiana fell into place at the rear of the small column. She barely noticed the steep descent or the rapidly cooling air. Her entire being focused on the man ahead of her, and on the night to come.

What a fool she'd been to jerk away like that! How stupid to shy from his touch! He'd been gentle, astonishingly so, and kind to give her his hat. Had she kept her wits about her, she might have played on that kindness to make the night ahead easier.

Her mouth tight, she studied the broad back ahead of her. By Saint Paul, he was big. Far bigger of frame than her husband had been. He carried a good deal more muscle than Aleksei had and a stone or more in weight, she guessed. Without warning, the image of Josiah Jones after he'd dropped the basket in the sweat house flashed into her mind.

Holy Mother, he would rend her in two!

Angrily Tatiana scolded herself for her foolishness. She was no untutored virgin. No giddy, love-struck bride. She knew that the smallest of women could accommodate the largest of men, given the right preparation. It was only the thought that…that she might have to prepare herself that carved a small, empty space just under her heart. Whatever other fatal shortcomings her husband had possessed, he'd known just how to ready a woman for pleasure.

Her mouth twisted. Look where such pleasure had brought her. To the slopes of a snow-swept mountain, trudging along behind a bearded stranger like a docile, well-broken mare, filled with worry about the night to come.

Pah! She was done with worrying. She'd think of

home. Of the ballads she loved to play on the pianoforte. Of the pink clouds of cherry blossoms that covered the hills of her father's estate in the spring, and let the night take care of itself.

It would have eased Tatiana's turmoil considerably to learn that the American paced ahead of her in much the same frame of mind.

With every step, Josh castigated himself for a fool. He'd had no business touching her like that, or responding to her obvious distress by giving her his hat. Neither one of them would survive the wilderness if he let her soften him or cloud his senses.

She could all too easily do both, he acknowledged grimly. With each painful, rasping breath she'd drawn, he'd had to fight the urge to slow his pace and give her rest. Every gentlemanly precept his mother had pounded into him had nagged at him to reach back and help her over this steep, slippery slope or that yawning crevasse. He'd refrained, knowing she had to toughen for the even steeper climbs ahead, but the effort had frayed his nerves more than he wanted to admit.

Then he had to hunker down beside her and touch her! Even now the back of his hand tingled from its brief contact with her creamy skin. Smart, Jones. Real walloping, tiger-toed smart.

If she hadn't jerked away, as though she feared fleas would jump from his sleeve onto her skin, he might have given in to another, even more powerful urge. He might have bent his head and taken another taste of that full, ripe mouth. It had been so close, and so damned tempting. Instead, he'd set up her back as much as she'd set up his.

In Russia, it is not done.

Ha! He'd bet his trusty Hawken that *it* was done in Russia as much as it was done anywhere else. The Countess Karanova didn't kiss like a woman who'd never had a man's hands laid on her. Nor had she appeared the least disconcerted by the sight of a lodge full of men skinned down to their hide. She didn't have a shy, maidenly bone in her all too tempting body.

Maybe he should think again about letting her out of their bargain. Maybe he should shake off the last remnants of his civilized upbringing. He'd gone too long without a woman, as his reaction to their fiery kiss last night had demonstrated. If the Russian put so little value on her respectability that she'd barter it away for a trip through the mountains, why the devil should he turn down what she'd offered?

He'd make camp as soon as they reached a lower elevation, Josh decided in a mood of tight, angry arousal, and let the night take care of itself.

His anger eased with the miles, if not his physical awareness of the woman behind him. Her heaving breath lashed at his back. Her little grunts as she clambered around granite outcroppings pounded at his ears. Futilely Josh tried to close his mind to her as he went sideways down a steep slope. The pony skittered behind him, seeking purchase under the snow. The countess made shorter work of the descent. Halfway down, her feet went out from under her, and she slid the remaining distance on her bottom. To her credit, she got up, dusted off the snow clinging to her dress and resumed her march.

They gained a stretch of level terrain just as the sun sank behind the western peaks. Squinting through the purple shadows, Josh searched the horizon for familiar landmarks. If he remembered rightly, there was a high alpine meadow tucked behind the round-topped crag just ahead. The last time Josh had camped there, he'd felt as though he'd bedded down in a patch of sky dropped to earth. The entire plateau had been covered in blue lupines and the little purple violets the low-landers called Johnny-jump-ups.

This time of year, he knew, the meadow would be a sheet of pristine white, broken only by the tracks of the animals that fished the stream that cut through its center. With luck, Josh might be able to snare a mountain trout or two for their supper.

The thought of feeding the hunger rumbling in his belly quickened his pace. Only after he'd scanned the small meadow for signs of possible occupation, stomped a patch of snow beside the stream into a hard-packed surface and started on the ropes that held the pony's pack, did he admit the true nature of his hunger. It had little to do with trout, and a whole lot to do with the countess.

She knelt beside the stream to pound a hole in its thin, icy crust. Her dark hair spilled from under his hat to trail like silk ribbons over her shoulders. When she leaned forward to scoop out a skinful of water, Josh's fingers froze on the pack ropes. The damp patches on her dress, made when she slid down the slope on her behind, drew his eyes. From where he stood, her bottom looked just about the right size to fill a man's palms. His palms, anyway.

His hunger spiked, then tumbled through his insides like loose stones rolling down the mountainside. With a wrench, Josh tore his gaze from the perfectly rounded damp patches and yanked at the ropes. What the devil was the matter with him? He'd been reacting to the Russian like an unbroken stallion on the scent of a mare since the moment he'd laid eyes on the woman. He didn't even like her…much.

Maybe he'd gone more wild than he realized, Josh thought, sobering. Maybe he'd been too long in the mountains. He'd never lusted after Catherine like this, nor had to clench his fists to keep from reaching out to stroke her generous curves. Unlike this Russian, Catherine Van Buren had called to all that was good and gentle and fine in him.

Deliberately Josh summoned the image of his betrothed. Just as deliberately, he accepted the pain that came with it. Hurt settled just under his breastbone as he unloaded the pony, staked it close to the stream and dug several handfuls of barley grain out of a pack for its dinner. Like an old, familiar friend, the ache stayed with him while he built a fire and set a handful of coffee beans to boiling. He'd lived with the hurt for so long, it had become a part of him.

Leaving the countess to tend the fire, Josh took his net to the stream and returned some time later with two fat trout. He gutted the catch with a few swift slashes and speared them on forked branches sharpened to points. Handing one branch to the countess, he settled cross-legged across the fire from her to cook his dinner. Flames hissed and spit as juices dripped, and soon the tantalizing aroma of seared trout teased at his nostrils.

"Is it now done, do you think?"

He glanced across the fire at her intent face.

"Not yet."

She nodded, wetting her lips in anticipation of the feast to come. The woman had a contrary mouth, Josh decided. The kind that looked sweet and sounded tart. It invited a man to kiss it, then puckered up all tight and disapproving when he did. He wondered what she'd look like when she smiled, really let loose and smiled in—

The acrid scent of singed fish snatched his attention from the woman across from him to his dinner. Cursing under his breath, he flipped the blackened filet over. He'd better keep his mind off the Russian and on something safer. More comfortable. More familiar.

He stared into the flickering flames and searched for the combination of gold and red that always reminded him of Catherine's lush curls and ripe, rosy lips. For the first time, she eluded him.

"Is it now done?" the Russian asked impatiently.

"Done enough, I'd guess. Better give it a chance to cool, though, or the juices will scald your mouth."

"I cannot wait," she muttered.

Josh hooked an elbow on his knee and held his own dinner away from the flames. Amused, he watched the woman pick at the sizzling trout with thumb and forefinger, her pinkie elegantly extended as though she'd just sat down to high tea. She should have looked ridiculous in her furred leggings, bulky fox cloak and Josh's floppy hat with the wild turkey feather stuck in its woven band. Somehow she managed to appear elegant. She nibbled her way daintily down to the bones.

Abruptly she discarded her nobility along with the fish bones. One by one, she licked her fingers. Then she swiped at the juices trickling along the back of her hand. Against his will, Josh found himself mesmerized by that small pink tongue.

She glanced up, flushing a bit when she caught him staring. "That was most good. I had the hunger."

Josh had the hunger, too. It burned a hole right through his gut.

Her gaze flickered to his untouched trout. To the pony. To her hands, and back to the spitted fish. She wet her lips once more. Watching the small, incredibly erotic act, Josh felt a groan rolling around in the back of his throat.

"Do you not eat?" she asked casually.

Too casually. The offhand question didn't disguise the hunger in her eyes. Josh rose without a word. Circling the fire, he thrust the branch into her hand.

"I'd just as soon feast on the smoked salmon I traded with Cho-gam for. I build up a craving for it whenever I come through these parts."

She sneaked a sideways glance at the trout. "Truly?"

"Truly."

While she attacked the second fish, Josh dug a good-size chunk of dried salmon out of one of the smaller packs. Flavored with wild seasonings and smoked over a slow fire, it made almost as tasty a meal as fresh-cooked mountain trout. He finished off his dinner and dusted his hands on the back of his pants.

"I'll gather more wood to feed the fire while you pick at the bones. Then we'd best bed down. We'll have to start out before dawn to make the next pass."

Her hand stilled halfway to her mouth. Slowly she laid aside the bite she'd been about to take.

"Yes. We must, as you say, bed down."

Chapter Five

Arms laden with wood, Josh followed the glowing beacon of the campfire. His breath steamed on the cold, and his blood pulsed from hard, vigorous exercise.

The strenuous activity of hacking up deadwood in this thin mountain air had cleared his mind. He'd worked off all traces of the raw hunger the countess had unknowingly fed with each lick of her fingers. He'd also come to a belated decision. It was time, past time, he set matters straight about their sleeping arrangements. He hadn't missed her sudden paleness when he'd mentioned bedding down for the night. He'd let her stew about the matter long enough.

He walked into camp, fully intending to set her mind at ease. And he might have done just that...if she hadn't scrambled to her feet and regarded Josh across a bed of pine boughs with the same enthusiasm she'd show a scaly-backed wood beetle that had just crawled out from under a rotten log.

Damnation! She could cut a man down to half his size with one haughty stare. Crossing to the fire, Josh dumped his armload of wood. He'd let her off the hook. He'd already decided that much. He didn't have to make the letting easy, though. Tucking his thumbs into his belt, he waited for her to make the next move in their prickly contest of wills.

She waited for the same thing. The fire crackled and sent a spray of glowing sparks into the air. The pony chuffed quietly a few feet away. In a nearby tree, a chickadee scolded as a comrade snuggled up to it for warmth.

Finally the Russian drew in a slow, martyrlike breath. "I have made a bed."

She was no coward. Josh had to give her that. She wasn't afraid to drag the matter right out in the open.

"So I see."

"I did not wish to open your packs, you understand, when you are not here, but..." Shrugging, she gestured to the scratchy pine boughs. "There should be blankets for the branches, or furs to cover these branches."

Declining her offer was one thing. Divvying up the tasks on the trail was another. She could pull her share of the load during the trek.

Josh jerked his chin toward the piled gear. "There's a capote in the smaller pack, and a buffalo robe tied to the frame."

She stared at him, her eyes shadowed and unreadable. For a moment Josh thought she didn't understand his reference to the hooded coat made from blankets that the French trappers had made so popular. Either that, or she was having second thoughts about this business of bedding down with a stranger.

"Countess..." Josh began, then halted abruptly. His American egalitarianism tripped over the title. "What did you say your name was?"

"Tatiana," she said stiffly. "Tatiana Grigoria."

Josh was still digesting that mouthful when she swept to the packs and went to work on the laces that attached the rolled buffalo hide to the wooden frame. She tugged the heavy rug free of the frame and dragged it to the makeshift bed. Pliant and just a touch rank, the buffalo robe weighed a stone or more. The countess...Tatiana...grunted once or twice, but got it spread across the pine branches. The fleecy, brightly striped capote was far easier for her to handle.

While she knelt to smooth the bed covering, Josh slipped into a routine that had become second nature to him. He answered a last call of nature, checked the pony and fed more wood into the flames. Survival instincts cultivated over the years would wake him at regular intervals throughout the night to keep the fire ablaze. When he returned to the pile of pine boughs, he saw that the Russian had already taken her place under the blanket.

She lay like a frozen deer carcass, all stiff limbed and unmoving. She didn't stir at Josh's approach, didn't acknowledge his presence by so much as the blink of an eye. She stared fixedly up at the stars, as though she intended to count every blessed one of them while he took his pleasure on her.

"You can rest easy, Tatiana," Josh drawled. "I'm not going to make you pay for your safe passage through the mountains. Not in that way, anyway."

She left off counting the stars. Her gaze slid sideways and fixed on Josh. If she was relieved by her reprieve, she didn't show it.

"Why do you not?"

The question flummoxed him. He couldn't imagine Catherine...or any other female of his acquaintance...calmly asking a man why he didn't lift the blankets and have his way with her.

"Because I don't choose to do the fandango with a woman who looks like she'd rather have a diamondback for a partner than me."

"What is this, this fandango? And this diamonds on the back?"

"A fandango is a dance." Carefully Josh positioned his Hawken, powder horn and possibles bag within easy reach of the bed. "A diamondback is a snake. A vicious, deadly kind of snake."

Her eyes narrowed as he eased his long frame down onto the springy bed. The branches rustled under his weight. The scent of pine and resin drifted through the pungent odor of buffalo. For several moments she didn't speak. When she did, her voice was as low and smoky as the campfire.

"Do you mock me, Josiah Jones?"

"No. Go to sleep. We have a harder trek tomorrow than today."

Tugging a fold of the capote over his body, Josh rolled onto his side. Within moments, he fell into the light half slumber of the woodsman.

Tatiana stared at the massive shoulders a few inches from her nose, thoroughly disconcerted. She had intended to pay her debt! She was *prepared* to pay her debt! True, she'd shivered at this man's approach like the tall grasses of the steppe in a high wind. She'd stared up at the stars as though she could lose all feeling, all sense of despair, in their silvery splendor. But, by all the saints, she was ready!

Hot, liquid shame rushed through Tatiana as she realized that she'd done as the coarsest woman of the streets and readied herself to receive a man who did not even want her. At this moment, she wasn't sure whom she hated more...the American whose body blocked the heat from the fire, or the woman she'd become. She lay rigid and dry-eyed, and tried to find surcease in sleep.

It came before she expected it. Exhausted by the day's march and her seesawing emotions, her limbs gradually relaxed into a limp, aching state. Tatiana closed her eyes and slipped into that velvety void between wakefulness and slumber. She twitched once, an involuntary spasm that pulled her back to consciousness for a moment. Then she drifted off once more.

She had no idea whether mere minutes or long hours had passed when a piercing cry ripped through the blanket of sleep. She jerked again, her knees coming up to whack against solid flesh. The American grunted at the impact of her kneecaps in the small of his back. Belatedly Tatiana realized she'd turned on her side and sought warmth from the body next to hers.

The scream came again, closer this time and terrifying in its savagery. The little packhorse whinnied in fright. Tatiana gasped. The American rolled off the bed, taking the wool covering with him. He snatched up his rifle and had it cocked before the first blast of cold air hit his quaking bed partner. Taut as a bowstring, he peered into the darkness.

A bleating, blood-chilling cry rose on the thin night air and ended in a deep-throated gurgle. After that, there was only stillness.

"What is it?" Tatiana whispered when her nerves could no longer stand the eerie quiet.

"Mountain lion," the American murmured. "They don't usually hunt at night, but it sounds as though this one just got himself a bighorn sheep."

He eased the rifle hammer partway down, still staring into the darkness. "The big cat's particular in his feed. He prefers warm blood for every meal. I suspect we'll find the remains of a—"

He broke off, his jaw dropping as he gaped at Tatiana. She huddled in the middle of the buffalo robe, naked and shaking with fear and cold.

"Cover yourself," he snarled. "Now."

He turned away. Legs spread, spine stiff, he stood facing the fire.

Although the frigid air had raised huge goose bumps on her uncovered flesh, Tatiana flushed. His tone left no doubt of his disgust. Had he forgotten his so crude order that she come to his bed bare-skinned and naked? An order he did not see fit to rescind before he calmly announced that he did not want her services, after all?

Her cheeks burning, she yanked the soft, supple buckskin down around her legs, then pulled on the long-sleeved, fringed jacket and, finally, the fur cloak. Fully clothed, she sat in the center of the bed. She longed to remain there, to never again move, but she knew she didn't have that luxury. She had to face the American. Had to understand what it was he wished of her for the rest of this damnable journey.

Feeling more ancient and gnarled than one of her father's precious apple trees, Tatiana pushed to the edge of the buffalo robe. The rigid, wide-shouldered man turned at the sound of her approach. She flinched, expecting more censure or insult. He caught the movement, and his face turned ruddy above the golden brown of his beard.

"I offer you my apologies," he said, his voice stiff. "I've treated you with less than the dignity you should expect from one you've asked for aid."

Tatiana stared at him, doubt heavy in her mind as she turned his words over. Had she misheard him? Had she missed his meaning?

At the outright suspicion on her face, Josh's conscience took another twist of the screw. He didn't blame her for not believing his apology was sincere. He'd told her flat out the price she'd have to pay for his escort. All day he'd let her worry about paying it. As a result of his mule-headedness, she'd stripped down and crawled into his bed to await his pleasure like a two-penny whore. Thoroughly and completely disgusted with himself, Josh tried to convince her.

"Despite what I said this afternoon about the fandango, I never intended to lie with you. Not in the way a man lies with a woman."

His conscience suffered another sharp prick. All right! For a few hours, he'd contemplated more than just lying with her. He'd tramped a good many miles thinking about her taste and her feel, and ached with wanting her. Even now, with disgust at his behavior weighing heavy on his conscience, Josh couldn't completely banish his regret at refusing what she offered.

His confession didn't seem to allay her fears. If anything, the suspicion in her face intensified.

"But in the sweat house you said that you would...that we would..."

"I was just trying to scare you. To keep you from the mountains."

She stared at him for long moments, then a slow flame lit in her eyes and she let loose with a stream of Russian. Josh didn't have to speak the language to know she was calling him every name a woman could call a man.

He deserved the tongue-lashing, and stood it without flinching. To take his mind off the sparks flying from her magnificent eyes, Josh tried to decide just how the hell he'd regain her trust. In the days ahead, her survival would depend on the faith she placed in him and his abilities. If she doubted every order or suspected his motives, she could well place herself...and him...in jeopardy.

"How do I know this is true, what you tell me?" she demanded. "How do I know you will not...you will not..." She spit out another Russian phrase, one Josh didn't need translated.

Frowning, Josh walked back to the pine bed and scooped up his fringed possibles pouch. He fumbled through the contents and extracted a small object wrapped in a piece of folded oilskin. He stood still for a moment, fingering the packet. He hadn't unwrapped it in months. A year maybe. Just looking at it pained him too much. Now he had no choice.

He returned to the furious woman. Holding the packet in the palm of one hand, he unfolded the oilskin and revealed a small painted portrait in a gilt frame.

"This is Catherine." His voice held a quiet reverence. "I wouldn't betray her or shame you by making you keep to our bargain."

Distrust clouded the Russian's eyes as she glanced from his face to his hand. Josh didn't press her. Nor did he pass her the miniature. It hadn't left his possession since Catherine handed it to him, the day of his graduation from West Point.

After a moment, curiosity overcame her suspicion and anger. "Is she your wife, this Katerina?"

"No. She died six years ago. A few months before we were to marry."

"How...how did she die?"

Absorbed in his memories, Josh paid no attention to the hitch in her voice. "We went for a carriage ride and got caught in a spring rain shower." His fingers closed over the portrait. "She took an inflammation to the lungs. She was dead within a week."

"Ahh."

The low exclamation brought Josh's gaze from his tightly clenched fist. Tatiana slowly lifted her eyes to his.

"I, too, have watched someone I once loved die, Josiah Jones. It causes the hurt to the heart, which never goes away."

The simple words pierced Josh's absorption with his own past and shifted his attention to hers.

"Your husband?" he guessed.

She dipped her head in a nod so slight he almost missed it and stared beyond him into the darkness.

"I think I did not love Aleksei as you loved your Katerina," she whispered. "Nor did he so love me. But still it gives one pain to remember the dying."

Josh almost asked her how she'd lost her Aleksei, but stopped himself just in time. He'd revealed too much of the past already, more than he'd ever shared with anyone outside his family. Besides, there was still the matter of the immediate future to settle with this woman. Refolding the oilskin, he returned the portrait to the pouch and faced the Russian across the nest of pine boughs.

"I won't tell you that we shouldn't share a blanket," he said with blunt if overdue honesty. "We should do whatever we can to keep warm at night. When we climb higher, we'll be grateful for any source of heat, even the pony's. The choice is yours, though. If you don't feel right, or safe, or comfortable bedding down beside me, I understand."

She lifted a hand and let it drop. Josh winced inwardly at the small, tired gesture. He'd pushed her hard today. Too hard.

"I want only to get to Fort Ross. To complete this journey, I will sleep where and beside whom I must, whether you or the horse, it matters not."

That put him right where he belonged, Josh thought with a tight inner smile. Having finally set matters straight on one issue, he wanted to make sure she held no misunderstandings on another.

"I can't promise to take you all the way to Fort

Ross. I told you before we started that my path goes north once we clear the mountains. But I'll get you through the passes and arrange safe escort for you to the fort, if that's what you wish.''

"It is what I wish."

Josh rubbed the back of his neck. They'd settled what needed to be settled. Talked out this business of sharing a bed. Agreed that they'd go their separate ways when they cleared the passes. The only thing left to do now was to get on with it.

"We'd better get some sleep. We have a hard climb ahead of us tomorrow.''

"*Da.*"

Assuming the tired murmur signaled acquiescence, Josh retrieved the blanket coat from where it had fallen and spread it atop the buffalo robe. Pine branches rustled as first he, then Tatiana, resumed their places. She held herself away from him, sharing the covering but not his warmth. That would come later, Josh knew, when sleep and the predawn cold drew them together.

He folded his hands under his head, listening to the uneven pattern of her breathing. Above him a thousand stars shimmered in the night sky. As was his habit, he courted sleep by mentally preparing himself for the next day's march. Slowly, inevitably, his thoughts spun from the trek to the woman who would make it with him.

She hid a surprising vulnerability behind that prickly exterior of hers. Josh hadn't missed the sadness in her voice when she spoke of her husband, or the bitterness. Why hadn't she loved him? Why hadn't the man loved her? Had theirs been a marriage of convenience, a merging of titles and properties? Even so, Josh couldn't imagine her nameless, faceless husband not desiring her. For all her forward ways and irritating hardheadedness, Tatiana Grig...Grigor...Whoever... could start a man's blood to pounding. She certainly wasn't lacking any feminine charms. His brief, startling glimpse of her full breasts and slender waist had confirmed that.

Josh rolled his eyes, cursing under his breath. The last thing he needed to do was think about the Russian's body! His own went hard as he fought to banish the image of her pale skin and rounded hips. In desperation, he tried to focus his thoughts on his memories of Catherine. His remorse over the way he'd treated Tatiana. The lost husband who had left those shadows in her eyes. Anything!

He was still trying to shove the image of her sleekly curved form from his mind when the branches beneath him sagged. Muttering in Russian, Tatiana burrowed into his side. The breasts that Josh had just been trying not to visualize pressed into his rib cage.

He closed his eyes. Opened them. Started counting the stars, as she'd done earlier. Gave up at 107, when she muttered again and nudged his shoulder with her chin. Resigning himself to a long, sleepless night, Josh brought his arm down. She sighed and cushioned her head in the hollow of his shoulder. Her breath washed his neck in warm, moist heat.

Josh started counting once more.

Tatiana woke to the rank scent of buffalo and a chorus of small, foreign sounds. Wrinkling her nose, she dug her face out of the curly, ticklish fur and breathed in a draft of cold air.

While her sleep-blurred eyes adjusted to the dimness that still blanketed the mountains, Tatiana identified the sounds that had teased her into wakefulness. The little stream trickled through its narrow, ice-encrusted channel. The pony huffed a short distance away. A faint chink confused her, until she recognized the sound of metal on metal. A spoon hitting a tin plate, she thought. Or the lid of the pot the American used to boil coffee beans.

The thought of the dark, steaming, bitter brew spurred Tatiana to movement. She thrust off the fleecy blanket and sat up, tilting sideways in the shifting boughs. Righting herself with one hand, she shoved her tumbled hair out of her eyes with the other.

"Mornin'."

The American's deep drawl came to her from the shadows. Blinking the last of the sleep from her eyes, Tatiana watched him move toward the fire in an easy, noiseless stride.

"God give you good morning," she murmured.

He knelt on one knee beside the banked fire and balanced the battered tin pot on the embers. "The coffee will boil in a few minutes. Keep warm until it does. You'll have time enough to tend to your needs while I pack up."

Tatiana had no objection to a few more moments in the bed's warmth. Bunching the fleecy blanket coat around her shoulders, she propped her chin on her knees and studied the confusing, confounding man she'd slept beside.

The fire's glow cast his face into sharp relief. Perhaps she'd been too hasty in her first assessment of the American's appearance, Tatiana admitted silently. He had not Aleksei's heart-stealing handsomeness or roguish charm, but neither was he quite the great hairy beast she'd first labeled him. Above his beard, his clear, gold-flecked brown eyes looked out on the world as though he owned it. His skin was weathered to a tanned, supple leather and carried no pocks or pits from the pox that afflicted so many of the sophisticated courtiers of Tatiana's world. And his smile...

She bit her lip, thinking of that unexpected and altogether disturbing smile. Thinking as well of the quiet pain in his voice when he spoke of his lost love, and of his refusal to hold Tatiana to her bargain.

Perhaps she'd also been too hasty in her assessment of his character. Perhaps...perhaps this journey would not be the voyage into despair she'd imagined. Buoyed by a new, tenuous hope, she crawled out of the nest of pine boughs and joined the American at the fire.

Her brief surge of hope lasted only until noon.

Chapter Six

With an eye to the graying clouds, Josh set a punishing pace.

Just before noon, he led the way around a spindletopped peak and headed for the bald upper slope of an otherwise impassable crag. Suddenly the temperature dropped and the wind began gusting in awful surges. Roaring and booming through the gorges like cannon fire, it stirred the snow and threw it up in the travelers' faces.

They were halfway across the bleak, desolate stretch above the tree line when the clouds dropped and obscured all landmarks from view. Cursing, Josh picked up the pace as much as he dared. After only another mile the pony's labored breath and heaving sides forced him to call a halt. The little packhorse would never make it with the load it carried. Grimly Josh went to work on the ropes securing the heavy packs.

Tatiana stumbled up beside him. The violent gusts whipped her hair until the tendrils danced around the tied-down beaver hat like dark, writhing furies.

"What do you do?" she shouted.

"We've got to get down to the timberline, and fast," he yelled back. "I'm going to lighten the load."

"Can we not..." The wind snatched her words away. "...here until the storm passes?"

"What?"

"Can we not stay here?"

"No. Without the trees to break the wind, the cold will cut right through to our bones. We'll be dead before morning."

Josh reached for the basket. Tatiana's face went rigid with alarm.

"But..."

"No buts." He dumped the heavy container onto the snow.

"But we cannot leave the basket!" Her mittened hands clutched at his sleeve. "We must not!"

He shook her off. "We must and we will. You've got two minutes to get out of it only what you need to survive for the next few days."

The smaller of Josh's packs landed beside the basket with a dull thud. He reached across the wooden support poles to even the remaining load. He hated to abandon the extra supplies he'd traded with Cho-gam for, but if he didn't get himself and his charge below the tree line before the storm broke, they wouldn't have much use for smoked salmon and coarse-ground acorn meal.

"You must...leave...another pack and take...the basket. Please."

He almost missed Tatiana's frantic plea in the shriek of the wind. He couldn't miss the way she planted herself in front of him, blocking his reach for the pony's reins. The desperation in her face brought Josh up short. Blue lipped with cold and staring a blizzard in the eye, she still wouldn't abandon her belongings.

He stared at her through eyes half-closed against the wind and whipping snow. A few female fripperies wouldn't cause this urgency.

"Just what's in this precious basket of yours?"

"I told you! All I could save of that which came with me on the ship. I must take it to Fort Ross."

Josh turned and strode back to the objects in the snow. Panting, she hurried alongside him.

"The basket is perhaps a little heavy, it is true. But I must...what do you do? Stop! Stop at once!"

Ignoring her screeched command, Josh drew out his knife and went down on one knee. In two fast slashes, he sliced through the rawhide thongs securing the basket's top. A quick wrench sent the lid skimming across the snow.

Incredulously Josh gaped at the contents. Sticks! Nothing but sticks. In neatly bound bundles, tagged and identified in Russian script. His mittened hand fumbled through several layers, searching among the brittle twigs for something that made sense of Tatiana's desperation. He found only more sticks. Disbelieving, he drew out one of the tagged bundles.

She snatched it out of his hand. "You must not expose them!"

Like a mother putting a child to bed, she knelt and carefully tucked the bundle back in the basket. "They were in the sea. I don't know..."

Josh wrenched her around so hard she almost toppled over. "What in the hell are these?"

"They are cuttings."

"Cuttings?"

"From the trees my father has nurtured."

"You're hauling *trees* through mountains covered with stands of virgin timber?"

"Yes!"

She tried without success to pull free of his hard grip. Josh tried without success to rein in his soaring fury.

"You're risking your life and mine for *trees?*"

"These cuttings came from most special trees!" She blinked rapidly to clear her wind-teared eyes. "From the peaches, and the pears and the apples of a most hardy kind. My father himself developed this apple. He named it in honor of…" Her mouth twisted. "He named it in honor of Nikolas, the Tsar of all Russias. It is called the Tsar's Treasure."

Josh surged to his feet, yanking her up with him. The absurdity of the situation staggered him. They were standing on top of the world, caught in a sea of wind, moments away from a blinding blizzard, and this addlepated female worried about a basket of dried, twisted sticks.

"I don't care who the hell they were named for," he roared in a voice to match the howling wind. "Those twigs are staying here."

"No!"

Without another word, he shoved past her and grabbed the pony's reins. He'd taken three stiff-legged strides across the snow-covered slope before Tatiana caught up to him. Her feet slipping and slithering on the steep incline, she dragged at his arm.

"Wait! You do not understand! I must get this stock to Fort Ross before the sap begins to rise in the trees that are there. Only then can I..."

"*You* don't understand!" Josh hurled at her. "If we don't get to shelter, and quickly, you're not going to make it off this mountain, much less to Fort Ross. Make tracks, Countess. Now!"

Pulling free of her frantic grip, he put his head down and stepped into the stinging flurries. The pony followed, its hooves muffled on the snow. They were still five miles to the timberline on the west slope, Josh estimated. Once there, he could fashion a shelter under the branches of a tall pine. If only the damned clouds would lift for a few moments so he could get his bearings.

Instead of lifting, the grayish light merged with the snowy surface until a hazy, shimmering luminescence coated everything and created dangerous false illusions. Large stones that Josh went out of his way to skirt around weren't even there. Others, he whacked right into. Once he stepped high to avoid what looked like a drift and fell flat on his face when his foot went down into a deep depression. Swearing, he dug himself out. He was brushing the snow from his face and beard when he noticed that Tatiana was nowhere in sight.

His hand froze in midair. Sudden, pounding fear clawed in his throat. Had she wandered off the path in this treacherous light and gone into a crevasse? Had the wind swallowed up her scream? An instant later, another, far more likely possibility hit him.

She'd gone back for her damned basket! He knew it as surely as he knew his own name.

Eyes narrowed to slits, Josh stared back into the hazy grayness. If she was so pigheaded, so insane, as to risk her life for a few bundles of kindling, that was her choice. He wasn't going back for her. No way in hell he was going back for her. If she didn't show up in the next ten seconds, he'd leave her. He'd damn well leave her.

One…two…three…

The flaps of his capote lifted in a gust of icy wind. The packhorse shivered and nudged its face against Josh's shoulder.

Eight…nine…ten!

The opaque whiteness remained an unbroken, impenetrable curtain.

Damn it! Damn it to hell and back!

With a vicious yank on the pony's lead, Josh plowed back the way he'd come. The icy wind should have heated from the searing curses he poured into it. Instead, it slashed at the skin above his beard like a thousand tiny knives.

After five minutes, the trail he'd made in the snow such a short time ago disappeared. After ten, his fury had settled like a cold lump in his gut and fear once more pulled at his chest. Had he missed her in this eerie light? Had they passed within a few yards of each other and not realized it? He shouted her name again.

"Tatiana! Damn you, where are you? Tatiana!"

Head down, heart pumping, he plowed on.

"Tatiana!"

"Here!"

The cry sounded thin and high above the roaring wind. His blood pounding, Josh pushed forward. Moments later, a blurry, indistinct figure staggered toward him through the swirling haze. She was bent double against the force of the gusts and the weight of the burden she dragged.

Josh halted in his tracks. Under his beard, his jaw clenched so hard it cracked.

She came closer, her breath shooting white puffs into the air with each step. "I...I could not...leave the Tsar's Treasure, Josiah Jones."

Exhaustion added a sharp, brittle edge to her words. Far from softening Josh's anger, the utter weariness in her voice stoked him to a hot, deadly fury. He was beside her in two strides. One hand twisted up her wrist. The other tore the makeshift thong handle from her mittened fingers. Yanking her unceremoniously behind him, he hauled her to the pony.

"No!"

Josh ignored the shrill screech, just as he ignored her fierce struggles. But when her free hand swung through the air and connected with the side of his jaw, he'd had enough. Fumbling at the pack, he ripped off one of the rawhide ties. She grasped his intent when he pulled her around and brought up her wrist.

"No! You shall not bind me!"

"You'll be lucky if that's all I do, lady."

While he looped the strip of hide around her wrist, her uncaptured fist pummeled his head and shoulders. Josh hunched a shoulder to ward off the blows. In the process, he inadvertently gave her an opening. Her hand went to his knife. Quick as a flash of summer lightning, it was out of the scabbard and at his throat.

"You shall not bind me!"

"Or what?"

"Or I shall slit your throat," she hissed.

When he didn't loosen his bone-crunching hold, she dug the tip of the knife deeper into his throat. A warm trickle traced a path down Josh's neck. His lips drew back in a slow, feral smile.

"Go ahead. Carve out my windpipe. Then get yourself through the mountains."

Josh saw her thoughts turn inward, as if weighing her chance of surviving without him. Realizing she was crazy enough to take that chance, he put an end to their standoff. With an agility born of countless wrestling matches, some friendly, some not, he hooked a heel around her ankles. His head jerked away from the knife tip at the same moment her feet went out from under her.

She landed with a bone-jarring thud. Josh followed her down, straddling her hips almost before they hit the ground. He had the knife out of her hand before she'd drawn a single breath.

He didn't waste time celebrating his victory. He had none to waste. If they found shelter before the skies opened up, the Russian would learn the consequences of pulling a knife on him. If not, it wouldn't matter.

Shoving the blade into its scabbard, he grabbed the end of the rawhide thong and lashed both of her wrists together. She screamed protests and threats in Russian, French and English, all of which Josh ignored. With a final tug on the knot, he clambered up. A yank on the thong pulled her up as well. Wrapping a hand around the back of her neck, he drew her forward until her breath pearled with his.

"If you drag your feet or try to slow us," he warned savagely, "I'll come back and burn every one of your precious twigs. I swear it."

She read the promise in his eyes. Her protests subsided into silence and a despair Josh refused to acknowledge. His only concern now was survival. Looping the end of the rawhide thong to his belt, he grabbed the pony's lead.

If he could find a path across the slope in this blinding, iridescent haze, and *if* the full fury of the storm held off for another hour, and *if* the Russian didn't pull any more stupid tricks, they might make it to shelter. When they did, Josh decided, the countess was going to regret this piece of work. Mightily.

Head down, he started off.

Tatiana threw a last, desperate glance over her shoulder to imprint the basket's location on her mind. A sharp yank on the hide tether pulled her forward. She stumbled after the American, twisting her wrists together in a futile attempt to loosen her bonds. The thick beaverskin mittens that protected her flesh from the cruel knots also frustrated all attempts to pick them loose. Inside the warm protectors, her fingers curled into claws.

With each step, she repeated a fierce, silent vow. *If* she survived this nightmare of cold, white light, she would reclaim the Tsar's Treasure. *If* she had to crawl through the snow on her hands and knees, she would so crawl. And *if* the American tried to stop her, she would do what she could not do a few moments ago and plunge the knife into his throat!

Rage and determination sustained her for the first mile. Youth and resilience for the next. By the third, the fury of the wind and sting of snow began to drain the reserves of strength Tatiana had built during her weeks with the Hupa. By the fourth, only fear kept her moving.

Holy Father, would this white hell never end? Icy snow swept up by the wind crusted her eyebrows and lashes. Cold numbed her cheeks, her lips. More than once, she stumbled. With her arms pulled taut by the rawhide tether, she couldn't break her fall and landed awkwardly on her knees. The first time, the American jerked her up with a curse and a warning to watch where she put her feet. The second, he shortened the link between them until her wrists were tucked under his arm and she trod almost on his heels. To her silent relief, his bulk blocked some of the wind and made the going easier.

Ever afterward Tatiana would wonder whether a capricious nature or a merciful God kept the clouds from dumping all of their heavy load. Snowflakes skittered and whirled through the air like sharp-bladed knives, but didn't descend in a suffocating blanket of white. Even without the snow, however, the swirling gray mists obscured all visibility. She plodded behind the American through the blinding haze for what seemed like two lifetimes.

They reached the timberline just as the iridescent light began to fade. Short, stunted trees provided intermittent relief from the biting wind. The American pushed on until the trees grew taller and thicker. Suddenly darkness descended with the finality of an ax.

At last they halted in a stand of towering pines. Too weary for words, Tatiana started to crumple in the snow where she stood. A tug on her bound arms kept her upright. In the icy darkness, she couldn't see the American's expression, but the coldness in his voice rivaled that of the air.

"If I untie you, will you stay put?"

"Yes."

She would stay wherever she dropped...until she'd regained her strength and decided how next she would proceed. She was too tired, too frozen, to think clearly right now.

She held out her hands, expecting him to sever the bonds. Instead, he yanked her over to the pony. A hand in the small of her back shoved her against the pack. Her arms were stretched up and over the bulging sacks and skins.

"What do you do?" she gasped. "I said I would not leave."

"I don't believe you, and I'm damned if I'm going chase after you again."

A few quick loops secured the rawhide thong to the crossed poles of the support. Tatiana's angry tugs caused the pony to stamp nervously.

"I do not lie!"

A snort of derision sounded above the swish of pine branches. "I don't believe that, either."

"Bastard! Evil-eyed horehound!"

Since she didn't know the English words for her curses, they served no purpose, Tatiana knew, except to vent her frustrations. She ran out of breath before she progressed much beyond the American's resemblance to several disgusting barnyard animals. Unutterably weary, she pressed her face into the deer-hide pack covering to escape the stinging wind. Bristles scraped her nose and cheeks. Whoever had cleaned this skin did a poor job, she thought dully.

The sounds of heavy labor rose behind her. A series of grunts. The thump of something hitting the snow. The swish of branches and, once, a sudden crack and a curse. Tatiana gave up trying to distinguish the sounds. The pack captured her breath and warmed her frozen face. Moments later, her knees gave. She sagged in weariness, then jerked upright at the wrench to her wrists. The packhorse turned in a half circle, as if to escape this unaccustomed pull. Tatiana followed, her arms aching.

When she thought she could bear the shooting needles in her shoulder joints no longer, a dim shape materialized beside her. The ropes came free, and she collapsed in a shapeless heap. The American ignored her to remove the pony's burden and lead it away. Tatiana couldn't find the strength to move. When he returned, a hand under her arm pulled her up and led her through the darkness.

"Duck your head. Lower."

His splayed palm went to the back of her neck. Bent double, Tatiana stumbled out of the whistling wind into a black hole of silence and, mercifully, warmth. The sharp tang of resin told her that it was a cavelike shelter under the swooping, snow-laden branches of a pine tree. The pungent odor of horse indicated that the pony shared the sanctuary.

Once more she collapsed, this time onto a layer of pine boughs. Shoulders hunched, head bowed, arms and legs aching, she let exhaustion roll through her in crushing waves. Blackness surrounded her, seeped into her soul.

The pine boughs rustled. A small thud sounded close to Tatiana. She felt rather than saw the American ease himself down beside the pack he'd dropped. The harsh grate of their breathing filled the small cavern. After a few moments, a hoarse command came to her through the black void.

"Tell me why you risked your life for a basket of tree cuttings."

Wearily Tatiana lifted her head. "Will you not untie me first?"

"No. Tell me."

How changeable he was, she thought. Was it only last night that he'd shown her the portrait of his lost love? Only a few hours since she'd awakened to find him crouched beside the fire and admitted that perhaps she'd been too hasty in her assessment of his person and his manner? Now she sought to find the strength to hate him, and failed dismally.

Tomorrow, she thought, propping her shoulders against the mounded snow behind her. Tomorrow she'd hate and beg and threaten and cajole. Tonight she was too weary to do more than close her eyes and respond to his demand.

"If I do not save the cuttings, my life is forfeit, as is my father's."

Silence greeted her low, husky admission.

"Even if I save them," she whispered, "I do not know if they will stay the tsar's wrath. I salvaged so little of what was on the ship. Only a small portion of what I brought from Russia."

Shivers shook her at the memory of those terrifying hours clinging to the top of the huge chest while the sea roiled around her.

"Go on." There was no pity in the deep, relentless voice.

"Before I go on, I must first go back."

"Go wherever you will. Just get on with it."

Sighing, Tatiana marshaled her thoughts. How could she explain? How could she find the words to voice her own vanity, her fatal blindness?

"My father is a renowned scholar," she began tiredly. "He is most famous, in Russia and elsewhere, for his knowledge of horticultural matters. When he was ambassador to the Court of St. James, he presented learned papers to the Royal Academy. He and the great earl of Lansdowne became fast friends. Always, they puttered in the orchards and the fields."

Her mind drifted back to those brief, halcyon days in the lush gardens of the earl's manor house. While her father and the stooped, balding Lansdowne indulged their passion for fruit trees and vines, Tatiana had giggled and splashed in the fountains under her chaperon's watchful eye and enjoyed the English predilection for picnics with the earl's grandchildren.

"When we returned to Russia, my father remained at his estates in the south, where he has many orchards. Like other young girls of my station, I went to serve the tsarina. To gain polish and a husband, you understand.''

Her fingers curled inside the furred gloves.

''I gained a husband, but not the one that the tsar had chosen for me. I was young. Foolish. I ran away with a captain of the Imperial Guards. I believed that Nikolas would relent once Aleksei and I were wed. Perhaps...perhaps he would have, had my husband not involved himself in a plot with other young, stupid officers to curb the tsar's power. Aleksei was executed, as were the other officers.''

Tatiana swallowed, trying to blank the horror from her mind. As always, the images proved too strong to keep at bay. Her husband's frightened face. Nikolas's implacable one. The black, cold eyes of the colonel who'd held her immobile, his fingers digging into her flesh, while the executioner placed a knotted rope around his traitorous subordinate's neck.

The man beside her shifted. The movement was a mere whisper of sound, only the smallest rustle of pine boughs, but it was enough to pull her from the black pit of her memories. Although he said nothing, she sensed a lessening in his cold anger. She wanted not his sympathy, Tatiana thought. Only his help. Gathering her thoughts, she finished the sordid tale.

''I was spared only by my father's most urgent pleas. He beggared himself to pay the price the tsar demanded for my life. When even the mountains of gold he raised did not satisfy Nikolas, my father made a last, desperate offer. He would save Fort Ross, which the tsar had decided must be abandoned.''

This time the shift was more abrupt. Pine boughs

swished as he turned toward her. "The tsar has decided that Fort Ross must be abandoned?"

"It is not widely known. Only among a few of Nikolas's most trusted advisors. So much has been invested in the venture, you understand, that no one wants to voice aloud its failure. Heads will roll if the fort fails. Vast fortunes will be lost. One of my father's friends whispered to him about the situation, and thus he made the offer to save the fort."

"With apple tree cuttings?"

She bridled at the disbelief in his voice. "It is the only way! The otters played out long ago in the seas around Fort Ross, you understand. Without the furs to ship back to Russia, the outpost has no use except to grow grains and foodstuffs for the settlements in Alaska, where yet they hunt the furs."

Instinctively Tatiana tried to raise her hands to augment her recital with the expansive gestures that were so much a part of her nature. Her bound wrists frustrated her. With an irritated frown, she let them drop.

"Unfortunately, the grain harvests have been most poor," she told her listener. "And the trees brought up from the Spanish settlements have yet to bear heavy harvests. These trees, they are too tender to survive the rains and the cold. The cuttings I bring will join with them at the base, and create a new, more hardy stock."

Tatiana finished in a breathless rush. She'd come so far. She could not fail now. She had to convince this man to take her back, to retrieve the precious cargo entrusted to her care.

"These cuttings, they are the only hope to save the

fort. There are not enough to join with all the trees in the orchards at Fort Ross, of course. I lost too many to the sea. But they will show what is possible, you understand." She leaned forward, searching the blackness. "You *must* understand."

Josh understood, all right. His mind raced with the understanding. The tsar had decided to abandon Fort Ross! President Van Buren was going to be mighty interested in that bit of information.

Josh had only visited the settlement once, some years ago. The wooden fort housed some sixty Russians and around eighty Aleuts who'd come down with them from Archangel to hunt the seas in their watertight kayaks. Even then, the otter population in the waters around the fort had thinned. The Aleuts were having to paddle farther and farther offshore to bring in the pelts. Josh hadn't realized that the fur take had dwindled to the point that the fort had turned to agriculture as justification for its existence.

This was going to take some thinking. Some deep, serious thinking.

Shifting his weight to make a nest for himself in the prickly boughs, he stretched out beside his rifle. The pony stamped and huffed a few feet away. The woman was silent for a few moments before voicing a puzzled question.

"What do you do?"

"I'm going to sleep."

A startled silence greeted that pronouncement. Then she stuttered a disbelieving protest.

"You...you sleep now? After all that I have told you."

"Now."

"But...but what of my cuttings!"

"I'll have to think about those."

"And these bonds? You cannot mean to leave me tied like this!"

"I can, and I do."

"They are too tight," she protested indignantly. "I shall not sleep in such discomfort."

The branches rustled as Josh found a better position. "You should have thought of that before you stuck a knife in my throat."

Chapter Seven

A fierce growling in her stomach and a burning need to relieve herself brought Tatiana out of an exhausted stupor. Her lids lifted, scraping over dry eyes blurred with sleep. She stared blankly at the grayish white wall before her until her sluggish mind made sense of it.

She was burrowed under a pine tree, she remembered slowly. Buried in a cavern formed of the snow and roofed by the tree's sagging branches.

Like an avalanche gathering speed, the events of the night before came rushing back. Life pumped into her aching limbs. Curling her legs, Tatiana tried to sit up. At that point, she discovered that she couldn't move her arms. Frowning, she remembered that she was still bound. She glanced down at the rawhide around her wrists. Its trailing end was trapped under her body and held her arms anchored to the ground.

With a twist that tangled the ties of her cloak around her neck, Tatiana flopped over onto her other side. She expected to find the American asleep beside her. Instead, she saw only the pony. It stood a few feet away,

Merline Lovelace 107

steam rising from its shaggy coat as it regarded her curiously through liquid brown eyes.

Relief skidded through her. She didn't have to face the American just yet. Within an instant or two, relief gave way to a more pressing need. He must release her. She must relieve herself, most immediately. She craned her head toward the small round opening that showed a patch of lighter gray.

"Josiah! Josiah Jones!"

Her shout made the pony dance, but brought no other response. She called again, louder and longer. Her shouts sank into the thick snow walls. Muttering curses under her breath, Tatiana struggled onto her hands and knees and crawled across the scattered boughs toward the opening. The fox cloak twisted beneath her and tugged painfully at her neck with each jerky movement. Her bound hands played havoc with her balance. Twice she toppled onto her side. Once, she went facedown in the snow.

Choking from the pressure on her throat, she finally crawled into a patch of dappled sunshine. She crouched half in and half out of the cave and glanced cautiously around her.

The howling winds of yesterday had died. The steep granite crags she and Josiah had descended in the blinding whiteness had gentled to a sweeping, tree-covered slope. Snow so pure it hurt the eye lay like a down-filled counterpane over the land. And the trees! Holy Mother, these towering trees! So straight and tall and dark a green beneath their lacings of white. Her father would be astonished at their height, and at the circumference of their massive trunks. When she took in the silent majesty of the scene, she sank back on her heels.

How could it be so beautiful, this land of savage seas and brutal mountains?

Suddenly the fact that she was alone in this magnificent wilderness sank into Tatiana's consciousness. She swept the area around the snow cave's entrance again.

She saw no sign of Josiah. No sign, either, of a morning campfire. Not even the battered tin pot he boiled his coffee in. Only a set of footprints in the snow, winding away from their subterranean shelter to disappear among the trees.

A queer little sensation darted down Tatiana's back. Not quite fear. Not exactly alarm. Still, when she spotted the packs under the concealing sweep of a snow-laden branch, she let out a slow, shaky breath. He wouldn't leave the pony and his packs, she reasoned. After what occurred yesterday, he might well leave Tatiana to her fate, but he wouldn't abandon his supplies.

Would he?

She struggled to her feet. Pushing her tangled hair out of her eyes with both hands, she reached awkwardly behind her for the hat that dangled by its cords and dragged it onto her head. A few strenuous tugs righted the heavy cloak. Tatiana gasped in relief when the cutting pressure on her windpipe eased.

Those basic needs attended to, she raised her arms and attacked the rawhide around her wrists with her teeth. The tight knots defied her every effort to work them loose. Nor could she gnaw through the tough, unyielding strands. Jaws aching, she bit down on a fur mitten and tried to pull it free of the thong. If she could tug the mitten off, the bonds might slacken enough to slip her hand through the loops.

After several moments of futile effort, Tatiana gave up. Spitting fur from her dry mouth, she resigned herself to relieving the pressure on her bladder as best she could with her hands still bound. She spent an awkward session behind the tree, then attended to the pony. With much coaxing and tugging on its lead, she got the beast out of the snow cave and tethered to a low-hanging branch. The poor thing looked as hungry as she felt.

She decided to search for something to feed them both. The bindings on the packs almost defeated her fumbling, mittened fingers. A film of sweat dewed her upper lip by the time she dug both fists into the pony's feed. Dumping a pile of the mixed grains and crushed acorns onto a cleared patch, she left the horse to its breakfast and dug into another pouch for her own.

Retreating to a fallen log, she held a strip of dried deer meat firmly in both hands and tore off a bite. It tasted like old, salty leather, with only a hint of wild onion to temper its bitter tang. Slowly Tatiana masticated the small bite to soften it and release its juices. While she chewed, she watched the trees where the American's footsteps wound away.

He would come back. He'd gone to hunt. To get their bearings. Perhaps…her jaw stilled. Perhaps to find her basket. He would come back.

She finished the dried meat and quenched her thirst

with clumps of snow. Her bound hands clenched uselessly in her lap.

He would come back.

Sunlight slanted through the trees and warmed the
air. As it had before, the fur cloak grew heavy and
hot. Tatiana brushed a mitt of snow across her heated
face.

He must come back.

The minutes slipped by. Her uneasiness mounted
and with it a trapped, frightened feeling. She fought
the fear for what seemed like hours. Finally her cour-
age deserted her. She bent over her hands and gnawed
on the bonds like a trapped wild animal. Her teeth
slipped and scraped against each other. The inside of
her lower lip split. Blood added its salty residue to the
taste of the deer meat. She was so consumed by the
desperate need to free herself that the sound of a thud
brought her springing to her feet in panting, stom-
ach-churning fear.

Josiah stood a few yards away, his face ruddy from
exertion. The packs he'd abandoned yesterday lay at
his feet...alongside Tatiana's basket.

She stared at the intricately woven container, knowing that she should feel grateful. That relief should roll
through her in great waves. At the moment, though,
the only emotion that consumed her was a heaving
resentment at having been left tied like a beast. The
American read her feelings in the tight, angry face she
turned to him.

"You'll fare worse if you pull a knife on me
again," he promised quietly. "Far worse."

Unspeaking, Tatiana held out her hands. She'd do what she must. Surely he understood that by now.

He regarded her steadily, then reached for his knife. The blade slipped free of its scabbard and sawed through the tough, unforgiving bonds. Removing her mitts, Tatiana rubbed her sore wrists and reassessed the man who stood before her.

In the bright light of morning, he seemed as tall and as solid as the trees. He'd thrown back the hood of his capote. The sun glinted on the burnished strands in his honey-colored hair and beard and gave his tanned skin the patina of polished oak. His golden brown eyes showed no hint of friendliness, nor yet of the anger that had risen like a live thing between them last night.

"Why did you go back for the cuttings?" she asked, struggling to keep her voice even.

He shoved his knife into its fringed holder. "I didn't. I went back for the extra food supplies. But I promised you we'd carry your basket as far as we could, and I hold to my promises."

"I thank you."

The words were stiff and forced, but the American didn't seem to take offense at their ungraciousness. Hooking his thumbs in his belt, he regarded Tatiana thoughtfully.

"Do you really believe these twigs will make a difference to the future of Fort Ross?"

"My father believes so. Me?" Her shoulders lifted. "I can only hope."

"If we make it through the mountains without slitting each other's throats," he said slowly, "I'll take you to the fort."

"But..." She stared at him, confounded. "But I thought your way went north."

"It does. I'll make a detour."

For one of the few times in her life, Tatiana was at a loss for words. After the events of the preceding day, she would never have anticipated such a change of face.

"Why would you do this after I...after I..."

The tension in his shoulders eased. "After you tried to carve a totem on my windpipe?"

"Why do you do this?"

"Let's just say you made me realize how important this matter of Fort Ross is."

She shook her head. Never would she understand him. "You're a most confusing man, Josiah Jones."

A brief, elusive smile pulled at his lips. "That's what Catherine used to say. Only she always called me Josh."

Ah, yes. His adored Katerina. She of the gilded curls and plump red lips.

Suddenly, inexplicably, Tatiana felt the full weight of two days and nights on the trail. Her eyes itched with the grit of sleep. Her scalp crawled with the need to pull the bone comb Re-Re-An had given her through her tangled hair. The tip of her nose, she was sure, glowed red from its exposure to the sun. She longed to shed the American's hat, her bulky fox cloak, and her several layers of buckskin and cleanse herself from head to toe.

Tonight, she promised herself. When they made

camp tonight, she would scrub herself with boiled snow. Assuming, as he said, she and this strange, confusing man did not slit each other's throats before then.

Josh waited for the Russian to ready herself, then set off at a steady pace, one he maintained throughout the day. As the miles passed, the wary truce between him and the countess slipped into the familiarity of two travelers who had grown used to each other's ways.

He didn't fool himself into thinking that she'd learned her lesson. The events of the preceding day had given him a good measure of her desperation. She'd carve him or anyone else up in little pieces if she had to, to get herself and her damned basket of twigs to Fort Ross. Now that he'd agreed to take her there, she walked with a quicker step and an eagerness that made light of the steep climbs and long miles.

Josh had his own reasons for detouring south, and they didn't have anything to do with apple tree cuttings. Ever since last night, he'd been thinking of nothing but Tatiana's startling disclosure. The Russians might abandon their toehold in California!

Fort Ross was the only fortified coastal settlement between the Spanish presidios to the south and the British Fur Company fort at Vancouver. Who would move into the area if the Russians left?

Not the British or the French, if President Van Buren had anything to say about it. He wouldn't tolerate further European expansion on the American continent. Just the rumor of incursions by the British Fur

Company into Oregon Territory had been enough for him to send Josh on this urgent mission to scout the northwest area.

Catherine's uncle would be as interested as Josh was in the startling news that the Russians might pull out of California. As president, he'd made repeated offers to purchase "higher California" along with Texas and other Mexican territories, and been refused. But now that the Russians were thinking about leaving the area, Mexico might be more willing to negotiate with the United States for the wild, unsettled stretch of land above San Francisco, if only to keep the French and British out.

The possibilities had tumbled around in Josh's mind from the moment Tatiana let fall about the fort's uncertain fate. With the swiftness of a man used to adapting to the unexpected, he'd unilaterally amended his orders. Oregon could wait. Fort Ross might not. He'd check out the situation for himself.

The fact that the detour would mean another few weeks in Tatiana's company had nothing to do with Josh's decision. Despite his scraggly beard and stained buckskins, he was an officer in the army of the United States. He had a duty to perform.

That duty occupied his thoughts well into the afternoon, when Tatiana's sudden exclamation shoved it right out of his mind.

"Look! There, to the right!"

Whipping his rifle from its leather sheath, Josh spun around. Muscles coiled, nerves snapping like the tip of a bullwhip, he searched the narrow gorge off to their right. Nothing moved among the snow-covered rocks.

"There!" Tatiana cried, running to his side. "There it is again."

She pointed to a thin vapory ribbon that rose from the ravine floor, folded back to the earth, then shot into the sky like a silver arrow.

"What can it...?" She broke off, her nose wrinkling. "Pah! It has the smell of the spoiled egg."

Josh brought his rifle up, grinning. "It's a geyser. A hole in the earth where hot water shoots out. This area is full of them."

She swung to face Josh, her eyes huge. "The water is hot?"

"Boiling, when it spouts out of the ground like that. It cools off when it drains into a pool or stream. It loses most of its stink then, too."

"I will bathe in this pool or stream," she announced breathlessly, "if you will make the camp here."

"Bathe?"

The idea of the countess stripping down for a bath caused a sharp kick of interest just below Josh's belt. A sudden vision of long legs, curved hips and lush breasts darted into his mind.

Sternly he repressed it. He'd already gone down this road once with her. He wasn't going to let lust get mixed into their volatile relationship again.

He threw a quick glance at the sun. They could travel a few more miles yet today. Maybe make the crest of the next pass. Or they could stop here, with the protection of the high-walled ravine at their backs.

The expression in Tatiana's eyes stopped just short of pleading, but it was close enough to decide the matter.

"We'll make camp at the mouth of the gorge."

She was in a fever of impatience by the time they'd selected a site beside the stream that twisted out of the ravine. After unpacking the pony and scavenged enough deadwood for the fire, Tatiana tucked her fur cloak under her arm and headed for the shallow, steaming pool formed by the geyser.

Josh called her back. "Hold on a minute."

He dug into one of his packs. Somewhere under the half-empty sack of coffee, his spare shirt and the wooden case that held his writing pens and several folded sheets of parchment was a bit of lye soap. He fished out the coarse bar and handed it to Tatiana. She clutched it in both hands, her face alive with eager anticipation.

"Stay within shouting distance," Josh advised. "Yell if you need me."

"I will."

"And don't get too close to the source of the geyser."

"No."

"If it shoots out again, the water could scald you."

"Yes, yes, I understand."

Josh watched her hurry upstream, the precious soap clasped to her chest. From past experience, he could have warned her that the bottom of the mineral-encrusted pool would be as smooth and slick as the inside of a shell. That the hot water would feel like heaven, but icicles would form on her hair the moment she stuck her head out of the pool. She'd find out for herself soon enough.

He'd never met a more impatient, impulsive, intrepid female. Josh tried to imagine another woman of his acquaintance traveling across Russia in the dead of winter, taking ship for an unfamiliar land, and putting herself in the hands of a complete stranger for a trek through the mountains, all for the sake of a few bundles of sticks. She had grit, this contrary, stubborn Russian. If nothing else, she had grit.

He busied himself with the mundane tasks of readying for the night. Sure enough, a small shriek carried on the cold air some moments later. Josh tensed at the sound of a splash, then relaxed when more splashes led to sputtered laughter. He added more wood to the small fire, knowing she'd need to dry her wet hair when she finished.

If she ever finished.

The minutes slid by. Josh kept one ear tuned to the faint sounds from inside the ravine while he readied a meal of salmon and mush cakes flavored with dollops of hardened bear grease. From the sounds of it, she was cavorting around in the pool like a playful seal pup.

The idea of Tatiana's lithe body gliding through bubbling waters curled the muscles in Josh's belly. Despite his best efforts, he couldn't seem to keep at bay a mental picture of her pale, white thighs. Her narrow waist. Her full, rounded breasts. Sweating a little, Josh tried to replace these too vivid images of Tatiana with older, more familiar memories of Catherine.

His betrothed's face hovered just beyond his mental range of vision. He didn't force it. She'd come to him. She always did when he needed her. She'd never left him, really, even in those moments when he'd taken his pleasure with another woman.

Josh hadn't remained celibate all these years. Far from it. Like most other men, he was firmly convinced it went against man's nature to go too long without release. Nor had he felt any guilt about pleasuring a willing partner. But none of the women he'd shared his bed with had ever taken a hold on his heart. That belonged to Catherine.

Still, the thought of bedding down next to Tatiana tonight stirred all kinds of contradictory feelings within him. He experienced a vague sense of disloyalty, and more than a touch of wariness. Sharing a blanket with the Russian was like sleeping with a curly horned mountain goat. There was no predicting which way she'd leap if riled.

Take that incident with the knife, for example. How far would she have gone if he hadn't knocked her feet out from under her? Smiling wryly, Josh fingered the tiny crusted cut on the side of his neck. For both their sakes, he hoped he didn't have to find out.

His smile twisted into a grimace as he encountered the blood caked in his beard. The knifepoint had stuck deeper than he realized. His fingers combed through the thick bush, dislodging the dried blood and a few pine needles. The countess wasn't the only one who needed to scrape off a few layers of trail dirt, he acknowledged.

He glanced over his shoulder at the mouth of the

ravine, then decided against stripping down. That wasn't a good idea, given the way his body reacted to Tatiana without a whole lot of direction or guidance from his head. He could get rid of some of his dirt, though. And maybe…he raked his fingers through his whiskers again. The thick, bushy beard and drooping mustaches had served him well this winter, but his own mother wouldn't recognize him under this hair. Besides, the blasted thing itched.

He shot a glance at the flaming red sun that hung just above the jagged peaks. Its clarity and color promised a night free of storms, maybe even a couple of nights. In two days, three at most, they'd be out of the mountains and starting their descent to the more moderate climates along the coast. He wouldn't need the protection and warmth of a beard anymore this winter.

Josh headed for the stream that trickled from the ravine. Pulling off his shirt to keep it from getting a dousing, he slapped water on his face and went to work. He was kneeling beside the narrow ribbon of water, dabbing at the nicks left by the scrape of his hunting knife across his jaw, when Tatiana returned from her bath. He heard her pause, then cross through the camp to stand a little way behind him. He splashed water over his bare, stinging cheeks and grabbed his buckskin shirt.

He turned, expecting surprise, or maybe just a hint of feminine approval at his clean-shaven countenance.

Hair slicked back with wet, she stared at him with wide eyes. Then her mouth thinned to a tight straight line.

So much for feminine approval.

She nodded to his chin. "Is that because of me?"

"No." Swooping, Josh retrieved the leather belt. "It itched."

"It itches?"

He rubbed a hand over his fresh-scraped jaw. "It did itch. Past tense."

"No, no!" she exclaimed. "I do not speak of the beard."

"Then what...?"

"Here." She stepped forward, bringing with her the faint scent of lye soap and minerals. Her fingertip lightly brushed his neck. "This mark. Is this because of me and the knife?"

Josh jerked at the contact.

"It pains you?" she asked, her eyes darkening.

No, it didn't pain him. But the touch of her hand, as light as it was, caused his muscles to jump. To cover his reaction, Josh gave her a small, nasty smile.

"Feeling guilty, are you?"

"I have not the least guilt," she returned tartly. "Neither do I have the desire to see the wound fester before you bring me to Fort Ross."

She dusted the snow off a boulder with an edge of her cloak. "Here, sit on this rock and let me tend to it."

"It's just a scratch. It doesn't need tending."

"I have no patience with foolishness. Sit, I say, and let me see to it."

For a moment, Josh was tempted. It had been a long time since a woman had fussed over him. He might have given in to her curt order if she hadn't issued it from whitish lips, with vapor curling all around her wet head.

"You're far more likely to need seeing to than me if you don't dry your hair. Come on, let's get back to the fire."

She didn't argue, probably because her teeth were starting to rattle like the shell necklaces of the Hupa during the leaping, stomping White Deerskin Dance.

"I shall dry my hair," she announced. "Then I shall see to your neck."

That sounded safe enough. By the time she finished with her heavy, waist-length mane, Josh would have himself in hand. By then, the mere touch of her fingers wouldn't knot his stomach. Or so he reasoned.

He soon discovered that he'd forgotten...or maybe he'd never known...how the simple act of watching a woman comb her hair could set a man's blood to pounding and push his breath clear down his throat.

She sat cross-legged before the fire, her head bent as she performed the timeless feminine ritual. Her fingers speared and separated the thick dark strands. The comb followed, jerking and tugging through tangles at first, then descending in a smooth sweep.

Mesmerized, Josh cradled a chipped blue enamel mug in both hands. The sludgelike coffee went untasted. Melted bear grease congealed in the pan he'd set out to fry the mush cakes. The sun disappeared behind the peaks, and night dropped like a blanket.

In the light of the fire, Josh studied the angle of her arm as it rose and fell. The curve of her neck. The dark, silky sheen of her hair. By the time she gathered the gleaming mass at the back of her neck and tied it with a strip of rawhide, he didn't figure he could get any more uncomfortable.

He was wrong.

A few moments later Tatiana knelt beside him and put her hands to his jaw to tilt it upward. At the feel of her warm hand on his skin, Josh got stiff and hard and so damned uncomfortable that it was all he could do not to jerk away from her.

Two more days, he told himself. Three at the most. If the weather held, they'd clear the last of the rugged peaks within four days and start the descent to the coast. Another week of easy trekking after that, and he'd be rid of his charge and the unsettling urges she roused in him.

He should have remembered that nothing ever came easy in the mountains.

Chapter Eight

The attack came just after noon on the fourth day.

The travelers had been climbing all morning through gray, chilling clouds. Josh stopped at the summit of a granite bluff. Despite the poor visibility, he recognized enough landmarks to know they'd come through the last of the high peaks. Relief jolted through him, followed by a spike of fierce primal satisfaction. Once again, he'd bested the mountains. Once more, he'd come through snows that kept less intrepid men huddled by their warm, safe hearths throughout the long winter months.

"Why do you stop?" Slushy snow squished under Tatiana's boots as she trudged up to stand beside him.

"I'm just getting my bearings."

She pushed the flat-crowned beaver hat back and swept the gray, hazy panorama with a critical eye. "They are not so high, these hills ahead."

"How can you tell?"

"The snow lies thinner, even on the eastern slopes. And there." She pointed to a long slash of muddy brown. "There, the white is gone entirely beneath the trees."

She had a good eye, Josh thought, and a keener sense of her surroundings than most whites he'd trekked beside. More than once in the past few days she'd surprised him with her stamina and her quick understanding of the rugged terrain they traveled. What was more, she seemed to share his respect for the soaring, silent peaks. She didn't disturb the serenity or jar Josh's nerves with constant chatter as they walked, nor did she complain about the pace. At night, she pulled her share of chores about the camp. Each morning, she got up ready and eager to push on. If the intimate press of their bodies had caused her even half the number of sleepless hours it had caused Josh, she sure as thunder didn't show it.

She would have made a good wife for a mountain man, he admitted with a wry, inner smile. Although he'd paid the bride-price Cho-gam demanded for her with great reluctance, the idea of keeping her slipped into his head at the damnedest moments.

Like when he remembered the slow, sensual movement of her arm as she combed her hair.

Or when she curled her body into his at night.

Or now, when her violet eyes trained on the distant horizon as though it held the same mystery, the same allure for her as it did for Josh.

"Are we through them at last?" she asked softly. "The high mountains?"

"Almost. It's a downhill trek from here to the coast."

"How long then to Fort Ross?"

"A week, give or take a day."

She tipped him a sideways look. "And so this journey shall be finished, Josiah Jones."

"And so it shall."

They were halfway to the bare patch of ground Tatiana had pointed to when Josh's senses picked up the first danger signals. Birds that should have resumed their twittering after the travelers' passage remained silent. A gray squirrel nattering at them from the safety of a tree limb broke off in midscold and darted away. Moments later, the pony lifted its head. Nostrils flaring, it tugged nervously at the end of the lead.

Josh slipped his rifle out of its deerskin case and motioned Tatiana to a safer position between himself and the skittish packhorse.

"What is it?" she asked, her voice low.

"Wolves. They've been with us for a couple miles."

She swept the surrounding trees with a quick, nervous glance. "In Russia, the wolf is the most feared of all wild creatures. It can bring down the sheep and the horse and even the brown bear."

"They've been known to do the same here," Josh replied, then kicked himself when her face went pale. "Near as I can tell, this isn't a large pack. Probably a male and its mate and a few of their offspring. We'll just keep moving."

The fact that they were being trailed by wolves didn't unduly alarm him. The timber wolves that prowled these parts preyed mostly on deer, moose and mountain sheep. They rarely attacked humans unless driven to it by near starvation. Experience had taught Josh that they'd devour the fresh-killed carcass of one of their own as readily as the wild game they hunted. If this pack turned menacing, he'd bring down the first predator he spotted and get Tatiana away while its companions tore the kill apart.

Only gradually did Josh realize that they weren't being stalked by a band, but by a solitary hunter. That alone was enough to make his skin begin to prickle. The fleeting glimpse of a gray shadow racing through the trees did more than prickle his skin. It raised the hair on the back of his neck.

Wolves were highly social animals. Even a male the size of this monster wouldn't hunt alone unless driven to it. It must have somehow lost its mate, or been chased from its pack by a more aggressive, dominant male. In either case, it had to be crazed with hunger to come after them. Grim faced, Josh passed Tatiana the pony's leading rein.

She glanced over her shoulder nervously. "Do you see them?"

"It. I see it. Hold tight to that rein."

Nodding, she wrapped the lead twice around her wrist and grasped it in a folded fist. Josh shifted the Hawken in the crook of his arm and moved slowly down the slope toward a stand of white pine. Eyes straining, he searched the surrounding trees for another glimpse of the gray shadow.

A low, deep-throated rattle set the pony's head to jerking crazily. Josh spun toward the sound.

Beyond their immediate circle, nothing moved. Not a bird, or a branch, or even the drift of a cloud across the snow. Pulling the rifle hammer to full cock, Josh searched the thick stand of pines.

The rattle sounded again, closer this time. Moments later, a snarling, yellow-eyed creature came crashing out of the trees. Foam trailed in long ropes from lips pulled back over bared fangs.

In the half second it took to bring the rifle up, Josh's blood turned to ice in his veins. He'd heard enough tales of mad dogs and wild creatures gone crazed to recognize the signs.

The Hawken roared.

Tatiana screamed.

The wolf spun in midair and crashed to the ground. Then, incredibly, it rose. Trailing blood and spittle, it went down on its haunches.

Cursing, Josh pulled the percussion pistol from his belt. The shot exploded in a blast of gunpowder and smoke at the same instant the wolf sank its jaws into the pony's throat. Terrified, the packhorse rose up on its hind legs. Tatiana shrieked and clawed at the reins wrapped around her wrist.

Snatching out his knife, Josh lunged under her arm. He dodged one flailing hoof and had a fist buried in the wolf's thick, mottled ruff when the pony gave an agonized squeal and threw itself sideways. Yanked into the fray by the pony's frenzied efforts to dislodge its tormentor, Tatiana slammed into Josh.

He lost his balance. Went down. Saw the pony rear above him. Twisting violently, he tried to avoid its razor-edged hooves.

The last thing he heard was Tatiana's shrill scream.

* · * · *

Ever after, Tatiana would break into a sweat every time she relived the seconds that followed.

As frantic as the pony, she smashed a shoulder into its heaving side and shoved it away from Josiah's sprawled body. The packhorse dragged her through the snow for several yards. She freed herself just as the little horse pitched forward onto its knees then toppled to the ground. It stared sightlessly at the sky while blood spurted from its severed jugular and crimsoned the snow. The wolf carcass draped obscenely across its withers like a shaggy fur mantle.

Sobbing with horror and shock, Tatiana turned her back on the carnage. Fear pounded at her with great, hammering blows as she ran back to the man sprawled in the snow and sank to her knees beside him. Her hands shook so badly she could barely get a grip on his arm to turn him onto his back. When she saw the huge, ugly swelling on his temple, she tasted terror.

"Josiah!"

His name was a shrill plea that echoed in an eerie stillness. After such a torrent of shrieks and screams, the quiet terrified Tatiana almost as much as the violence just ended.

"Josiah! Josiah! Do you hear me?"

He didn't respond.

Another sob rose in Tatiana's throat. Choking it back, she pulled off her furred mittens. With one hand, she eased the awkward angle of his neck. With the other, she slid the mittens under his head so that it rested on warmth instead of snow. Then she sat back on her heels and fought to control her spiraling panic.

She must not succumb to the hysteria that welled in her throat. She must think. She must act. She must tend to Josiah.

Shaking violently, she examined the swelling on his temple. The distended, reddish purple bulge seemed to grow even as she watched. Should she lance it? Release the blood gathering under the skin? Or leave it to drain naturally?

She knew nothing of head injuries. Less than nothing. Her ignorance terrified her almost as much as Josiah's utter immobility.

"You will not die," she promised the injured man, praying it was true. "I shall not allow you to die."

Since she had no idea what else to do, Tatiana decided to prick the massive swelling and release the pressure on his skull. Hands shaking violently, she tugged the fringed pouch where he kept his most precious possessions from under his hip. It was in this bag that he carried the picture of his Katerina and here, Tatiana had learned in the past few days, he stashed his tobacco, his extra shot, flint for starting a fire, and the whetstone he used to sharpen his knife. Surely, surely he would carry also that most useful and necessary tool, a bone needle.

She gave a cry of relief when her fumbling fingers uncovered not a bone needle, but one of steel. A good three inches in length, its eye was large enough to thread with a thin strip of rawhide. No doubt he used the implement to stitch his clothing. Cradling his head on her knees, she bent over the ugly purplish mass. It took all of her will to press the tip into the swelling flesh.

Josiah's whole body jerked at the cruel bite of steel.

"Be still," Tatiana pleaded as hot blood poured over her hand. "Be still."

Hours later, she cradled his bandaged head to her breast and alternately cursed and thanked God for this man's great strength. It helped him battle the demons that held him in their grip, but it made the task of tending to him a monumental challenge. Her arms ached from trying to hold his restless body immobile. Her throat was raw from singing the same refrain, over and over.

"Be still," she murmured hoarsely. "Please, Josiah, please. You must be still."

Holy Mother, why didn't he wake? How long would the blow to his temple keep him thus, not awake, not asleep, but tossing feverishly in between?

At the sound of her voice, he quieted for a few blessed moments. Wearily Tatiana sagged against the packs she had retrieved from the horse's stiff carcass. The mounded bundles provided her and Josiah protection from the wind sweeping down off the crags above. The thick buffalo robe protected them from the damp ground.

As the afternoon had waned and drifted toward dusk, Tatiana hadn't left her charge for more than the short time it took her to make a rudimentary camp. That done, she'd dragged the dead wolf as far away from their location as she dared. If other hunters came with the gathering darkness, she could only pray that they would satisfy their hunger on the predator's remains and not follow the blood scent to the horse. She positioned the American's rifle and pistol close at hand, just in case. Then she spread her fur cloak atop the snow, took Josiah into her arms and covered them both with his warm, fleecy blanket coat.

Thus they had stayed for more hours than she cared to count.

In all this time, Josiah had alternated between frightening stillness and a restless, almost frenzied thrashing. Just when Tatiana thought he had slipped into a natural sleep, his limbs would jerk and he'd almost come awake. As he did now!

"Lie still," she crooned. "Lie still."

She rocked him as a mother would a child, gently, soothingly, until her arms felt as though they would pull free of their sockets and her back ached with the strain of his weight.

His tensed muscles relaxed, and Tatiana eased back against the supporting packs once more. Wearily she studied the face nestled against her breast. Without his bushy beard to disguise him, Josiah Jones presented a most striking countenance. Square jawed and rough planed, his face carried the stamp of his mountains.

Like these thrusting granite peaks, he could be cruel. Tatiana hadn't forgotten or quite forgiven him for the night he'd left her in such discomfort, her hands bound and her imagination whirling with plans for revenge. Like the mountains, he could also surprise her with his swift changes. He'd gone back for her basket and altered his route to deliver her to Fort Ross. She didn't understand him, but after almost a week in his company, she trusted him with her life.

Strange, she thought, her gaze roaming his rugged

face. She had not thought she could trust, ever again.
Nor had she imagined she would again feel this slow
pull, low in her womb, when she looked on a man.
After Aleksei, she'd vowed never again to let desire
rule her head or her heart. Yet this rough, brusque
American stirred needs and longings she'd all but forgotten.

Lightly Tatiana traced her fingers along his chin.
The skin was pale where he had scraped the beard
away, and warm to her touch. The curve of his jaw
was now as familiar to her as her own.

What would it be like to be held tight in his arms?
To share more than his warmth when darkness blanketed the earth? To glory once more in her woman-
hood? How would it feel to be loved again, and cher-
ished, if only for a night?

Her fingertips followed the line of his lower lip. He
frowned at the light touch. Mumbling incoherently, he
turned his face into her breast.

"Shh." Tatiana rocked him gently. "Shh."

He muttered low, disjointed phrases. A single word
carried to Tatiana clearly.

"Catherine."

She stilled. Her eyes fixed unseeing on the darkness
beyond the fire. Slowly, wearily, she began to rock
him once more.

Her eyelids fluttered. She forced them up. Moments
later, they drifted down again.

Tatiana had no idea how long she slept before she
came to with a small start. For a confused, panicky
moment, she tried to identify where she was and why

she'd regained her senses so suddenly. The reason came to her in a crash of fear.

Josiah!

She no longer held him in her arms. They were empty, as was the makeshift bed the two of them had shared. Alarm lurched through her in great surging waves. She scrambled to her knees, only to crumple back to the fur at the feel of a firm, reassuring hand on her shoulder.

"I'm here." Josiah knelt beside her, his eyes clear and unclouded.

The fear and the worry that had built in her for so many hours burst. Sobbing, Tatiana flung her arms around him and clutched him to her bosom again.

"At last you are awake!"

Josh thought about telling her that he'd been awake for more than an hour. That he'd used the quiet time while she slept to subdue the ferocious hammering in his skull and cleanse himself of blood and gore. That the entire time he'd worked, her musky, womanly scent had stayed with him, until he'd developed an ache in his lower body a hundred times sharper than the one he'd chased out of his head. Instead, he stroked her hair and waited for her choking cries to dwindle to hiccuping sobs.

"I saw the carcasses," he said when at last she quieted. "What happened?"

She answered in a teary, shaking voice. "The wolf came, and then the pony, it kicked you. Most soundly. I made the camp and waited for you to wake."

The brief recital left out a few pertinent details. Like where she'd found the strength to tend to the camp and to him. And why a woman who'd tried to carve a totem on his windpipe a few days ago had taken to nuzzling him to her breast. At this moment, though, Josh wasn't concerned about those missing details. He'd get them later. Right now, he had to force out the question that had haunted him since he'd first opened his eyes.

"Did the wolf bite you, or scratch you, or mix its blood with yours?"

She shuddered. "No, no!"

"Are you sure?"

"I am sure."

Josh drew in a deep breath. He knew as well as any man of the mountains that there wasn't any cure for the madness that came from the bite of a crazed canine. While Tatiana had sprawled in exhausted slumber, he'd steeled himself for the worst and checked his body for puncture wounds. He'd found no injuries except the lump on his temple. He hadn't found any marks on Tatiana's face or limbs, either, but he'd needed to hear her confirmation to banish the tight coil of worry in his belly.

He wasn't the only one who'd worried, he discovered a moment later.

"I...I thought that you would never again wake, Josiah Jones."

Her eyes swam with tears. They traced silvery trails down her cheeks and brought home to Josh all she'd suffered in the past weeks. Reaching out, he brushed away a tear with his thumb.

"It would take more than a pony's kick to do any

permanent damage to my cast-iron skull, Countess Karanova.''

Smiling weakly, she curved a cheek into his palm. "But you were so still, and then so restive. I feared at times I must tie you down, as you tied me.''

The reminder of how he'd treated her made Josh squirm. "I'm sorry about that.''

She sniffed. "Me, also. It was most uncomfortable.''

Josh started to pull his hand away. Somehow it got wrapped around the curve of her neck. Gently he massaged her tight, knotted muscles.

"Ahh.''

The sigh slipped through her lips. Her head went back. Bonelessly she slumped against him. Using both hands now, Josh worked the stiffness from her neck and shoulders. He was only returning in small measure the care she'd just given him, he assured himself.

Which didn't explain why he drew her around some moments later and kissed her, but by then Josh had gone beyond explanations. He saw only the tracks her tears had left on her pale, smooth skin and her generous, all too seductive mouth.

Unlike their first kiss, he meant this one to be gentle. A soothing of her fears. A sharing of her burdens. A token of his thanks for her care. Just like the first, however, it took on a life of its own the moment his lips touched hers. What started soft and warm and tame built without warning into hard and hot and primitive.

Her lips opened under his. The fingers Josh had curled around her neck speared through her loose, silky braid and anchored her head. His tongue found hers with a hunger Josh had tried to deny for too long.

Abruptly he shifted. Ignoring the brief protest from his temple, he pulled Tatiana into his lap. Her arms threaded tightly around his neck. Straining, she pressed her chest to his.

By the time Josh remembered his promise not to take what she had offered in trade for his escort through the mountains, it was almost too late. Her dress had hiked around her hips. His shirt had pulled free of his belt, baring his chest to her eager hands. Desire tumbled through his veins like fiery, potent brandy.

"I'm sorry," he muttered.

He tried to put some space between them. She wouldn't be moved.

"Wait, Tatiana," he said raggedly. "I promised you that I wouldn't..."

"Do not!" She slapped a palm across his mouth. "Do not speak to me of promises! Or of lost loves. I don't wish to remember the hurt, Josiah Jones. I want only to feel as a woman feels. Just for tonight. Just for now." Tears brimmed in her eyes once more. "If...if it doesn't pain you, let me lose myself in your strength."

If *he* didn't lose himself in *her*, it would more than pain Josh. It would cripple him. He wanted this stubborn, contrary, seductive Russian as he'd never wanted another woman.

"Just for tonight, Josiah," she whispered. "Please."

He'd take her slowly, he vowed with savage intensity. Although his muscles knotted and his hands grew slick as he slid her dress up over her hips, he'd make her feel as a woman was supposed to feel or kill himself in the trying.

Her skin was like the finest, smoothest cream, warm to his touch until the cold air kissed it. Her belly rippled under his spread palms. Her hips curved to a narrow waist. Josh raised himself on one elbow and raked a hungry glance down the length of her slender body. Then a jerk of his arm pulled the capote over them both. Black, smothering darkness captured their heat.

Contorting his body to fit Tatiana's, Josh tasted her. She squirmed at the rasp of his tongue on her stomach. The movement raised her dress above her waist. Josh shoved it even higher and took a tight-budded nipple in his mouth.

Gasping, she cradled his head to her breast once more. Only this time, there was nothing of a mother nuzzling a babe in her hold. This time, she arched under him and offered herself as a woman does to her man.

Desire sliced at Josh like the cut of a bullwhip. Suckling, teasing, worrying the tender flesh with the edge of his teeth, he wrapped an arm around her waist and dragged her into the center of his own heat.

The feel of a hard knee prying hers apart roused Tatiana from a whirling vortex of sensation. She tensed in an instinctive and wholly futile attempt to deny the hand that delved between her legs. Momentary panic crashed through her. No man had ever touched her thus, except her husband. Even Aleksei had never pinned her with his weight and held her spread so wide and helpless while he opened her to his touch. Nor had he ever…she gave a strangled cry. Sweet heaven above, he'd never done that!

Her face burning, Tatiana felt her juices dew the fingers that slid in and out, in and out. Readying her. Claiming her.

When Josiah's thumb found the tight nub of flesh at her core, she forgot her embarrassment. Forgot her dignity. Forgot everything but the white-hot sensation splintering through her.

And when he thrust into her, she lost herself in his hard, muscled strength.

Chapter Nine

Josh awoke just before dawn with a single burning need. With everything in him, he wanted to roll Tatiana onto her back and bury his rigid shaft in her satiny heat once more.

He lay tangled in the furs, staring up at the fading stars as he fought for control. Wrenching his mind and his senses from the woman at his side, he forced himself to think about the ravages the wolf had caused. The sorting and repacking of supplies he'd have to accomplish. The day's journey. Anything but the feel of Tatiana's legs entwined with his!

They should clear the mountains today and start the descent to the coast. Tonight they'd camp within sound of the sea. They'd spend at least another week en route to Fort Ross...unless Josh took a slower, more circuitous route.

When he realized what he was thinking, he stiffened. He couldn't extend the trek just to spend a few more nights with Tatiana. They both had urgent, all-too-different reasons for wanting to reach Fort Ross as quickly as possible.

She hoped to save it, and her father, with her precious bundles of twigs.

Josh wanted to verify the details of the fort's uncertain future and, if possible, secure its possession for the United States.

The thought of Tatiana's anger if and when she learned of his real reasons for accompanying her to the Russian fort made Josh throw back the furs. Muttering a sleepy protest at the loss of his warmth, she curled in a tight ball. Fire speared through his loins at the sight of her long, slender legs and the gleam of one rounded hip. Gritting his teeth, Josh drew the covers up to her chin.

His jaw tight, he righted his clothing, fed the fire and put the coffee on to boil before digging through the packs for his ax. He needed to construct a travois to haul their supplies. Even more, he needed to think…and to shake this nagging sense of guilt.

Moments later he selected a tall thin pine and swung the blade. The ax blade bit into the trunk with a solid thud. Wrenching it free, Josh swung again. With each blow, he reminded himself of his mission.

He was an officer in the army of the United States!

Under orders from the president!

Van Buren would want him to follow up on the information Tatiana had let slip about Fort Ross.

Except…the ax stilled in midswing…he'd gone well beyond his orders last night.

By giving in to his mindless, rutting lust for Tatiana, he'd complicated an already uncomfortable situation. What was worse, Josh knew damn well he'd taken advantage of her temporary weakness to satisfy that lust. She'd been shaken by fear, by the aftermath of the carnage left by the wolf. Despite her pleas to him to love her, she'd really wanted comforting and reassurance.

Disgust with himself roiled through Josh's gut, and a determination to get Tatiana to Fort Ross before he scarred her far worse than any wolf.

The blade slammed into the trunk a final time. With a series of sharp cracks and groans, the tall pine began to fall. Grimly Josh started on the second tree.

The sound of the pine's crashing descent brought Tatiana awake. She lay still under the furs, trying groggily to identify the sound. A few moments later, she picked up the rhythmic bite of Josiah's ax.

Tugging the blanket down, she breathed in cold, crisp air. Faint streaks of pink and gold ribboned the dark sky above her. She stared up at the shifting, glowing ribbons, knowing she should rise. But for the first time since setting out from the Valley of the Hupa, she wasn't eager to resume her journey.

A curious languor seemed to weight her limbs. She longed to draw the capote to her nose and lie abed until servants miraculously appeared with a pot of hot chocolate and a plate of the rich, currant-filled pastries the Countess Karanova had always begun her days with.

Even stronger than her physical lassitude, however, was her reluctance to face Josiah. How *could* she face him, after what had occurred between them last night?

Her fingers clutched at the blanket coat as vivid, startling images darted through her mind. By Saint

Petr, had she really wrapped her legs around the man and begged him to love her? Was that really she, Tatiana Grigoria, daughter of a count and once wife to a captain of the Imperial Guards, who groaned and gasped and writhed in his arms like the veriest wanton in the throes of her passion?

But what passion it was!

Never, ever had Tatiana imagined herself capable of such shattering, shuddering pleasure. Or dreamed, for even a moment, that the American could bring it about. Despite the giggles and pointed comments the Hupa women had let drop about his talents under the blankets, Tatiana had never known anything to compare with Josiah Jones's impact on her body and her senses.

What had she been thinking of, to lose herself in his arms like that? She couldn't give herself over to mindless pleasure, not with so much at stake. She'd done that once, and nearly lost her head as well as her heart. She must conserve her strength and her energies for this endless journey.

Greatly troubled, she dragged herself upright and searched among the tangled furs for her clothing. To the steady, ringing whack of the ax, she dressed and cleansed herself with melted snow, then poured thick, bitter coffee into a tin mug. Sipping slowly, she contemplated just what she would say to Josiah when he reappeared. She was so absorbed in this difficult task that she didn't hear him approach.

"Are you ready to walk?"

Startled, Tatiana looked up to find him standing over her, hands thrust into his belt. She knew him well enough by now to see the wariness in his gold-flecked eyes. Slowly she set her mug aside.

"Yes, I am ready."

"I'll load the packs. Then we'll move out. I want to make camp in the lowlands tonight."

His brusque tone stung, as did his closed, guarded expression.

"I shall pack the eating utensils, then," she replied evenly. "And we shall unpack them tonight in these lowlands you speak of."

Tatiana rose, silently berating herself. What had she expected? That he would languish at her feet like a besotted courtier? That he would greet her with an ode to her beauty? Her womanliness? She herself had set the boundaries to their joining. They had come together for one night. For a few moments of breathless passion. That was all she had asked of him. All she wanted of him. That, and his escort to Fort Ross.

Evidently that was all he wanted of her, too, as his next words confirmed.

"It seems I'm always apologizing to you, Countess."

Tatiana stiffened. "For what do you apologize this time, Josiah?"

"For last night."

Pride lifted her chin. Hurt gave her voice a brittle edge. "You are sorry for last night?"

He looked away briefly, and Tatiana guessed that he was thinking of his Katerina. His precious Katerina. Her hurt sharpened into something she refused to admit was jealousy. She could not, she would not feel jealousy of a woman long dead!

"I'm not sorry it happened," he said after a moment. "No man in his right mind could be. But it can't happen again."

"Do not fear," she replied in a voice tipped with scorn. "It shall not happen again."

And the next time a horse kicked his thick head, she vowed, she would let the blood build in his skull until it burst!

The angry glitter in Tatiana's eyes warned Josh that he was bungling this badly. He wanted to tell her the truth. Even more, he wanted to pull her into his arms and kiss the scorn from her ripe, tantalizing mouth.

Instead, he watched her turn away to gather the scattered items. Forcing himself to move, as well, he laced the buffalo robe between the poles he'd just cut and began to load supplies onto the travois he'd drag behind him. The last item he added to the pile was Tatiana's basket.

By noon, the confining mountains gave way to rolling foothills. By nightfall, they reached a broad, almost level stretch of forest broken by occasional prairies. Rain fell in continuous sheets, making for a wet, cold camp that night. Tatiana shared a bed with Josiah, but she took little comfort from his body's heat. To her disgust, it disturbed her most greatly, and kept her stiff and rigid in a futile attempt to avoid contact.

The next day she heard the roar of the ocean through the rain and fog. Deep and ominous as a great, booming cannon, it crashed against a shoreline that Josiah informed her was yet many miles away. Tatiana shivered under her fur cloak, remembering her last encounter with the sea.

Late that afternoon the American led the way into a village of a people he called the Wiyot. The inhabitants who greeted them carried guns and swords and wore various pieces of sailor's garb with their own, exquisitely decorated skins. Many sported beads and brass trinkets that could only have come from traders, as well as long, pointed dentalium shells through their noses.

The men welcomed Josiah in a language he seemed to readily understand and offered food and drink. The women took Tatiana to a lodge where she gratefully steamed away long days of travel. After a meal consisting primarily of fried whale blubber, wild onions and a roasted, bulbous root the size of a hen's egg which Josiah identified as a swamp potato, Tatiana collapsed onto a pallet in the corner of the chief's lodge.

Josh spent most of the night trading news with his hosts, drinking bitter beer, and fighting his desire to join her in the soft, warm bed. His head ached as much as his groin when the fire burned low and the Wiyot chieftain nudged him in the ribs with a sharp elbow. Augmenting his words with signs and gestures, the headman nodded to the sleeping Tatiana.

"I see your eyes go often to the woman. Did she really walk with you through the mountains?"

"She did."

"She is strong, and brave, to make this walk."

"Yes, she is."

The headman grunted and held out a cup carved

from whalebone. "Drink, then go join your woman and take your ease of her so you may rest well this night. You have a long way yet to travel."

Josh's gaze slid to the recumbent figure. He wanted nothing more than to take his ease of her. His jaw working, he pulled his eyes away and took the cup.

"The woman can wait," he said tightly, downing the contents in two long swallows. "First, we must decide on a price for the horses you will sell me."

The headman waved a hand. "You need no horses for this journey. The Wiyot build great boats to hunt the whale and the sea lion. In one, maybe two days our boats shall carry you and your woman to the land of the Pomo and this Russian fort."

Josh's stomach twisted. One, maybe two days in the company of the friendly Wiyot and Tatiana's journey would at last end. He nodded slowly.

"I thank you."

"There!" Josh shouted. "On that bluff!"

Keeping a tight grip with one hand on the side of the huge, hollowed log that the Wiyot sent skimming over the waves with such skill, Tatiana dashed her wet hair out of her eyes with the other. Squinting through the whipping rain, she followed the line of Josiah's arm.

He leaned forward until his chest touched her shoulder. Even so, she could barely hear him above the boom made by the sea as it spent itself against a long line of gray cliffs.

"Do you see it?"

"No!"

"There, the round tower with the cross atop it."

Tatiana searched the rain-shrouded promontories high above the surging sea. Suddenly she saw it! The structure Josiah pointed to. It was set back from the cliffs, barely visible in the swirling rain. Yet the merest glimpse of the distinctive Russian Orthodox cross wrung a cry of joy from her lips.

It symbolized all she knew. All she was. With that double-barred cross came bearded patriarchs. Brilliantly painted icons. A religious faith that shaped Tatiana's every thought. She blinked eyes already teared by the wet, stinging cold and gave a fervent prayer of thankfulness for her deliverance.

The prayer still tumbled from her numbed lips when she saw another symbol of Russia whipping in the wind on a flagstaff some distance from the cross. Her fingers dug into the boat's side.

The double-headed eagle of Imperial Russia showed against a field of white. Below the eagle was a slash of red and one of blue. Nikolas's flag. The man whose fury and thirst for vengeance had brought her here, so far from her home and all she had held dear.

Damn him. Thrice damn him.

Her eyes stayed fixed on the snapping, curling flag until the boat drew closer into shore and the high palisaded wall of the fort cut it from view.

Tatiana clung to the boat's sides as pounding waves pushed it toward a small, rock-strewn cove some hundred or more feet below the fort's walls. She caught a fleeting glimpse of a bearded sentry leaning out a window of the fort's eight-sided log blockhouse. He waved an arm and shouted something, no doubt ascertaining their status as friend or foe.

Josiah shouted a reply, but Tatiana paid no heed to his brief message. Shoulders hunched, insides all aquiver, she gripped the boat's sides with both hands and cringed back, as though to escape the onrushing rocks and foaming surf.

Josiah's arms came around her. Strong. Sure. Steady.

"Don't fear." His voice was warm and reassuring in her head. "After bringing you this far, I won't let you come to grief now."

Absurdly Tatiana believed him.

Several short, stocky men from a tribe Josiah identified as Pomo met them at the base of the cliffs. They helped drag the great oceangoing canoe high onto the rocky beach. While the head Pomo conferred with the leader of the Wiyot crew, Josiah guided a still-shaky Tatiana to a set of wooden stairs. The steps switched back and forth across the cliff face, leading up...and up...and up!

Tatiana took the first stairs with a swift, eager foot. By the time she reached the top of the cliffs, her breath came in ragged gasps. Her sodden cloak dragged at her neck like a sack of stones and her slippery boots could barely hold to the treads. With a final boost from behind, Josiah propelled her up the last stairs and she stood at the top of the cliffs.

Fort Ross rose before her. A palisade of tall, straight redwood logs sharpened to spikes at their tops surrounded the entire fort. The small gate in its western wall was guarded by cannons bristling from the portholes of the eight-sided blockhouse and by sentries who peered through the rain to watch Tatiana's approach.

Although the Russian inhabitants of the fort had coexisted peacefully for more than twenty years with the Spanish and the Pomo tribesmen who populated the area, it was readily apparent that its governor, Alexander Rotchev, allowed no slackness in security.

Tatiana drew in several gulping breaths, then marched toward the small gate. It opened while she was yet some yards away. A tall, thin young man in spectacles and a black frock coat came forward to greet them. His shoulders hunched against the rain, he ignored Tatiana and offered Josiah a courteous welcome. His English was broken but easily understandable.

"My greetings, sir. I am Mikhail Pulkin, acting *prikashchiki* to Baron Alexander Rotchev, the manager of this outpost of the Russian Fur Company. In his absence, I welcome you and your..." He gave Tatiana a tentative smile. "Your, ah, wife, to Fort Ross."

Belatedly she realized the picture she must present. Her wet, straggly hair, drooping fur cloak and buckskin leggings were bad enough. The turkey feather poking from the band of the hat that dangled down her back only added to her disreputable air.

"I am not this man's wife," she informed Pulkin in swift, flowing Russian. "I am Tatiana Grigoria, Countess Karanova, and I wish to speak with the Princess Helena immediately."

The clerk's pale blue eyes bulged behind his rain-spattered spectacles. "Count...Countess Karanova?"

"Yes, it is I."

"But...but you were lost overboard!"

"Yes, yes, I was lost, and I am sure you all thought me dead. But I am here now, and—" she lifted a brow "—I am *most* chilled."

Her aristocratic tone decided the matter instantly. Bowing up and down like a child's toy on a string, the stammering, stuttering young factor ushered Tatiana to the gate.

Josh grinned. Although he hadn't understood a word of the exchange, he'd caught the down-your-nose stare Tatiana had turned on this Mikhail fellow. The poor man all but fell over his feet to get out of her way as she swept into the compound.

Josh followed at a more measured pace. His trained eye cataloged the fort's defenses, noting changes since his only visit years ago. The stockade was as well built as he remembered, with blockhouses in opposite corners to control every approach. He counted at least four cannons in each tower.

The high walls enclosed some seven or eight buildings, all constructed of redwood timber aged to a drab brown by time and the weather. A large two-story warehouse stood against the north wall of the compound, and a long barracks-type dwelling against the south. The chapel dominated all other buildings. Occupying a rise in the northeast corner of the compound, it lifted two squat, round towers to the rainy sky. Each tower was topped by the curious Russian crosses.

A fierce determination filled Josh as he surveyed the sturdy, well-maintained fortifications. Whatever it took, he'd keep them from falling into the hands of the British or French.

Tatiana's progress across the grassy compound caused a great stir of interest. Clerks and artisans and one or two women in long dresses and aprons spilled out of buildings. Heedless of the rain, they were as anxious as any isolated settlers to greet visitors. They gaped at Tatiana, evidently unused to the sight of a woman in native garb regally striding ahead of men. Mikhail Pulkin's whispered asides as he hurried along behind her raised a buzz of exclamations in Russian.

Mounting the shallow steps to the front entrance of the single-story dwelling, Tatiana rapped on the door. Some moments later, the wood panel opened to reveal a short, slender blonde in an elegant gown of blue wool. Her eyes rounded at her first sight of her visitor. They rounded even more when Tatiana sank into a graceful curtsy and uttered a soft, flowing phrase in Russian.

"Ta...Tatiana?"

Rising, the younger woman essayed a shaky smile. "*Da*, Helena."

With a shrill screech, the blonde threw herself through the doorway. Laughing, sobbing, exclaiming volubly in Russian and French, the two women fell into each other's arms.

Josh and the clerk stood patiently, the rain pounding down on their heads and shoulders as they watched the joyous reunion. Finally a laughing Tatiana pulled free.

"Come, let us get out of this wet," she said in English, including Josh in the conversation for the first time. "And then I shall introduce you to my escort. He brought me from the mountains, Helena, where I was taken after I washed into the sea."

Chattering like a magpie, she went inside. In her excitement, she didn't notice that her friend's initial, spontaneous joy had faded. Her eyes now troubled, the older woman followed the countess in buckskin through the open door.

With the clerk a half step behind him, Josh stepped over the threshold into a room that might have been transported from a stately town house in one of the world's capitals. Gold velvet draped its glass-paned windows. A thick Turkish carpet in brilliant jewel tones covered the plank floor. Heavy furnishings in a dark wood were arranged before an ornate brass fire screen that caught the sparks leaping from a bright fire. A pianoforte took up one corner of the room. In the other corner, gilt-edged books filled floor-to-ceiling shelves.

"This is the Princess Helena Palovna Rotcheva," Tatiana announced, claiming Josh's attention. "Niece to the Tsar of all Russias, wife to Baron Alexander Rotchev, and a most particular friend of my youth. Princess, may I present Monsieur Josiah Jones."

Josh propped his Hawken against a wall and crossed to the dark-eyed, stunningly beautiful woman. Her face grave, she held out her hand. He took it in his, bowed at just the proper angle and dropped a light kiss on the back of her fingers.

Helena didn't appear the least surprised at the

smooth, polished gesture from a man in travel-worn deerskins. Tatiana, on the other hand, stared at him in some indignation.

"Why did you never accord me such courtesy?" she demanded tartly.

Josh shot her a brief, slashing grin. "Maybe because you never earned it."

"Pah!"

With a flip of her wet hair, she turned her back to her friend, who'd listened to the brief exchange with some surprise.

"Despite this…this seeming lack of respect, Monsieur Jones provided me safe escort through the mountains, Helena. It was the most fantastical journey, but now it is done. I've brought the Tsar's Treasure with me. What I could salvage from the sea, that is. My father will be saddened to hear so much was lost."

The princess's face tightened into stark lines. "Tatiana…"

"No, no! Do not fear. I know my father wrote your husband that he was sending many bundles of cuttings, enough to propagate a full orchard. I saved only a small portion of the treasure, it is true, but even these few will show the tsar how we can increase the yield here. We can yet save Fort Ross, and lift the yoke of his vengeance from my own and my father's neck."

"Tatiana, dearest."

The concern in the princess's voice communicated itself to Josh, if not to the bedraggled younger woman. Something was wrong here, and he sensed that it didn't have anything to do with fruit trees.

Making her own interpretation of her friend's worried countenance, Tatiana rushed on. "These cuttings shall take, Helena, I swear! My father knows whereof he speaks. He sent some of the same cuttings to the Royal Horticulturist at the court of King Rudolph and the king himself—"

"Your father is dead."

Silence dropped over the room like a hammer. Stunned. Disbelieving. Anguished.

Taking Tatiana's hands in both of hers, the princess poured out the news in an agonized rush. "A ship sailed from Vladivostok just weeks after yours to bring you the news. It dropped anchor almost the same day we learned you were lost. I'm sorry, my dearest friend. I'm so sorry. I know how much you loved him."

For long moments, Tatiana didn't move, didn't speak. Nor did Josh. He couldn't help her. No one could, as he knew all too well. She had to suffer through this in her own way.

But at that moment he would have given his arm to spare her the pain he saw in her white, pinched face.

"How...?" She closed her eyes and dragged in a ragged breath. Her lids lifted slowly to reveal pools of torment. "How did he die?"

"We were told he had a cough." Helena said brokenly.

"Da," Tatiana whispered. "He did."

"He started bringing up blood soon after you left. He died in his own bed. He...he used the last of his strength to call a blessing upon his daughter."

With a small animal moan, Tatiana crumpled.

Josh caught her just before she hit the floor.

Chapter Ten

"**B**ring her here!"

Her face white and stricken, Helena shoved open the door to a room just off the central living area. Issuing a series of short staccato orders that sent Mikhail Pulkin scurrying, she hurried into the bedroom. Ruthlessly she swept a collection of dolls and toys from an elaborately carved sleigh bed and yanked back the feather-filled counterpane.

"This is my daughters' room," she said distractedly while Josh placed his limp burden on the bed. "They're with their father and my son, and will return soon. In the meantime, I shall tend to the countess. Oh, the poor, poor dear! She's so wet, and chilled."

She bent over Tatiana and fumbled with the strings of her fur cloak. The tough, wet rawhide strands defied her efforts.

"I'll do it," Josh told her. Shrugging out of his coat, he edged the princess aside. "You'd best dry yourself before you take a chill, too. And stir up something hot to drink."

"Yes, yes, it is already ordered." Helena pushed

her hair back from her forehead with a shaking hand. "I've sent Mikhail to rouse the servants from their quarters behind the house."

"Go change," Josh ordered brusquely. "I'll take care of Tatiana."

Helena stared at his broad back, as surprised by his curt instruction to a princess royal as by his use of her friend's given name. At the tsar's court, either could cost a man his tongue, if not his head. Even here, where everyday life demanded strenuous labor from princess and commoner alike, Helena was careful to maintain the distinction of her station.

Unaware of her scrutiny, the American pulled off Tatiana's cloak and tossed it aside, then eased the hem of her fringed dress up to her thighs. Frowning in concentration, he went to work on the laces of her furred leggings.

Helena eyes widened. By Saint Sophia! Her friend wore nothing but those leggings under the dress! And this man's hands moved over her body with a most startling familiarity.

Good! A fierce satisfaction shot through Helena as she turned and hurried to her own bedroom. Good! With all the grief the handsome, charming and so *very* irresponsible Aleksei had brought Tatiana these past years, Helena sincerely hoped that her friend had finally had a taste of a real man on this fantastical journey of hers.

Just a taste. Just enough to rid her once and for all of any memories of her despicable husband.

Helena slammed the door to her room, not a little shocked by the vehemence of her feelings. In love with her own husband to the point of idiocy, she had never once been tempted to break her vows. When her Uncle Nikolas had sent clever, loyal, hardworking Alexander to this farthest reach of the Russian Empire in an attempt to make it once again a profitable enterprise, Helena had packed up her babies, her servants and her belongings and accompanied him without a backward glance. Before she'd left St. Petersburg, though, she'd tried to warn a young, laughing Tatiana of Aleksei's shallow character.

She'd failed, as everyone must fail who attempts to speak sensibly to a person in the passionate throes of first love.

Helena's heart had ached when she'd learned of Aleksei's part in the disastrous, failed plot against the tsar. She hadn't spared a flicker of sympathy for the traitorous officer who lost his life as a result, but she'd known that Tatiana, too, would suffer for her husband's acts.

Which she had. Holy Mother, she had. Word of the tsar's vengeance had reached even Fort Ross.

Now her friend was here, without husband or father. And here she would stay, Helena vowed silently, throwing aside her wet dress. Here she would work out her grief and regain her strength and, the princess prayed, learn to laugh once more.

Perhaps even to love again.

An image of the tall, broad-shouldered American sprang into Helena's mind. She remembered the heart-stopping grin he'd turned on the countess, and their careless, somewhat shocking exchange. Despite his rough clothes and so great size, he possessed a smooth address. He'd kissed her hand with as much polish as any aristocrat. Helena wondered who he was. She would instruct Alexander to find out, she decided, pulling on a dry gown.

But first she must tend to her friend.

After a swift detour to the kitchen to hurry the servants, she raided her husband's private stock of spirits. Bottle and goblet in hand, she bustled back into her daughters' room and shooed the American away from the bed.

"Go with Mikhail. He will take you to the men's quarters, where you may change from your wet clothes. I'll see to the countess."

He relinquished his place with obvious reluctance. "She's starting to stir."

"So I see."

"She needs something hot inside her."

"Yes, yes, the samovar is already heating. I shall give her green tea infused with herbs. In the meantime, she shall have a touch of spirits."

He hung over Helena's shoulder. "What kind of spirits?"

"Kvass."

Worry gnawed at Josh like a hungry wolf. With all Tatiana had endured on the long trek, she'd never fainted or shown the least physical weakness. Now she lay so still, and so damned pale.

The glass bottle clinked against the goblet. Helena poured a generous measure of cloudy liquid, then thrust the decanter into the American's hands.

"Drink heartily yourself. It will warm you. Then, please, go with Mikhail."

He tipped the bottle to his lips and took a long, deep pull. The colorless liquid released its fire halfway to his gullet. Suddenly Josh's eyes widened. His throat seized, and beads of sweat popped out all over his body.

"Hellfire and dam-nation!"

He held the bottle out and regarded it with awe. He'd downed some potent liquor in his time, made from just about every substance that could be mashed, boiled or buried in a crock to ferment. None of those concoctions had a kick anywhere close to this one.

"What did you call this?"

"Kvass," the princess replied. "Vodka, it is known here."

"Vodka, huh?"

Cradling her friend's head against her bosom, Helena poured several small sips into her mouth. Almost instantly, the fiery liquor produced a similar effect on the unconscious woman.

Tatiana swallowed. Choked. Jerked awake. She stared at Helena's face for several seconds, then burst into tears. The princess dropped the goblet and wrapped her arms around the weeping woman. Soothing, rocking, sobbing herself, she comforted her friend.

Josh's fingers gripped the bottle as a swift, irrational need rushed through him. He should be the one holding Tatiana, as she'd held him. He should be rocking and murmuring to her, as she'd had with him. He should comfort her.

Frowning, he gathered his wet coat and left the room. The young clerk met him in the hall, his blue eyes tragic behind the round spectacles.

"The poor countess, to suffer such loss! First her husband, and now her father."

Nodding, Josh strode toward the rifle propped against the wall.

"At least she is once again with her own people to give her comfort," Mikhail commented.

"Yes, she is."

Josh wondered why that fact afforded him so little satisfaction. Tatiana was safe and warm and among her own kind. She'd reached Fort Ross, as she'd been determined to do.

Tucking the Hawken into its niche in the crook of his arm, he headed for the door. The clerk accompanied him out into the cold drizzle.

"Baron Rotchev should return before the dinner hour," Mikhail said, pulling his collar up against the rain. "He will wish to speak with you."

Mention of the baron brought Josh's mission slamming back to the forefront of his mind.

"I wish to speak to him, as well."

Some hours later, Mikhail Pulkin escorted the American to the manager's residence once more.

Mikhail, Josh had learned, was the second son of an admiral of the Russian Imperial Fleet. Having shown little military inclination as a boy, he'd been sent to Fort Ross to make his fortune and his future with the Russian Fur Company. He'd started as a lowly company scribe and worked his way up to his current title of acting chief clerk.

"I fill this position only temporarily, you understand," he confided to Josh as they crossed the compound. "If I prove myself, perhaps it shall be mine permanently." His eager smile faded. "Or perhaps a similar position in Archangel, if we...if I must leave Fort Ross."

Josh picked up the quick correction, but they arrived at the manager's residence before he had time to probe further. A tall, balding man with shrewd gray eyes and a kind smile, Baron Alexander Rotchev greeted him warmly.

"Please, please come in, Monsieur Jones. You are most welcome in my home. My wife has told me of your great services to Countess Karanova."

"How is she?"

The baron shook his head. "Most saddened. They were very close, she and her father."

"Yes, she told me."

"She sleeps now. My wife stays with her, you understand, in case she should awaken. If you please, let Augustine take your coat."

Josh shrugged out of his coat and handed it to the waiting servant. He'd traded his travel-stained buckskins for his only cloth shirt and a pair of borrowed trousers. Several of the Russians had offered the loan of a broadcloth coat, but none of their garments would stretch across his shoulders. He settled for tying a white stock around his throat and knotting it in a neat fall.

The baron gestured courteously to the chairs arranged in front of the fire. "Come, join me for a drink. Then you must tell me how you came to serve as the countess's escort on her incredible journey. Mikhail, you will pour, if you please, and join us."

The clerk went to a tall, carved sideboard and returned with three goblets. Josh eyed them warily. He couldn't take much more of the fiery vodka on an empty stomach. To his relief, the aromatic scent of fine aged brandy rose from his cup.

Baron Rotchev offered a toast to their safe arrival at Fort Ross, and to the tsar. Josh offered one to his host's gracious welcome. The civilities out of the way and their bellies sufficiently warmed, they settled back in their chairs.

"So, Monsieur Jones..."

"Josiah, if you please, sir. Or, if you have a mind to it, just Josh. We don't hold much with formalities east of the Sierra Nevadas."

Rotchev smiled. "So I have discovered. You will tell me, Josh, how it was that you became escort to our countess."

Josh figured he could answer that question any one of a dozen ways. He could relate Cho-gam's determined efforts to sell off his unwilling, uncomfortable bride. Or Tatiana's startling offer to share Josh's blankets in exchange for his services as a guide. Or her desperate determination to haul her basket of twigs to Fort Ross, even if she had to slit Josh's throat to do it. He settled for a shrug.

"I found her in the Valley of the Hupa, where she'd been taken after her rescue from the sea. I tried to persuade her to wait there until the snows melted before attempting the high passes, but she was determined to get to Fort Ross with her bundle of sticks."

"Ahh, yes. The Tsar's Treasure." The baron swirled the brandy in his goblet. "Her father is...was a most renowned horticulturist. He wrote to me of his experiments with apple and pear trees. He believed that he'd developed a new, most hardy variety which would flourish in the sandy soil here.''

"His daughter believes it, too." Resisting the urge to finger the fresh-healed cut on his neck, Josh added an offhand comment. "She seems to think that a more bountiful fruit harvest is important to Fort Ross's future.''

Rotchev exchanged a look with his chief clerk.

"Well," the baron admitted slowly, "I suppose it is no secret that the tsar is displeased at how much has been invested in this colony, with so little return.''

"Most displeased," Mikhail put in unhappily.

"Those who sank great sums of moneys into the Russian Fur Company lost heavily when the sea otter population fell," Rotchev continued. "The tsar among them.''

Josh probed with careful casualness. "I came through here some years ago. The otter had already played out, but there was talk of a shipbuilding enterprise to increase the Company's transpacific trade. That should have brought in a tidy profit.''

Rotchev fingered his goblet. "Sadly, that enterprise also met with less success than was hoped. The forests here provided abundant materials, you understand. Our shipbuilders cut bay and oak for the hulls, and redwood for the crossbeams. Unfortunately, they didn't cure the wood sufficiently. Or perhaps it is not curable in this damp climate. In any case, rot set in almost as soon as the ships launched. They still ply the coastal trade, but can't be trusted for the longer sea voyages.

Which leaves farming as our main enterprise," he concluded.

"And ranching," Mikhail added gloomily. "Not that our rancheros bring in much income. The tariffs imposed by the Mexican government make trade with us too costly for the Californios. Our tannery produces fine hides and much tallow, but..."

Shrugging, he pulled off his spectacles and wiped them on the tail of his coat.

"These tariffs have worsened the situation," the baron admitted. "For years, we traded arms and hides and cloth made by our weavers to the Californios for wheat and other foodstuffs to supply not only our fort, but the outposts in Alaska. Now, only the more wealthy, like Captain Johann Sutter, can afford to trade with us."

"Captain Sutter?"

Rotchev smiled. "A most remarkable man. Of Swiss birth, and soon to become a citizen of Mexico. He obtained a grant of land to the south, along the Sacramento River. He chafes even more at the tariffs and restrictions on trade imposed by the Mexican government than do we."

The baron set aside his goblet.

"Enough of the affairs of Fort Ross. Tell us what news you bring from the East. Did you attend the fur trappers rendezvous last year? Is it true that the price of beaver has dropped so low that the trappers are leaving their mountains to escort wagon trains of settlers across the plains?"

"It's true," Josh replied, willing enough to change the subject. Although the baron hadn't come right out and admitted that the Russians were considering pulling out of Fort Ross, he'd given Josh plenty to think about. He'd take the next few days to see with his own eyes the state of the Russian settlement...and to make sure Tatiana recovered fully from her journey.

Shrugging aside the thought that he was coming perilously close to confusing duty with his personal desires, Josh supplied his host and the young clerk with the specifics of the declining beaver trade. After twenty years, the top hat that no civilized gentleman would be seen without was fading from the fashion scene. Hunters and trappers were leaving the mountains, and settlers were pushing farther and farther west.

Gradually the conversation turned more personal. Rotchev inquired politely of Josh's home, his family. The American admitted what others knew of him... that he'd worn the uniform of an officer for several years before the mountains called to him. He kept his current detached status to himself, however.

Sometime later, the sound of feet running down the hallway cut him off in midsentence. Josh jumped up, every muscle in his body tensing.

A small child darted into the room, guinea gold ringlets flying. She skidded to a stop before the baron. Casting huge sideways glances at Josh, she poured out a spate of breathless Russian.

"English, Irina," Rotchev admonished with a shake of one finger. "You must speak English in front of our guest."

The little girl stumbled over the words. "Mama...

Mama says we are to...to..." Blushing, she scooped invisible food into her mouth.

"We are to eat?"

The bright ringlets bobbed vigorously. *"Da!"*

"Without Mama's company this night?"

"Da, Papa."

The baron rose. "So we shall. Come, Josh, let me show you to the table. Mikhail, you will escort Irina, if you please."

Josh bedded down in the single men's quarters that night. For the first time since leaving the Valley of the Hupa, he was warm, dry, clean and well fed. His stomach rumbled contentedly from the mountains of black bread, potatoes and hot, spicy meat patties he'd consumed. The brandy he'd downed should have sent him into instant sleep.

Instead, he lay wide-awake, his hands folded under his head. He stared at the bottom of the bunk above him while snores from the other men rose in a snuffling, whistling, snorting chorus. As one sleepless moment slid into the next, Josh admitted what kept him so edgy and restless.

He missed the feel of Tatiana's body curled into his. Even more, he missed Tatiana. After the long days and nights they'd spent together he felt suddenly...cut off. She'd been his concern for so long now that he almost resented having the burden taken from his shoulders.

Which made no sense at all, Josh admitted wryly. He'd wanted to get her to Fort Ross as much as she'd wanted to arrive at its gates. Damn it, his small role in her life was done. He'd served his purpose.

If they'd both lost sight of their separate purposes for one mindless night, they'd recovered their senses the next morning. Now Tatiana had reached her destination, and Josh had to decide what he was going to do with the information he'd gleaned from Baron Rotchev.

With war threatening between Mexico and the United States over the status of Texas, the discontent of immigrants like this Captain Johann Sutter could make a difference in northern California...as much as the disposition of Fort Ross. In the noisy darkness, Josh swiftly amended his orders once again. He'd head south. Talk to Sutter and other settlers. Relay his findings to the United States vice-consul at the presidio in Monterey.

But first, he'd spend a few days at Fort Ross...only to ascertain its exact state, he told himself firmly.

With that goal in mind, he rose with the first faint streaks of dawn the next morning. Pulling on the durable fringed shirt and leggings that had dried beside the woodstove overnight, he shook Mikhail awake. The young clerk poked his nose out of the covers.

"Why do you rise so early?" he asked groggily.

"I'd like to look around the fort and the outlying areas."

"Go look," he mumbled, jerking the feather ticking up over his ears.

That was good enough for Josh. Pulling on his fleecy blanket coat, he headed for the door.

Cold clean air and the tangy scent of wood smoke greeted him. With most of the fort still bathed in dim shadows, Josh followed the smoky scent to the west gate. The two sentries lifted the bar at his approach and the massive wooden portals creaked open. Josh strode through and made for the lodges built a short distance away.

He soon located the Wiyot who had transported him and Tatiana south. Hunkering down beside the leader, he entered into a lively debate over exactly how much had been asked and how much promised for the canoe trip. Their Pomo hosts enjoyed the dickering hugely, laughing and adding their advice to both parties. Soon they were joined by several Aleuts, the native Alaskan hunters who'd accompanied the Russians south to hunt otter.

Ears tuned, Josh picked up more subtle hints about the Russian's increasingly tenuous hold on Fort Ross.

"The wheat rots at the root in the damp soil," one Pomo told him.

"The crows eat the barley seed before it can sprout," another put in.

"These Russians know not how to work the soil, as do the Spanish to the south," a wrinkled old man said sagely. "They are workers with wood, not tillers of the earth. Only their orchards bear fruit." He waved a bony hand toward the distant rows of bare, stunted trees. "But with even these, the wind and the sea take their toll."

Josh swiveled on his heel to survey the orchards that spread across the rolling plateau and climbed up the hillsides to the east. Suddenly his eyes narrowed.

A lone figure moved among the trees. Head bowed, skirts lifting in the early-morning wind, she walked slowly, almost aimlessly, as though lost and not aware of it. As Josh watched, she seemed to stumble. She sank to the earth and sat there, shoulders slumped in utter despair.

Cursing, Josh surged to his feet. Abandoning his surprised companions without a word, he loped across the low, rolling hills. His heart hammered with the force of a drum by the time he reached her.

"Tatiana!"

She lifted her head. Josh's chest contracted at the sight of her pale face and red-rimmed eyes. He stopped and hooked a hand under her elbow to pull her up.

Once on her feet, she flowed against him as though she belonged there. Instinctively his arms folded around her. Josh buried his face in her hair. Still slightly damp from a washing, it smelled of lilacs.

"I'm sorry about your father, sweetheart," he murmured into the soft fragrant mass. "I didn't get a chance to tell you last night, but I grieve for you."

She clung to him, her nose buried in his neck. A shudder started at her chin and worked its way down her shoulders, past her hips, to her knees. Josh tightened his arms.

They stood locked together, heedless of the wind whipping from the sea or the birds twittering in the gnarled, leafless trees. At last, Tatiana pulled free.

She wore a long black dress and a knee-length coat of gray wool, Josh saw. A collar trimmed with black braid stood up under her chin like a sentinel. In her European attire, she seemed at once different, and achingly familiar.

"I welcome your condolences," she said in a ragged voice. She drew in a deep, shuddering breath, then her violet eyes lifted to his. "I was most...most distraught last night and did not show the gratitude I should have. I thank you, Josiah, for bringing me to Fort Ross. From my heart, I thank you."

Tell her! The urge slammed into Josh like a fist. *The president's orders be damned! Tell her now why you brought her to Fort Ross!*

Before he could shape the words, she bent and scooped up a canvas bag that lay at her feet. Her hands shaking, she pulled out a bundle of twigs.

"I have come to do as my father sent me to do."

"But I thought...that is, I figured..."

Her mouth curved in a tight smile. "You thought perhaps that my father's death would alter things? No, it only makes me more determined than ever to prove him right. If only one cutting takes, if only one tree bears an abundance of fruit, it shall make the difference to Fort Ross, you shall see. All shall see!"

Josh's hands curled into fists as she sank to her knees once more.

"I shall begin here, to test my skill. Once I am sure of what I do, I shall work my way up the slope."

She pulled a small knife from the canvas bag and attempted a cut halfway up the trunk. The blade sawed uselessly against the tough bark. Frowning, Tatiana tossed aside the kitchen utensil and held up her hand.

"Give me your knife, if you please. It has the sharpness that is needed...as I well know."

Silently Josh pulled the blade from its sheath. Tatiana took it and laid it against the gnarled trunk.

"I make the cut, here, just above this swelling bud. My..." Her voice faltered. Swallowing, she continued in a low, shaky tone. "My father said that was of the most importance."

The razor-sharp blade made a deep slash in the bark. That done, Tatiana selected one of the small twigs and whittled its end to a flat vee. Fingers trembling, she inserted the wedge-shaped end into the cut and held it in place with a palm.

Her other hand fumbled awkwardly for the bag. When she couldn't reach whatever it was she sought, she raised her eyes to the man standing rigidly beside her.

"Will you help me, Josiah? Please? Just hold the cutting in place while I wrap it with cheesecloth."

Slowly Josh went down on one knee.

Chapter Eleven

During the next few days, the backbreaking work of inserting her precious cuttings into endless rows of apple and pear trees soothed Tatiana's grief like a healing balm.

She could almost hear her father's gentle voice instructing her where to slash. How deep to insert the little twig. How much rich mulch to wrap around the joining. Almost see his eyes shine as he waxed eloquent about his passion. Gradually Tatiana's pain at his loss gave way to an acceptance based on an unshakable faith in God's mercy.

She worked steadily from dawn to dusk alongside the Pomo and Russian laborers Alexander sent to assist her. Josiah knelt beside her throughout the first day, and only relinquished his place on the second when the baron invited him to ride out to visit the fort's tannery and gristmill.

"Go," Tatiana urged, brushing a grubby hand across her brow. "I have plenty to help here, and Alexander will welcome your company."

His expression closed, he nodded.

Shading her eyes with her hand, Tatiana had watched him stride away. Long legged, lean hipped, he carried himself with a sinuous grace surprising in so large a man. The swaying fringes on his shirt drew her eye to the wide planes of his back and muscled shoulders. Unbidden, Re-Re-An's words came back to her.

He was much a man, this fringe person.

Very much a man, Tatiana admitted silently.

To her surprise, Helena echoed the same sentiment some days later.

Insisting that Tatiana take a break from her labors to join in the celebration of the feast of Saint Sergius, founder of Russia's greatest monastery, the princess ordered a bath and an afternoon of rest. Just before dusk, she swept into her daughters' room with a bundle draped over her arm. Shooing the giggling girls from the room, she surveyed Tatiana from head to toe.

"No, no, you shall not wear that black gown to the feast tonight. It is too old and unfashionable."

Tatiana blinked. Helena had given her the dress, and the princess was nothing if not fashionable. Even here, at the farthest outpost of the tsar's empire, his niece changed her sturdy wools and linens each evening and sat down to dinner in velvet and lace.

"I'm in mourning, Helena. This will do."

The older woman tilted her head to one side. "When did you leave St. Petersburg?"

Tatiana thought back over the long, wearying weeks of travel by coach, by sled, by ship and foot. "In October, just after the feast of Saint Berens."

"It is now March," Helena said gently. "Although you could not know it, your father has been dead for almost six months. It's proper that you wear mourning, but not such smothering black. I've brought you another dress."

She shook out the gown draped over her arm and held it up. A spill of lavender silk trimmed with black lace and sparkling jet beads caught the light.

"Helena, I cannot!"

"The tsarina herself declared gray and lavender acceptable for mourning after three months," the princess stated firmly. "Besides, your American leaves Fort Ross tomorrow. Will you send him off remembering you only in stained buckskin and crowlike black?"

Tatiana felt a painful catch just below her heart. "He's not my American."

Helena gave a most unroyal snort. "He all but eats you with his eyes. What's more, I noticed how his hands moved over you with a most interesting familiarity the first night you arrived, when you fell into his arms."

"I did not fall into his arms. I fainted."

"I know you, Tatiana Grigoria! Do not try to tell me you shared nothing but polite conversation those days and nights in the mountains."

Heat rushed into Tatiana's face. She looked away, unable to meet her friend's eyes.

"Ahh, I embarrass you. I'm sorry." Helena wrapped an arm around her shoulders. "I only hoped that you had found joy, however brief, with a real man after all the pain your cursed Aleksei gave you."

"I found...something."

"I knew it! Sit down and tell me all."

Sighing, Tatiana sank onto the edge of the sleigh bed. "There's nothing to tell. He desired me, and I...yes, I desired him. Once. Only once."

"Why?"

"Well," she said with a defensive lift of one shoulder, "he's passing handsome without the awful beard he wore when I first saw him, and he treated me gently. Most of the time," she added on a disgruntled note.

Helena let that interesting aside pass. "I meant, why only once? Were I stranded in the mountains with such a man, I might be tempted to forget my marriage vows many times over."

"Ha! You would never do so! You think the sun rises and sets at Alexander Rotchev's express wish. You would never forget yourself, especially with this too gruff woodsman."

"Yes, well, Alexander told me some interesting bits about this woodsman who kisses a lady's hand with the most precise correctness. Did you know he was an officer in the American Imperial Guards, or some such?"

"Like Aleksei," Tatiana echoed in a small, faint voice.

"*Not* like Aleksei!"

No, not like Aleksei. Thinking back, Tatiana recalled how Josiah had stood toe-to-toe with her in the Hupa sweat house and adamantly refused to take her into the treacherous mountains. When he'd dropped his silly basket, everyone present had seen evidence of his thrusting desire. Yet still he'd refused her company.

Nor, once she'd forced herself upon him, would he take her body in trade for his services. Even after he'd given in to her pleas and brought them both to searing, shattering pleasure, he'd not followed that act with demands for another. As he himself had told her, he reserved his heart for only one.

Quite unlike Aleksei.

Staring down at her laced hands, Tatiana admitted the stark truth to Helena. "We shared but one night by his choice as much as mine. He does not want me. Not really. He loves the woman he once hoped to marry."

The princess plumped down beside her, still clutching the silk gown. "What woman?"

"She is called Katerina. He carries her portrait with him always."

"Why did they not marry?"

"She died." Tatiana's brow wrinkled. "Some six years ago, if I remember correctly. Before he lost himself in the mountains."

A silence settled over the room while both women pondered the precariousness of life.

"Do you want this Josiah Jones to want you, my friend?" Helena asked softly.

"No! Yes! I don't know!" She threw the older woman a tortured glance. "What would it matter if I did? He is of America. I am of Russia. He will go his way tomorrow, I mine."

"Listen to me, Tatiana. If I've learned nothing else with Alexander, I've learned that where one comes from and where one travels to matters not when the heart guides the steps."

"But..."

"But me no buts. Do you love this man?"

"I...I desire him," Tatiana admitted. "Most fiercely. But I will not lose my head with my heart again, Helena. It hurts far too much. Besides," she added after a moment, "he loves his Katerina."

"Bah! If you cannot make a man forget a love six years dead, you're not the woman I remember. Stand up, Countess Karanova. Stand up."

Yanking Tatiana to her feet, she measured the gown against her shoulders. "Yes, yes. This will do nicely. Tonight the American shall see you in something other than buckskin or black wool. Tonight, my friend, he shall see you as the woman you are. Now change, and quickly, while I go fetch my box of perfumes and paints."

The silk clutched to her bosom, Tatiana stood unmoving long after Helena rushed out. Her friend's question echoed in her mind. Did she want Josiah to want her?

She had only to think about his departure on the morrow to know the answer. After so many days and nights in his company, sharing so many travails, the thought of watching him walk away left a hollow, panicky feeling in her stomach.

She'd never met a man so sure of himself. So at one with the world he inhabited. He was strong enough to be gentle. Gentle enough to bring her to a passion she'd never known.

But desire was not enough, she'd learned all too painfully. She must think with her head, not her heart!

Josiah was a wanderer, with no lands, no roots.

Her lands, what remained of them, spread along the Volga. If her father's great gamble failed, she could expect to suffer mightily at the hands of the tsar. If the cuttings saved this far-flung outpost, she could go home with her head high and expect some measure of restitution. Take up again the life she led before Aleksei.

Quite unexpectedly, the prospect chilled her.

Was that what she desired? To return to the court of the tsar who'd executed her husband? To see again the cold black eyes of the colonel who'd held her arms and forced her to watch? To spend her days dancing attendance on the tsarina and her nights with another husband, this one chosen for her by Nikolas?

Her fingers crushed the silk as the future loomed dark and bleak ahead of her.

What choice had she?

None, she realized. Except perhaps...

Her gaze dropped to the gown in her hands.

Josh made his way through the noisy, laughing throng crowded into the lower rooms of the two-story warehouse. In the short time he'd spent at Fort Ross, he'd learned the names of a good number of the sixty or so Russian residents. They now greeted him cheerfully, as did the Pomo and Aleuts who'd joined tonight's celebrations.

They were a hardworking, industrious group, Josh had discovered, but far more suited to clerking and woodworking than to agriculture or animal husbandry. No wonder their tsar had grown disenchanted with Fort Ross's inability to resupply the Alaskan settlements. It could barely provide for itself.

The larders showed no evidence of any lack tonight, however. Trestle tables groaned as women in white blouses and bright-colored skirts loaded them with platter after platter of steamed sea bass, boiled potatoes, and vegetables simmered in a flavored stock. The mouthwatering scent of spiced beef rolled and fried in a flaky dough filled the air. In the past few days Josh had developed a real taste for these delicious piroshki, if not for the vodka that flowed so freely from earthenware crocks.

Music rose in tinkling, merry notes over the din. Oblivious to the noise all around him, a musician rested one foot on a stool and plucked away at a many-stringed instrument. Josh stood listening quietly until a flushed, grinning Mikhail pushed a cup into his hand.

"To your health, Josh, and to our blessed Saint Sergius."

The others in the room picked up his refrain. "To Saint Sergius!"

The celebrants emptied their cups in great noisy swallows. Swiping their arms across their mouths, they eyed Josh expectantly.

He took a deep breath. Braced his shoulders. Lifted his cup. "To Saint Sergius."

Prepared as he was, the combustible brew nevertheless brought tears spurting into his eyes. He blinked rapidly as a chorus of ribald laughter rose all around

him. Even Mikhail, looking boyish and unclerklike
with his sandy hair all askew, doubled up.

"To the tsar!" a short, stocky, bearded craftsman
shouted a moment later.

Josh swallowed a groan and another swill.

Ever the proper host, Baron Rotchev signaled for
silence. Politely he lifted his cup. "To His Highness,
the President of America!"

Heads went back. Cups tilted.

"To the sea," a dark-eyed Aleut offered. "And the
otter it…"

Josh muttered a prayer of thanksgiving as the storehouse door opened and Princess Helena's light, merry
laugh interrupted the round of toasts.

"La, my husband! Do you begin the festivities without us?"

Sailing into the room, she dragged off her cloak.
Golden hair upswept, rubies at ears and throat, her
bosom white above a low-cut gown of bloodred velvet
dripping gold lace, she generated a collective gasp of
admiration.

The baron bowed over her hand. "No, my dearest
wife, I would never dream of beginning anything without you. We only get the preliminaries out of the way.
Now that you—" he smiled to a figure at the door
"—and the Countess Karanova have arrived, the party
truly begins."

Josh stood rooted to the floor as Tatiana glided
through the crowd. Her hair was a tumble of shining
sable curls, her lips a deep, rosy red. Holding herself
as regal as any queen, she bestowed a brilliant smile
on the baron. He bowed again, beaming.

"My dear countess, you look quite like your old self. If the Princess Helena did not already hold the title, I would declare you the most beautiful woman in all the Russias."

She gave a gurgle of laughter. The merry, tinkling sound hit Josh with even more of a wallop than the cloudy liquid in his cup.

"You're too kind, sir, and too besotted with your wife to notice any woman in the room but her."

Her hand went to the strings of her black velvet cloak. Stumbling over his feet, Mikhail rushed to take the garment from her hands.

If the princess glowed in red and gold, Tatiana glittered in shimmering, sensuous lavender silk and glistening black jet. A high, weblike collar of black beads banded her neck and spread over her bare shoulders in an intricate pattern of loops. A huge tear-shaped amethyst hung from the lowest loop. It drew every man's eyes, Josh's included, to the shadowy valley between breasts bared by the low-cut gown.

"We will give thanks," the baron proclaimed, leading the ladies to benches set at the head table. "Then we shall eat and sing and show our American guest how Russians celebrate the feast of Saint Sergius, no? Here, my friend, sit here beside the countess."

Slowly Josh moved to the seat indicated. Make no mistake, the Countess Karanova had returned to her own kind. This glittering, elegant woman bore little resemblance to the tangle-haired shrew who'd accosted him in the Hupa sweat house. Even less to the writhing, passionate creature who haunted his every waking hour and most of his sleeping ones, as well.

He'd felt her withdrawal from the moment they'd arrived at Fort Ross. Now he barely recognized her.

Just as well he was moving on tomorrow, Josh told himself. He'd delayed his departure too long as it was. It was time, past time, to get on with his mission. For reasons he preferred not to think about at this moment, the prospect of resuming his solitary wandering didn't hold the lure it once had.

Thoroughly disgruntled, he took his assigned seat and drew upon the manners he hadn't used in years.

"May I pour you some wine?" he inquired politely. "Or perhaps beer?"

Tatiana threw him a startled look. "Vodka."

"As you wish."

An hour later, Tatiana was forced to admit that the evening wasn't going at all as she had planned. She'd thought to dazzle Josiah with her charm. Perhaps stun him just a bit with her borrowed paints and perfumes. She'd certainly never intended to make him stiffen up like a poker and treat her like a stranger.

Of a sudden, he'd grown so...so polite! Throughout this interminable feast, they'd carried on a stilted dialogue, each awkward with the other. Now the sound of voices raised in song and the stamping feet of the exuberant dancers put an end to their stiff conversation.

This would not do. This would not do at all. Frowning, Tatiana nibbled at the remains of a flaky pastry coated with honey and debated how best to break through the American's so strange reserve. When her tongue flicked out to catch the sticky sweetness that ran down her fingers, Josiah stiffened. She glanced up to find him regarding her intently.

"What is it?" She raised her voice to be heard over the music. "Have I honey on my nose or chin?"

"No."

She popped the last crumbs into her mouth, then took another swipe at her sticky fingers. To her surprise, a slow, breath-stealing grin etched its way across Josiah's face.

"Why do you smile at me in such a way?" she demanded.

"What?"

"Why do you smile at me so?"

He bent and brought his mouth closer to her ear. Tatiana's nerves took fire when his warm breath tickled the fine hairs at her temple.

"I was remembering the night we roasted mountain trout over the fire. You licked your fingers then, too."

She blinked. "And that causes you to grin?"

"Yes, ma'am, it surely does."

Actually, the sight of Tatiana running her tongue around her fingers caused Josh to do a whole lot more than grin. It also blew away his vague, uneasy notion that the woman who'd walked through the mountains and this shimmering, sophisticated creature were somehow different beings.

"You are a puzzlement to me, Josiah Jones," she said, shaking her head. "Shall I ever understand you?"

"I'm not sure the good Lord meant for men and women to understand each other."

"Oh, so? What, then, did He intend for them to do?"

Tatiana read the answer in his eyes. Swift heat poured into her face. Sweet Virgin above, she could not believe that she blushed like the veriest schoolgirl!

"Among other things," Josiah replied with a wicked grin, "He intended them to dance."

Rising, he stepped over the bench and held out his hand to her. "Will you take a turn about the floor with me?"

"They're doing a Ukrainian *hayivka,*" she replied doubtfully. "Do you know this dance?"

"No, but it can't be much harder to learn than the Hupa White Deerskin ceremonial."

"Ha! You shall see!"

Gathering her skirts, Tatiana rose. A stately gavotte or even a graceful waltz would have accorded more with her dignity than this rollicking folk dance. She feared greatly for the delicate kid slippers she'd borrowed from Helena among the forest of stomping boots. Yet she wouldn't have missed the chance to put her hand in Josiah's for all the gold in the tsar's treasury.

The contact was all too brief. He led her to the floor, and Tatiana found a place in the noisy, laughing circle of women. Hands on hips, she dipped a shoulder to every second beat and took a gliding step to the right on every third. Arms looped over each other's shoulders, the men moved in the opposite direction. The wooden floorboards shook under their heavy, pounding thumps.

"This isn't so difficult," Josiah commented when they faced each other once again.

Tatiana threw back her head. "Oh, so? Wait until we make another turn or two."

Luckily she was only a few feet away from him when the tempo abruptly doubled. She couldn't miss the surprised expression on his face as the men suddenly dropped to a squat and thrust out first one leg, then the other. Dragged down with the others, Josiah landed on the floor with a resounding whump.

Laughter erupted from all sides. Grinning sheepishly, he was pulled to his feet and swept along in the energetic dance. After a few more clumsy tries, he managed to catch the rhythm. He thrust out his legs with some energy, if not skill.

Many believed the *hayivka* was intended to lighten hearts after the long, dark Ukrainian winters and stir the blood for the spring ritual of choosing a mate and bringing forth new life. Even here, so far from the land of its origin, the dance served its purpose. Tatiana couldn't help but notice the way Josiah's muscled thighs bulged with each bend and thrust, and the stretch of his linen shirt across his shoulders as he swept past. She dipped and swayed and felt her blood heat with each glimpse of his lean hips and broad chest.

And when the whooping, stomping men broke their ring to claim their partners, her womb contracted like a vise. Josiah stood before her, his chest heaving from his exertions and his amber eyes gleaming as he encircled her waist with both hands.

Breathing every bit as hard and as fast as he, Tatiana

put her hands on his shoulders. They stared at each other for long seconds before the dancers pushed them into movement. Taking his cue from the others, Josiah swung her around, then lifted her high in the air.

Laughing, breathless, her blood roaring through her veins, Tatiana gave herself up to the dizzying dance and to the feel of his hands on her body. When the music finally ended, she could only cling to his shoulders while the room spun around her and a single thought drummed in her head.

By Saint Igor, she wanted him! With everything that was female within her, she wanted him!

And he wanted her. She could feel it in the bite of his hands at her waist. See it in the skin stretched taut across his cheekbones.

"Tatiana..."

Her heart thrilled at the harsh, urgent note in his voice. Her head tried to warn her to go cautiously.

"Yes?"

"I need to talk to you."

Talk was not what she saw in his eyes. Nervously she wet her lips.

"So we shall sit, and you shall talk."

The sight of her small pink tongue drove the last rational thought from Josh's head. His blood pounded from the exuberant, primitive rhythm of the dance. His body pulsed with the need to claim the woman he held captured in his hands. He ached to pick her up, throw her over his shoulder and storm out of the warehouse to find a bed. A pile of hay. A nest of furs. Anywhere they weren't watched by a hundred curious eyes!

"Not here," he muttered hoarsely.

He didn't sling her over his shoulder, but he did drag her to stand before their hosts.

"Will you excuse us?" he asked brusquely. "We have…unfinished business yet to discuss."

Alexander Rotchev lifted a surprised brow. Before he could comment, however, his wife intervened.

"You may use our parlor," Princess Helena declared loftily. "We shall remain here with the children for at least another hour or more, so you need not fear to be disturbed during this—" her dark eyes slid to Tatiana "—discussion."

Josh used the short trip across the compound to gain a measure of control over his galloping, riotous senses. He lost it again the moment the door to the Rotchev residence closed behind them and Tatiana flung off her cloak. She stood silhouetted against the glow from the banked fire. If she was wearing any petticoats under that thin, shimmering silk, Josh sure as thunderation couldn't see them. His throat closed at the outline of her rounded hips and long, curved legs.

He reached her in two strides and pulled her into his arms. His head went down to claim her mouth. She rose up to meet it, locking her arms around his neck. Their kiss was a rough, greedy fusion of two hungry bodies.

Josh dug his fingers into her hair and held her head still while he plundered her mouth. He tasted the honey she'd licked from her fingers. Her tongue danced with his. All too quickly, he was close to forgetting who he was, who she was.

"Tatiana," he said raggedly against her lips.

She angled her head, her mouth moving hungrily over his. "Yes?"

"I have to leave tomorrow."

"Do you, Josiah?"

"Yes."

"Why?" She tore her mouth from his, breathing hard. "Is the call of your mountains so strong that you must answer it always?"

Duty and desire fought a short, ferocious battle. Josh wanted to tell her. Ached to tell her. Loyalty to the uniform he once wore so proudly kept him from crossing the line.

"I have business I must conduct," he said gruffly, "but I'll come back. I swear it. Before your precious twigs begin to sprout."

Tatiana believed him. God help her, at that moment she believed him. Even worse, her weak, foolish, so very *stupid* heart urged her to give him something to speed his return.

Wrapping her arms around his neck, she canted her hips into his. The intimate contact brought a glint of laughter to her eyes.

"These twigs are not all that sprout, I think."

Groaning, Josiah swept her into his arms and carried her to the massive settee. In a flurry of frantic hands, he raised her skirts while she worked the ties of the front flap on his buckskin britches. They were both panting by the time their flesh came together, and on fire with need by the time their bodies joined.

Chapter Twelve

An hour later Josh escorted Tatiana back across the compound. As they approached the noisy, still-crowded warehouse, his steps slowed. He had little desire to rejoin the festivities, and none at all to end his moments alone with Tatiana.

He'd promised her that he'd return, and he fully intended to as soon as he relayed his findings to the United States vice-consul in Monterey. But what then? What could a half-pay officer with no roots and no future offer this dazzling Russian? What would she want from him when she learned his real reasons for escorting her to Fort Ross?

Cursing the president's express instructions to keep his mission secret, Josh pulled Tatiana to a halt some yards from the storehouse entrance.

She turned to look up at him questioningly. Light spilled through its glazed glass windows and painted her face in a soft glow. Dark curls tumbled about her face, less ordered now than when they'd left some time ago. Josh tucked a soft, silky curl behind her ear.

"I must leave in the morning."

"So have you said."

"I'll return within a month, six weeks at the most."

She smiled. "Yes, before the twigs sprout."

It wasn't a declaration of love. Far from it. For now, though, Tatiana decided, it would do. It would do nicely. Josiah would return, and by then her head would have sorted through her heart's foolish reaction to his slightest touch.

"What will you do while I'm gone?"

"I shall water the cuttings and pray that my father's work bears fruit."

"If it doesn't?"

"It must," she said simply. "It is his legacy to me, all I have left to..."

The sound of an agonized moan cut her off. Startled, Tatiana jerked around and peered through the darkness.

"Stay here," Josh ordered softly.

Moving on soundless feet, he rounded the corner of the warehouse. A dim figure knelt in the mud just outside the glow from the windows. Shoulders hunched, arms wrapped across his middle, the man gave another long, wretched groan.

Josh recognized the lank, sandy hair at the same moment Tatiana brushed past him, clucking like a hen roused from the henhouse late at night.

"Mikhail! What do you do here, in the cold and the mud? Have you been hurt?"

A pale face turned up to hers. Swallowing convulsively, the young clerk tried to answer. "No, not...not hurt. Just..."

He gave another groan and hunched over. When he

lifted a bleary face once more, Josh gave him a sympathetic grin.

"Too much kvass?"

Mikhail tried to nod. The movement caused his eyeballs to bulge behind his spectacles. He bent over and retched repeatedly.

"It matters not what caused the sickness," Tatiana scolded when his heaving subsided. "Take his other arm, Josiah. Aid him to rise."

Between them, they got the rubber-kneed clerk to a bench set against the storehouse wall. When he sank onto the seat and dropped his head into his hands, Tatiana perched beside him and patted his back.

"Go inside," she instructed Josh. "Fetch a cloth and some water."

Resisting the urge to salute, he complied with her curt orders. Moments later, Tatiana tipped water onto a folded kerchief.

"Here," she said softly. "Lift your head."

"No, Countess. You must not sully…"

"Come, come. Let me bathe your face. You'll feel much better."

"No, I…"

"Cease this foolishness. Lift your head."

Reluctantly the clerk complied. While Tatiana dabbed at his face, he threw a silent, agonized look over her shoulder.

Josh understood the unspoken plea. The last thing any young man wanted was for a beautiful woman to tend to him in such humiliating circumstances. Hiding a smile, he moved to the bench.

"I'll take care of him. You go inside."

"No, no, he is most ill."

He hooked a hand under her arm and raised her to her feet. "Go inside. I'll see that he gets cleaned up and finds his bed."

Tatiana stood irresolute, her glance shifting from the hunched-over clerk to the tall man before her. She felt the strangest need to spin out these moments with Josiah as long as possible. God help her, she would even grasp at poor Mikhail's wretchedness as an excuse to delay rejoining the crowd.

The truth of the matter was that she didn't want this night to end. Even less did she want the morning to come. She knew Josiah's ways. He'd be gone as soon as the gates opened at dawn. She'd not see him again for a month, perhaps six weeks. Her weak heart ached at the thought.

"I may not have the chance to speak privately with you again before you leave," she said softly. Her fingers brushed down his cheek and traced the shape of his chin. "May God keep you safe, Josiah Jones."

"And you, Tatiana Grigoria."

She dropped her hand and turned away.

"She's so beautiful," Mikhail mumbled, following her with bleary eyes. "And so kind."

Kind and ferocious and stubborn and brave, Josh thought as he hauled the clerk to his feet. The youth staggered along beside him.

"And so tragic," he added. "Did you know...?"

He stopped and burped mightily. Looking rather surprised that he could emit such a burst of sound, Mikhail swiped his sleeve across his mouth.

"Did you know the tsar made her watch her husband's execution?"

Josh shot him a quick look. "No."

"The commander of the Imperial Guards himself held her while the executioner strangled the man. Right before her eyes."

"The bastard!"

"Yes, he was. And stupid, too, to get himself involved in a plot against the tsar."

The surge of fury that swept through Josh didn't center on Tatiana's dead husband, but on the man who would force a wife to watch such a horror.

"Now she has lost her father," Mikhail said mournfully. "And soon she will lose what is left of her estates, if not her head. We will all lose everything." He belched again, then slapped a hand across his mouth. "Your pardon, sir. Oh! Ohh!"

Hastily Josh lowered his burden. Leaving the wretched clerk on his knees in the center of the compound, he strode to the well. The wooden bucket dropped into the pit with a splash and came up full. When the cold water hit Mikhail full in the face, he floundered like a mountain perch on the end of a line.

Tossing the bucket aside, Josh yanked him to his feet. "What is this about Tatiana losing her head?"

Mikhail goggled at him, clearly unsure what had caused his benefactor to become so ferocious. His befuddled mind fixed on an extraneous detail.

"You should not address the countess by her given name. It is not done."

Josh grabbed the lapels of his frock coat. With one jerk, he pulled the whey-faced clerk half off his toes.

"Why did you say that you'll lose everything? I thought these cuttings Tatiana brought with her were supposed to save Fort Ross?"

Mikhail floundered helplessly in his iron grip. "It's...it's too late. It was too late when she arrived with them."

"What the hell are you talking about?"

The clerk shook his head in a futile effort to clear it. "No, I must not speak of it."

Josh lifted him a good foot in the air. "Think about the woman who just wiped the spew from your face. And about the fact that I'll peel your scalp back inch by inch if you don't tell me why the hell it's too late."

Mikhail's mouth opened, closed. Opened again.

"Talk," Josh snarled.

"The...the ship that brought word of her father's death also brought a message from the tsar. He ordered Baron Rotchev to..."

"To what?"

"I should not..."

Josh gave the clerk a shake that rattled his teeth. "To what?"

"To draw up plans to dispose of Fort Ross."

Slowly Josh lowered his captive. Feet spread, mouth grim, he studied Mikhail's woebegone face.

"When?"

"No date has been set, but...but the Baron Rotchev was instructed to approach the British and French by the end of June, to see if they have interest in purchasing the properties."

"Why the British and the French, and not Mexico or the United States?"

Thoroughly miserable, Mikhail could only shake his head. "Tsar Nikolas will never deal with the Mexicans. They are peasants. There is not a drop of royal blood among them. Nor, if you will forgive me for so saying, among the leaders of your own country. No, he will sell Fort Ross to the French or the British."

"Over my dead body," the American muttered. "Does Tatiana know about this?"

"The countess? Yes, but she believes her father's precious cuttings will yet stay the tsar's order, if only they take hold."

"You don't believe they will, do you?"

"No one does," Mikhail said morosely. "For all his great wisdom, Count Karanov could not know how thin the soil is here, and how difficult it is to grow a decent crop. No, we shall all sail home this fall, or to Archangel...if the tsar doesn't order us all hung from the walls of Fort Ross first."

Josh was beginning to develop a powerful dislike for the ruler of all Russias. He had also developed an equally powerful determination to keep Fort Ross from falling into the hands of either the British or the French. In the process, he'd damned well make sure Tatiana didn't fall into the tsar's hands.

"I must tell Baron Rotchev what I have told you," Mikhail muttered abjectly. He turned on wobbly legs and headed back to the warehouse. "Now I shall never be first *prikashchiki*."

Josh caught him by the arm. He admired the youth for having the spirit to own up to his mistakes. The Lord knows, Josh himself had confessed a record number of transgressions during his years at West Point.

Experience had taught him, however, that confessions were better received if the culprit had worn a clean uniform when he made them.

"Come on. Let's get you into a clean shirt. Then we'll both go talk to the baron."

Hope that he wouldn't have to bear the full brunt of the baron's anger flared in Mikhail's pale eyes. "You will speak to him, also?"

"Yes."

Josh couldn't tell Rotchev of his secret mission. Not without higher authority. But he could damn well advise the Russian that the United States *might* have an interest in Fort Ross and get some idea of the price the Russians intended to ask.

He rode out the west gate just after dawn the next morning on a rawboned gelding with dappled hindquarters he'd purchased from the Russian American Fur Company.

Pulling up on the crest of a rolling rise, he looked back. Gray, swirling mist obscured the fort. Only the peaked roof of the storehouse and the crosses atop the chapel towers pierced the low-lying fog.

For the first time in longer than Josh could remember, he didn't feel a stab of relief at trading wooden walls and roofs for open skies. The hills ahead didn't call to him. Even the mountains were silent.

Instead, he felt the damnedest urge to turn his mount and ride back for one last word with Tatiana. One final promise.

What could he say to her?

That his feelings for her had slipped right past lust

into unfamiliar, uncomfortable territory? That the mere thought of her was enough to make him so damned tight he could barely keep his mind on the road ahead and his senses alert? What in the hell did he have to offer her, except a promise?

I'll be back. I swear, I'll be back.

A week later he rode through the gates of Sutter's Fort.

In his years of wandering, Josh had spent many a night within the walls of frontier fortresses, but none of them compared to the armed compound Captain Johann Sutter had constructed alongside the Sacramento River.

Baked adobe brick walls some two feet thick and eighteen feet high surrounded a huge compound that included several barracks buildings, a bakery, a mill, a blanket factory and various workshops. Cannons bristled from the battlements, and Indian troops armed with rifles patrolled the walls alongside Mexican vaqueros and beefy-faced, mustachioed immigrants from a host of other nations.

At the far end of the compound stood the main residence, an imposing adobe structure that combined home and headquarters. Josh pulled up before the tall wooden doors and dismounted. Handing the gelding's reins to a waiting stable boy, he pounded the travel dirt from his shirt and britches. He'd stomped out most of his dust when his host came striding out.

His face brick red in the unseasonably warm spring sunshine, Sutter extended his hand. *"Willkommen Sie."*

Josh returned the firm grip. "Thanks."

"*Ach,* so. You are American."

"Josiah Jones, out of Jonesboro, Kentucky."

"*Ja, ja,* I know this Kentucky. I ran a business in Independence before I come to California."

"That's what I heard."

"Please, come inside." With the graciousness of a frontier host, he ushered Josh into the cool, dim interior. "Vill you have beer to wash the dust from your throat, or wine pressed from the grapes of my own vineyards?"

"Beer, please."

"Maria!" Sutter bustled to a far door. "Maria!"

While his host issued rapid orders in Spanish to the slender, dark-haired girl who came running at his shout, Josh reviewed what he'd learned in his week of travel.

Having arrived in California only the year before with little more than the clothes he stood in, Johann Sutter had blustered and strutted and finally convinced Governor Alverado to sell him a substantial land grant, which he named New Helvetia in honor of his Swiss homeland. A talent for fast talking and a promise of fair wages had brought both Indians and immigrant settlers under his banner. Those natives who resisted, he conquered with the ruthlessness of earlier Spanish conquistadors. Now he ruled his fiefdom like a medieval lord and, if the rumors were true, chafed at the restrictions the Mexican authorities put on his boundless energies.

"It's true," the Swiss told Josh over dinner sometime later. "I have plans. Great plans. In a few months, I go to Monterey and become a citizen of Mexico."

He speared a chunk of spicy beef from the huge bowl making the rounds of the hungry men seated at the trestle table.

"Then I vill become a judge," he predicted, waving his fork to emphasize his point. "An official of the government. I vill present the concerns of the settlers in Alta California to Governor Alverado."

"Someone needs to," a red-haired, wiry Scotsman in tattered canvas trousers muttered. "Don Alverado never leaves Monterey. The bloody bastard doesn't have any idea how much these tariffs have hurt our trade, or the hardship they put on the other settlers."

Josh had picked up the same refrain over and over in the past week. Discontent with the Mexican government's heavy-handed attempt to control trade within its territories became the subject of discussion at every table sooner or later. That discontent was building to a flash point in California, as it already had in Texas.

"Only last month the Spanish tried to stop one of my fishing ships from landing in Bodega Bay," Sutter told Josh indignantly. "They claimed it carried contraband."

"It did," the Scotsman put in, grinning.

"That is not the point," Sutter exclaimed. "If my friend, Baron Rotchev, had not intervened, the Mexicans would have fired on my ship!"

"I stopped at Fort Ross on my way south," Josh said casually. "It's built up a lot since the last time I was there."

The Swiss nodded. "These Russians know little about working the land, but they have brought some master builders with them. I'd give much for their granary vith its great millstone and fine threshing floor. And for their cannon," he added darkly.

While the women cleared the tables, the men pulled out their clay pipes. Sutter treated all to a wad of Virginia tobacco from his personal supply. Soon thick smoke filled the room, as dense as the clouds of war that seemed to hang perpetually over the United States and Mexico.

"When var comes," the Swiss said with a meaningful glance at Josh, "not all vill be sorry if the Spanish lose their northern territories. Even I, soon to be a citizen of Mexico, have little respect for a government that ignores the velfare of its people."

Josh suspected Captain Sutter's antipathy to the government had more to do with the restrictions it imposed on his own enterprises than its attitude to the rest of its citizens. Wisely he kept his opinion to himself and probed deeper into the turbulent politics of the area.

He left his host in a fog of tobacco smoke some hours later. He'd heard enough, more than enough, to make his detour south worth every strenuous mile. What was more, the determined, almost fanatical gleam in Sutter's eyes when he spoke of his plans to expand his empire had planted the seeds of a daring idea in Josh's mind.

Now he had only to lay that idea before the American vice-consul in Monterey. Then he'd return to Fort

Ross to claim the woman he was coming to think of as his.

Josh boarded one of Sutter's ships the following morning. After plowing through rough, contrary seas, the schooner dropped anchor in San Francisco Bay.

There, he booked passage on a seagoing vessel heading south. Just when the captain was ready to raise the sails, a heavy fog rolled in and smothered the bay. To Josh's disgust, they sat at anchor for almost a week waiting for the weather to clear. Finally the fog lifted and the ship began its journey down the coast.

Caged and restless, Josh heaved a heartfelt sigh of relief when the ship finally rounded the tip of Monterey Bay. As soon as it had warped up to the wharf, he bid the captain goodbye, slung his gear over his shoulder and made his way to the adobe structure that served as the vice-consul's residence and place of business.

A servant showed him to a dim waiting room just off the central courtyard. Josh paced the chamber, anxious to talk to President Van Buren's designated representative. He'd met the vice-consul once, during a previous visit to California. Henry Wetherington was a good man, but possessed an inbred Yankee caution and hardheadedness. Josh would have to talk fast and hard to convince him to act quickly in the matter of Fort Ross. There wasn't time to send word to Washington and await instructions.

When the door opened behind him, Josh whirled, expecting to see the Right Honorable Henry Wetherington. Instead, a supercilious, thin-nosed individual in starched shirt points eyed Josh up and down.

"Yes?"

"I'm here to see the vice-consul."

The newcomer's nostrils pinched inward, as though it pained him to deal with individuals in travel-stained buckskins.

"I'm Percival Banks, first secretary of the consulate. How can I help you, Mr…?"

"You can't," Josh informed him curtly. What he had in mind didn't fall within the realm of authority for first secretaries. "Tell the vice-consul that Lieutenant Josiah Jones wants to talk to him."

Banks peered down his nose. "That might be difficult. Mr. Wetherington resigned his post and sailed home with his wife some weeks ago. The new vice-consul isn't expected to arrive for several months."

Josh stared at him, nonplussed. "Who's in charge here?"

"I am," the man replied with a smirk. "At the direction of Ambassador Kent, in Mexico City. Now if that's all, Lieutenant, I have business to attend to."

"No, that's not all." Josh thought fast. "Get me some paper and ink."

"I beg your pardon?"

His mind racing, Josh didn't bother with pandering to the bureaucrat's ego.

"You heard what I said. Move, man!"

Clearly offended, Banks nevertheless responded to the voice of authority. Josh scratched out two quick missives. He folded each, sealed them with hot wax and handed the first to the secretary.

"Give this to the new vice-consul if he arrives before my return."

He fingered the second, wishing he had time for more than a terse note informing Tatiana he'd be gone longer than planned. But the ship he'd just left stopped in Monterey only long enough to take on fresh water. If he was going to get back aboard, he'd have to move.

Passing the stiff-backed assistant the second note, he dug in his possibles bag for a five-dollar gold piece.

"The letter goes to the Countess Karanova at Fort Ross. This should cover the expenses."

Tossing the coin to Banks, he headed for the door. It slammed shut behind him with a bang.

The first secretary sniffed disdainfully. "Rude, unmannered woodsman."

Both notes landed on a pile of correspondence waiting attention by a lowly scribe. Pocketing the gold piece, Banks strolled out of the antechamber.

Chapter Thirteen

"No, no, Mikhail. Do not drench the band. Only dampen it."

Softening her admonishment with a smile, Tatiana took a tin cup from the clerk's hand, dipped into the bucket he held and poured a trickle of water onto the encrusted cheesecloth banding the tree trunk.

"Thus so."

Handing the cup back to Mikhail, Tatiana shaped a muddy hand around the cloth. Gently she felt for any loosening of the joint. The cutting held firmly, as far as she could tell.

Why, then, had it not sprouted?

The question gnawed at her. More than two months had passed since she'd inserted this twig into the slash in the bark. It should have put out leafy buds by now, or at least shown the start of them. Why had it not?

Perhaps she'd not kept the cloth band wet enough. Perhaps she'd kept it *too* wet. Saint Petr, why had the cutting not sprigged? Wearily Tatiana pushed herself to her knees.

"I understand how to do it. Let me finish this row

while you rest, Countess.'' Mikhail's pale blue eyes beseeched her from behind his spectacles. ''You look so tired.''

More than willing to yield to his entreaties, Tatiana sank back onto the pillow of her thick skirts. Her customary energy seemed to have deserted her of late. Each day she felt a little more of her strength seep away. Or was it her hope?

Two months had passed. More than two months.

The cuttings did not bud, and Josiah Jones did not return.

He'd said he would come back within a month, six weeks at most. But March had melted into April, and April into May, and she'd neither seen nor heard from him.

Now soft winds blew off the sea. Pink and white wildflowers carpeted the rolling hills around Fort Ross. The early-morning mists that rose like witches' breath from the trees gave way to cloudless, sunny afternoons...and still he didn't come.

For weeks, every schooner that sailed into the sheltered little bay had brought a leap of hope to Tatiana's heart. Each time the sentries shouted word of a stranger riding toward the fort, her breath had snared in her throat.

With every disappointment, she reminded herself of all that could occur to delay even the most intrepid traveler. Lame ponies. Unexpected rainsqualls. Rivers swollen by spring floods. Shuddering, she refused to let herself think of wolves that foamed at the mouth.

Keeping busy had helped pass the long weeks of waiting. Each morning, Tatiana assisted Helena in schooling the children. Each afternoon, she tended to the orchards. She'd spent backbreaking hours among the gnarled, leafless trees, wetting her precious cuttings and directing the laborers where to plow between the rows for the spring wheat planting. Whenever his duties allowed, Mikhail would join her there, as he had this afternoon.

The clerk had changed greatly since the festivities in honor of Saint Sergius. Helena had told Tatiana of his indiscreet disclosures to the American, and of Alexander's short-lived wrath. Unlike his vengeful tsar, however, the baron was far too shrewd a manager to dismiss a valued assistant out of hand for one mistake. Evidently Mikhail had learned a painful lesson that night, one he took to heart. Tatiana had not seen him touch a glass of vodka since.

And the saints could bear witness to the fact that she'd seen much of him these past months!

He seemed always at her elbow or just a call away. He adored her with his eyes, and stumbled over his feet in his eagerness to assist her. A few years ago, Tatiana might have teased and flirted and made light of his obvious longing. Three months ago, his slavish devotion might have soothed a spirit lacerated by her husband's betrayal. Now a scraggly bearded American consumed her thoughts, and her labors in the orchard drained her of the energy to do more than smile absently at the lovesick clerk.

Leaning back on her hands, she let the sun warm her face. Of their own accord, her eyes found the distant mountains to the north. The tallest, called Mount Helena by the inhabitants of Fort Ross in honor of their beloved princess, showed a cap of white against a startlingly blue sky.

It seemed only yesterday that Tatiana had struggled across steep, snow-covered slopes behind Josiah and the shaggy little packhorse. Yet now the snows had disappeared from all but the highest peaks, and the terror of their trek through the blinding, stinging blizzard of white had faded from her mind. Only softer, kinder memories remained. Of Josiah giving her his hat to shield her face from the sun. Of the coarse soap he'd handed her when she'd gone to bathe in the foul-smelling pool left by the geyser. Of his mouth on hers, and his arms banding her to his body while he surged into her with a powerful...

"Countess!"

Mikhail's urgent cry cut into Tatiana's all-too-vivid memories. Jerking upright, she scanned the sloping orchard for his tall, gangly figure. He waved to her from the bottom of the hill. The sea sparkled behind him, making it difficult to decipher his expression, but there was no mistaking the excitement in his voice.

"Countess! Come quickly!"

Tatiana scrambled to her feet, hope piercing her heart yet again. Perhaps Mikhail had spotted a ship coming around the curve of the cliffs! Or a traveler approaching the gate! From where she stood, she could see nothing but the long rows of leafless trees. Lifting her muddied skirts in both hands, she hurried down the slope.

"Look!" Mikhail thrust his forefinger at one of the trees. "There!"

Swallowing her crushing disappointment, Tatiana

dragged her gaze from the empty bay and focused on the cutting he pointed to. Suddenly the hope that had just plummeted like a stone thrown into an empty well shot straight up again. Her heart pounding, she sank to her knees.

"Holy Father above."

Scarcely daring to breathe, she examined the swelling nub. It showed only the faintest tint of green, just enough to bring a rush of tears to Tatiana's eyes. Furiously she blinked them back.

Swiveling on her knees, she studied the tree across the row. When she saw a similar coloration on the cutting that was joined to its trunk, she couldn't contain her tears any longer. Burying her face in her hands, she gave them free rein.

"Countess!"

Mikhail's voice spiraled to a squeak of dismay. He dropped to his knees beside her and groped in his pockets for a handkerchief. It dangled uselessly from his fingers while Tatiana sobbed.

"Shall I fetch the Princess Helena?" he asked in alarm.

She shook her head.

"The Baron Rotchev?" Helplessly he bent until his head hovered a few inches from hers. "Please, Countess, do not distress yourself so."

Gulping back her sobs, Tatiana raised her tear-stained face. "I do not cry from distress, but from joy. The cuttings have taken hold, Mikhail, as my father said they would."

He looked doubtful and vastly relieved at the same

time. "I did not believe they would," he confessed after a moment. "I was stunned to see the bud."

Tatiana snatched the handkerchief from his fingers and stabbed at her swollen eyes. Not for all the jewels in the tsarina's crown would she admit that she, too, had harbored secret doubts. These past weeks, while the air had warmed and the bushes had put forth the first chartreuse shoots of spring, she'd waited and worried and feared and questioned her father's wisdom.

She questioned it no longer. Two cuttings had taken hold. The rest would, also. The fall would see a harvest of juicy, yellow-striped apples and succulent pears from these special trees. So her father had promised. So it would happen.

They were months yet from bud to harvest, Tatiana knew. And several years must pass before the trees bore final testimony to the hardiness her father had so confidently predicted. For now, though, she had at least the promise of a rich harvest to offer the people of Fort Ross...and the tsar.

Damn and thrice damn Nikolas. He hadn't believed, either.

Resoundingly she blew her nose into Mikhail's handkerchief. "Go seek out Baron Rotchev and bring him here," she begged the clerk. "I must show him these trees most immediately."

He brought not only the baron, but his wife, as well. Helena hurried past her husband and dropped to her knees beside her friend.

"What is this that Mikhail tells us? Have your twigs really sprouted?"

Smiling, Tatiana pointed to the bud.

With her husband peering over her shoulder, Helena bent to examine the greenish swelling near the tip of the cutting. "That is it?"

"That is it."

"It's so...small."

"It will grow, Helena, and merge its core with that under the bark. In the fall, the branches of this tree will groan under the weight of their fruit. By next fall, you shall harvest enough to provide all the settlements in Alaska with fresh apples and pears. When the tsar sees that this land can yield such abundance, he will reconsider abandoning Fort Ross."

Her eyes met those of the baron. "Will you wait until fall, Alexander? Can you?"

"No," he replied gravely, reaching down a hand to help the women rise. "Nikolas has instructed me to approach the British at Fort Vancouver by the end of June."

Helena tossed her head angrily. "A supply ship is due next week. I have already written my so pigheaded uncle of what Tatiana does here. Now he shall learn that her twigs have surprised us all by sprouting. And you, my husband, shall delay your travel until the last possible minute. Even then, I foresee that these negotiations shall prove difficult and time-consuming."

The baron grinned at his imperious wife. "As you command, my princess."

"Go now," she said, her face softening into a smile. "Take Mikhail with you. I would walk with Tatiana in the sun for a while."

Alexander dropped a kiss on his wife's nose, congratulated the countess on her success and strolled off with the clerk. Helena watched him for a moment, then sighed and linked her arm through Tatiana's.

"Men must always follow orders so particularly. One wonders how they pull their britches on each morning without a written order telling them to do so."

Smiling, Tatiana matched her pace to Helena's brisk walk. The two women soon cleared the orchard and followed the line of the cliffs. The coastal breeze tossed their hair and their skirts and brought bright spots of color to Helena's cheeks. To Tatiana's, too, evidently.

"It's good to see life in your face again," the princess commented. "You've been looking so wan and pale of late."

"Have I?" Puffing a bit from the walk, Tatiana shrugged. "Perhaps I was more worried than I wished to show about the cuttings."

"Is that all you worried about?"

"Is that not enough?"

Helena stopped and swung around. Her brown eyes troubled, she searched Tatiana's face. "Do you also worry about whether the American will return to Fort Ross, as he told Alexander he would?"

"Pah! Why should I care whether he will return?"

"Perhaps because he is father to the child you carry."

Tatiana let out a slow gust of breath. "You know?"

"I've borne three children, my friend. I know how a babe saps a woman's strength. It did not take me long to understand why a woman who walked through the mountains must now drag herself out of bed. Why even a short stroll like this would cause her to wheeze and puff like an ancient crone."

"I'm not as familiar with such matters as you, Helena. I only realized myself a few weeks ago."

"This is my fault," the princess said bitterly.

Tatiana stared at her. "Yours?"

"I encouraged you to flirt with the American, and conspired to give you time alone with him."

Despite herself, Tatiana smiled. "I think perhaps this babe is more my fault, and Josiah's, than yours."

"That's not what Alexander will say." Helena heaved a heavy sigh. "So, my friend, what shall you do?"

Wrapping her hands around her middle, Tatiana faced the Pacific. Curls of white foam scudded along its blue surface. Sunlight sparkled like diamonds between the waves. Somewhere across that endless stretch of ocean was Russia, and Tsar Nikolas.

"I shall wait," she said slowly. "For as long as I can, I shall wait."

Her waiting came to an abrupt end some two weeks later.

She had taken the Rotchev children to walk and play on the rock-strewn beach below the fort. The dazzling sunshine had caused them to fidget and balk so much at their lessons that their exasperated mother had threatened to lock them in the root cellar for the rest of the summer. Taking pity on all concerned, Tatiana had swept the three miscreants out of the house and down to the beach.

A stiff breeze whipped their hair and salt spray

stung their cheeks, but none of the four minded. Enough of the day's warmth had collected in the rocks to chase any chill away. Following the children's example, Tatiana had shed her shoes and tucked up her skirts. She was on her knees, digging for shells with a wooden spoon alongside the chattering children when an excited shout sounded above the raucous call of the seagulls.

"Tatiana!"

The countess raised her head. Lifting one hand to push her wildly whipping hair out of her eyes, she squinted through the shimmer of the sun upon the sea. At her side, Irina gave a high-pitched giggle.

"It's Mama. She's getting her feet wet."

Her brother smacked the back of the youngster's head with his wooden spoon. "No, she's not. Mama wouldn't splash through the water like a silly girl."

Her eyes filling with instant tears, Irina stuck her thumb in her mouth.

Tatiana hid a smile at the children's squabbling. Indeed, the Princess Helena seemed to have forgotten her dignities. Holding up her skirts in both hands, she raced toward the four figures huddled together at the far end of the sandy cove. Whatever had sent the princess splashing through the eddies had put a look of excitement on her face. It was visible even at this distance.

"Tatiana!"

Pushing herself to her feet, Tatiana shook out the damp, sandy folds of her high-waisted dress. As yet, her pregnancy had resulted in nothing more than a slight rounding of her belly and a heaviness in her breasts. Still she was grateful that the new fashion for longer, tighter corsets and fitted bodices hadn't yet reached Upper California. She waited with mounting impatience for the princess to skid to a halt.

"Why do you run so, Helena?"

The older woman drew in a great, gulping gasp and grabbed the younger's hands. "A rider approaches. I was just starting to descend the stairs to the cove when the sentry called the news."

Tatiana's fingers clutched Helena's. Hope shot into her heart with the swiftness of an arrow. "Did the sentry say who comes?"

"No. Only that he comes from the south and..."

"The south? But..."

Her hope plummeted. From the first day they'd met, Josiah had insisted that his way went north.

Helena squeezed her fingers. "Tatiana! He rides the gray gelding! The one with the dappled hindquarters that Alexander sold to your American!"

Her momentary doubts disappeared in a burst of joy. Perhaps Josiah followed a more circuitous route back to Fort Ross. Or changed his itinerary. At that moment, Tatiana cared not a whit. Lifting her skirts, she started down the beach.

"I'll leave the children with you," she called over her shoulder to the grinning princess.

She made it to the top of the stairs with much puffing and gasping. Sweat rolled down her temples, and she knew her hair must look like a covey of quail had nested in it. For all of five seconds, she debated whether she should slip across the compound and compose herself.

Josiah had seen her looking worse, she decided. Far worse.

She was standing outside the men's quarters, attempting a conversation with Mikhail, when her eager ears picked up the clop of horses' hooves. The raw-boned gelding trotted through the open gate a moment later. Tatiana's joyful anticipation curled in on itself.

The rider sported worn leather boots, canvas pants and iron gray muttonchop whiskers.

"It's Robert Ridley, Captain Sutter's chief factor," Mikhail exclaimed. He hurried forward, eager for news.

Crushing, pain-filled disappointment kept Tatiana rooted in place. Why did Josiah not come?

Holy Father above, why did he not come?

She learned the answer to her question over dinner, when Ridley casually mentioned the American who had stopped at Sutter's Fort.

"Name of Jones. Friendly sort of fellow, but a bit of a loner, like most of those mountain men."

Slowly Tatiana lowered her fork. So Josiah had gone south after all? How strange, after his insistence that he must travel north.

"He seemed mighty interested in the Captain's operation," Ridley commented as he scooped peas onto his knife. "Asked all sorts of questions. We figured he might be thinking of settling in the Sacramento Valley."

Tatiana's heart skipped a beat. Scarcely daring to breathe, she met Helena's gaze. Excited speculation sparkled in her friend's dark eyes. Before either of them could frame the question that hovered in their minds, Ridley lifted his shoulders in a shrug.

"We were mistaken, though. Jones sold Captain Sutter his horse and took ship for San Francisco. We heard later that he booked passage aboard another ship heading for Mexico."

Tatiana wet suddenly dry lips. "Do you...? Do you say that Josiah Jones left California?"

"Yes, ma'am, or so's we heard." He shrugged again and rolled more peas onto his knife. "A wanderer like that's got the sky in his rifle sights and the wind in his blood. Guess we were foolish to think he'd want to put down roots."

"Yes," Tatiana whispered. "We were."

Chapter Fourteen

Josh gripped the stone balustrade edging the south portico of Chapultepec Palace and stared down at acres of lush green trees. The thick canopy obscured the road that led from the center of Mexico City to this citadel set high on a windswept promontory.

Behind him, a facade of crenellated gray stone rose several stories. Built by the Spanish conquerors atop the ruins of an Aztec emperor's palace, Chapultepec now housed Mexico's military academy, which, at this moment, was preparing to present a review of its cadet troop to the president. Among the guests scheduled to attend was the Honorable Hannibal Kent, United States Ambassador to Mexico.

This review was a calculated show of strength, designed to impress the representatives of the United States with Mexico's military zeal. Rumblings of war over the issue of Texas had grown too loud to ignore. It was time to rattle the sabers.

The shrill of fifes calling the cadets to order carried clearly to Josh. Drums pounded out a rapid beat. Idly he wondered how many times he'd tucked in his chin,

stuck out his chest and marched across the parade
ground at West Point in response to just such a martial
summons.

Moments later, his ear caught the sound of boots
hitting the flagstone balcony in cadence with the
drums. Turning, Josh watched the United States military attaché to Mexico stride across the balcony.

"I passed a note to the ambassador. He'll meet us
right after the parade."

Josh nodded to Major Rutherford Lee. "Thanks,
Ruff. I'm in your debt for arranging this meeting on
such short notice...and for the uniform."

"What are former classmates for, if not to lend their
only spare set of dress blues to scruffy-looking woodsmen who show up at their quarters unexpectedly?"
Lee ran an assessing eye over his property. "The uniform looks good on you, Josh. Damn good. But you
should be wearing major's epaulets, or even colonel's,
not those lieutenant's wings I borrowed for you."

Josh shrugged, which was about all the movement
he could manage in the tight blue jacket. Its stand-up
collar cut into his windpipe, and he didn't dare draw
a full breath for fear of popping the gold buttons and
black braid that frogged its front. The crimson sash
looped around his waist was comfortable enough, but
Ruff's dress sword felt strange every time it banged
against his hip.

"I'm satisfied with my scruffy buckskins," he replied easily.

The major reached inside his jacket and pulled out
two fat cigars. Handing one to Josh, he bit off the end

of the other and spit the plug over the railing. Josh sniffed appreciatively at the rich, rolled tobacco.

"I should have known you'd have a smoke in your pocket. You and your damned cigars almost got us both thrown out of the Point."

Unperturbed, Ruff scraped a match along the balustrade. Cupping the flame in his hand, he held it for Josh before applying it to the tip of his own. Clouds of fragrant smoke soon lifted on the breeze.

This was the first moment of quiet for the two men since Josh's sudden arrival a few hours ago. He'd caught Rutherford just as he was walking out the door to his quarters on his way to the review. The one-time roommates had barely had time to exchange greetings while Josh shucked his buckskins and pulled on Ruff's spare uniform. He'd explained as much of his mission as he could during the brief carriage ride to Chapultepec. Now he could only wait for a few moments along with the man he'd traveled some thousand miles to see.

"I heard about Catherine," Ruff said in his cultured Southern drawl.

His mind on the scheme he intended to present to the ambassador in a few moments, Josh didn't take in his friend's quiet words right away. The major mistook the reason for his silence.

"I'm sorry. I shouldn't have spoken of her," he said with a grimace. "I guess I still haven't quite got over the fact that she chose a clumsy-footed, oversize Kentuckian instead of one of Virginia's finest sons."

He leaned his elbows on the railing and stared at the trees below. Smoke curled from the tip of his cigar as he recalled the long-ago days when he and Josh and half the plebes at the Point had competed for the attention of the same woman.

"God, she was beautiful," Rutherford murmured.

Frowning, Josh blew out a stream of smoke. For the life of him, he couldn't fix Catherine's image in his mind. A hazy picture of golden curls and a red, pouting mouth hovered just out of reach. Each time he thought he had her, the unformed features would take on a firm, pointed chin, a generous mouth, and lustrous violet eyes. And each time he thought of Tatiana, regret ripped through his gut.

He shouldn't have left her without telling her that she'd got into his blood. That he craved the sound of her voice, even when it shrilled at him like a crow. That his hands itched for the feel of her skin.

Damn it, he should have told her how much he wanted her.

Whatever happened with her trees and her fort and her damned tsar, he wanted her. She'd given herself to him twice now. Once in the mountains, and once on Princess Helena's settee. This time, Josh wasn't about to let her take back the gift.

His head lifted as the drummers beat a long, rolling tattoo. Suddenly cannons boomed, one after another, in a continuous, earsplitting salute.

"Sounds like the president's about to arrive," Ruff commented. Taking a final deep pull on his cigar, he tossed it over the railing and tugged at the hem of his uniform jacket. "We'd better take our place among the lesser minions and see what kind of officers the

Republic of Mexico is turning out. We might be sighting down our rifle barrels at them in a year or two.''

Or less, Josh thought grimly as he followed his friend through the marbled halls of the military academy. He hadn't yet told Ruff how strongly the sentiments of the settlers swarming into California ran against the Mexican government. Or how ready men like Johann Sutter were to throw off Mexico's authority.

California was another Texas waiting to happen. If the United States didn't take some action to fill the gap when the settlers rebelled, as Josh was convinced they soon would, some other foreign power would claim the coastal territories.

Now he just had to apprise the United States ambassador to Mexico of that fact.

The moment Hannibal Kent joined the two officers in a small private reception room just off the main hall, Josh knew he'd made the right decision when he caught ship for Mexico. A career politician and dedicated patriot, Kent grasped the implications of the potential Russian pullout immediately. Clasping his hands behind his back, he paced the black and white tiles.

''The Hudson's Bay Company will want the fort, of course, although I doubt they'll pay what the Russians will ask. The thinning otter take in the Pacific waters has hurt their profits, too. The French might balk at the price, as well, especially since the Mexicans claim title to the land, if not the livestock and equipment.''

He halted and leveled a piercing stare at Josh. ''Are

you certain that the Russians won't entertain an offer from the United States?''

''My information is that Tsar Nikolas refuses to deal with a government run by commoners.''

Kent snorted. ''Since he won't even allow our emissary to St. Petersburg into his presence, I'd say that assessment is pretty close to the mark. So what do you recommend, Lieutenant? You must have a plan in mind, or you wouldn't have come so far to deliver this information in person instead of simply sending a message.''

''I do, sir.''

Josh ignored a swift, sharp stab of guilt. He wasn't betraying Tatiana. He wasn't the one who would decide whether the Russians would abandon Fort Ross. He was only looking out for his country's interests if that decision was made.

''The tsar won't deal with the governments of Mexico or the United States, but he might accept an offer from a private citizen. Particularly if that man is a personal friend of Baron Rotchev.''

''Who's this citizen we speak of?''

''Captain Sutter, Johann Sutter.''

Swiftly Josh detailed the Swiss landowner's mercurial relationship with the Mexican authorities, his grandiose plans to expand his empire, and, most importantly, his fervent desire to get his hands on the Russian's impressive arsenal.

''But you say this Swiss is about to take the oath of citizenship in Monterey,'' Kent objected. ''How will it aid the United States if a Mexican citizen obtains possession of Fort Ross?''

"From what I was able to pick up, Sutter has served under several flags and claims allegiance to none. Like the desert fox, he'll take on any colors necessary to survive and prosper...including ours."

"That doesn't particularly impress me," the ambassador commented acidly. "I have little regard for those who choose their nationality to suit their circumstances."

Major Rutherford entered the conversation for the first time. "With all due respect, sir, we don't have to hold him in high regard to make use of him."

Josh shot his friend a grateful glance and picked up his argument. "If we secretly provide Sutter with the funds to purchase the Russian fort..."

Kent's bushy gray eyebrows shot up. "If *we* provide him the funds?"

"Yes, sir," Josh said firmly. "We...or more correctly, you, in the person of the United States government. You'll have to act on your own authority. There isn't time to get the president's approval."

"You aren't making this easy, Lieutenant!"

"No, sir." Tersely Josh summarized the crux of the matter. "If we supply Sutter with the means to purchase Fort Ross, we accomplish two strategic objectives. First, we keep it out of the hands of the British and the French. Second, we make a staunch ally for the United States if...when...war with Mexico comes."

The ambassador turned his back on the two officers and stared out the glazed glass windows. Josh shot a quick look at his former classmate. Ruff shrugged his shoulders.

Gritting his teeth, Josh fought to contain his impatience. He'd had weeks to grapple with this issue. Too many weeks, damn it. Resisting the urge to yank at the choking gold-braided collar of his borrowed uniform, Josh waited for the ambassador to work his way through the problem.

Finally Hannibal Kent faced the two men. His brows formed a thick gray line across his forehead as he met Josh's intent gaze.

"How much?"

An hour later, Josh left the ambassador's presence with the authorization he needed to talk to both Captain Sutter and Baron Rotchev. The next day, he bid farewell to Ruff and started the long ride from Mexico City to the western coast. With luck and fair winds, he'd reach Upper California before the end of June.

He passed the dusty miles with thoughts of Tatiana. Had her cuttings sprouted? he wondered. Did she fill her time tending to them? Did she await his return with the same stomach-clenching impatience he did?

Tatiana lifted her voice to be heard over the tinkling notes of the pianoforte. "May I speak privately with you, Helena?"

The princess threw a quick glance over her shoulder. "But of course." Gathering her skirts, she rose gracefully from the piano bench. "No, no, you keep practicing, Irina. I will speak with the countess, and hear your scales when I return."

The tousle-haired little girl thrust out her bottom lip and hit a series of discordant notes that made both women wince. Shaking her head, Helena looped her arm through Tatiana's and steered her toward the open door.

"This warmth beckons to Irina. She longs to run outside and play. So do I, for that matter. Come, let us walk in your so green orchards and enjoy the sun."

Arm in arm, the two friends strolled through a compound ringing with the sounds of activity. A kerchiefed washerwoman used a wooden paddle to fish wet clothes from a huge cauldron, then slapped and pounded them against a washboard. The fort's armorer hammered on a wooden rifle stock. The barrel maker pulled a strip of heated metal from an open fire and plunged it, sizzling and spitting, into a tub of cold water. Returning the workers' greetings, the women made for the open gates.

As Helena and Tatiana passed through the community of lodges outside the gates, Pomo and Aleut women gave them friendly smiles. A trio of lean, lop-eared dogs raced by in pursuit of a startled jackrabbit. The dogs in turn were chased by a band of noisy children. By the time the two walkers gained the orchard, they both welcomed its dappled shade.

Flapping a hand to shoo away a swarm of buzzing gnats, Helena grimaced ruefully. "The sun is fiercer than I realized. We should have worn hats."

"Susannahs," Tatiana murmured, plucking a leaf from a low-hanging branch.

"What?"

"He called them Susannahs."

The princess slanted her friend a puzzled look. "Who is called Susannah?"

Sighing, Tatiana shredded the leaf between her fingers. "When we walked the mountains, Josiah gave me his hat since I didn't have a bonnet...a Susannah...to shield my face."

"Oh." The older woman's face settled into disgruntled lines. "A pox on the man! I can't believe I was so mistaken in him."

"Nor I, Helena. Nor I."

"To think that he would sail away like that, without a word to you."

"It is not the first time I misjudged a man," Tatiana admitted with only the faintest trace of bitterness. She could blame no one but herself for her folly, after all. "But it shall be the last."

"How so?"

Tossing aside the bits of green, she lifted her chin. "I'm going to marry Mikhail."

"What do you say?"

"I'm going to marry Mikhail."

"But...but..."

"I will hear no buts. I've made up my mind."

"Tatiana! He's only a clerk!"

"He is the second son of an admiral of the Imperial Fleet," she returned. "And what was Alexander when you married him, Princess?"

"All right, all right. I concede the point. What matters more is that Mikhail's but a lovesick boy! He has not the nerve to brush your hand with his lips, let alone untie your chemise and kiss you where a woman aches to be kissed."

"I shall instruct him in the matter."

"No, no, it will not do." Dismayed, Helena took

her by the shoulders. "You need a man, my friend. A man with the strength to match yours."

"They seem to be in short supply."

The princess opened her mouth, then shut it. She had no answer to that one. Softening her rigid stance, Tatiana admitted what had kept her awake these many nights.

"What I need is a father for my babe."

Sympathy poured into Helena's eyes. "Oh, my friend. You would not be the first woman to bear a child outside the bounds—"

"No!" Tatiana wrapped her arms around her middle. "My babe shall not be born a bastard," she said fiercely. "If I have nothing else to give my child, I shall give it a birthright without shame. No, I have decided to marry Mikhail, and so I shall inform him."

Once more, the princess gaped at her. "You've decided? You shall inform him? Tatiana, do you mean to tell me that the poor boy knows nothing of this plan of yours?"

"Not yet. I wanted to tell you first, and to solicit Alexander's assistance in drawing up the marriage contracts. Then I shall tell Mikhail all."

Perhaps not all, Tatiana amended silently. She'd tell him of the babe, and of the bleak future that awaited them in Russia if her father's experiment did not make the tsar relent. She'd also tell him of the wealth he stood to gain if, indeed, some or all of her estates were returned to her.

But she would not, could not, tell him of those shameful, wonderful hours in Josiah's arms.

The anger and hurt that had been building within

Tatiana since Robert Ridley's visit spilled hot and furious through her veins. She turned away from Helena, loath to let even her friend see evidence of her searing pain.

Damn the American! Damn him to a thousand hells! She'd thought...she'd believed...

She blinked back prickly tears. Pah! What did her stupid thoughts matter now? All that mattered was the babe that grew within her each day. She'd felt it move for the first time just yesterday, and the tiny flutter inside her womb had changed all.

No longer would Tatiana wait for someone else to decide her fate. No longer would she place her hope and her foolish, *foolish* heart at risk! She must think not of herself, but of the babe, and plan her future accordingly.

Mikhail was like dough in her hands. He worshiped her. Hung on her every word. Tatiana would see that he didn't stray from her side, as had Aleksei. Nor would he ride off into the mists, she vowed savagely.

Pulling in a deep, steadying breath, she turned back to her friend. "You must see that this is the best course, Helena. My child shall have a father, and Mikhail will gain much if your uncle returns even the least of my lands."

"Tatiana, should you not wait? We'll hear something from my uncle within a few weeks, I'm sure. You know not how he'll react to the news of your return from the dead, or of what you do here."

"That's the reason for my decision! I do not know what the tsar will do! What if he orders my return to Russia? Marriage to another. Someone who refuses to give my child a birthright? No, I dare not wait. Please, my friend, stand by me in this.''

"Of course, I will.'' Resolutely the princess banished all trace of doubt from her eyes. "Come, let us find Alexander and set him to work on the marriage contracts. Then you shall inform Mikhail Pulkin that he is to be your husband, and we shall plan a great feast to celebrate the event, yes?''

At first, Alexander adamantly refused to be party to such a hasty marriage. He yielded to Tatiana's insistence only after much argument and entreaty. His wife's determined face did much to secure his reluctant support. His pen scratched across sheet after sheet of foolscap while Tatiana dictated the conditions which would best protect Mikhail and her child if their union proceeded.

Contracts in hand, she then sought out her intended groom in his dusty office on the first floor of the warehouse. Mikhail could only gawk in stunned astonishment at the woman who marched in, firmly closed the door and offered marriage to him. Tatiana didn't spare him the truth of her desperate circumstances or that she carried another's child.

"Is it...?'' He swallowed convulsively. "Did the American...?''

"It matters not who fathered my babe,'' she replied stonily. "Once we are wed, you shall be my husband and father to my child.''

Stuttering, stammering, his Adam's apple bobbing up and down like a water buoy in a stormy sea, Mikhail accepted the countess's offer.

* * *

Their marriage took place the following week.

Sweating profusely in his black frock coat and tight white neckcloth, Mikhail stood beside his bride before the chapel's tall altar screen. Brightly painted icons of the Holy Virgin and a galaxy of saints filled the niches in the wooden screen. Sunlight glittered on the gold and jewels that decorated the icon shields.

In the Russian way, no musical instruments were allowed within the church. Instead, a burly shepherd with the voice of an angel chanted a single melodic line, while a choir of some ten other men added the approved variations. The scent of light, fragrant sandalwood and precious balm of Gilead drifted on the still, hot air.

Baron Rotchev performed the ceremony, which would have to be sanctioned by a priest at the first opportunity. Given the scarcity of priests at the farthest corners of the Russian Empire, such civil ceremonies had long been recognized as legal and binding on both parties.

Tatiana made her vows in a voice ringing with sincerity. "I swear by all that is holy to cleave unto my husband and honor him most faithfully."

She would! She *would!*

Mikhail wet his lips. "I…I, too."

His boyish face flushed at the ripple of laughter that greeted his squeaky pledge. From behind the glinting screen of his spectacles, his eyes sought Tatiana's.

She smiled encouragement at him. He swallowed, then took her hand in a damp grip.

"In the presence of God and these witnesses, I

swear to cleave unto my wife and treat her with all honor and respect. May God grant us the blessing of many children, and…and soon.''

Tatiana's throat closed.

He was young and most clumsy, but kind beyond words. After his initial stupefaction at her proposal, he'd sworn over and over again that he would cherish her babe as his own. That was all she had asked of him.

Now he was her husband.

Resolutely Tatiana banished forever the image of a crooked grin and broad, buckskin-clad shoulders.

Not five nights later, those same shoulders came crashing through her bedroom door.

Chapter Fifteen

Josh rode up to the gates of Fort Ross in a fever of impatience. Signaling his companions to wait, he reined in his exhausted mount a few yards from the gate and pulled off his hat to allow ease of identification.

"Hey, up there!" he shouted to the sentries in the corner blockhouse. "Open the gate!"

A dim silhouette leaned over the cannon barrel and peered down at the late arrivals. "Who comes?"

"Josiah Jones. I was here a few months ago, during the feast of Saint Somebody."

A deep chortle drifted through the stillness of the night. "Yes, yes. I remember. You are the American with the so big feet who dances the *hayivka.*"

"That's me," Josh confirmed dryly. "I have Captain Sutter and some of his men with me."

"Wait, I shall open the gates."

The small group dismounted, stretching and using their hats to pound the travel dust from their legs. As he waited with the others, Josh felt the anticipation that had been simmering in his veins this past week come to a fast, bubbling boil. He gripped his mount's reins in a tight fist and wondered if he'd gone moon loco.

It was late, past midnight. His small party could have stopped earlier at the farm just south of the Russian River, but he'd pressed them to ride on through the darkness. And now Josh stood before the gates of Fort Ross, in a hot shiver at the thought of the dark-haired, violet-eyed woman just a few yards away.

The massive gates creaked open enough for the four travelers to slip inside, then closed again. Josh's gaze went immediately to the manager's house nestled against the west wall. He'd expected to find the windows dark and shuttered. Still, disappointment ricocheted through him like a misfired minié ball.

Sutter, too, observed the closed shutters on the house he'd visited so many times before. "I see the baron and his family are abed. I don't vish to disturb them. We vill hold our business until morning."

Josh nodded. "I'll rouse Mikhail Pulkin in the men's quarters and have him point us to some empty bunks. Thanks for letting us in," he said to the guard as the travelers started for the stables.

"You are most welcome. But if you seek Mikhail Pulkin, you will not find him in the men's quarters. He and his wife now occupy the former manager's quarters, there, above the storehouse."

Josh swung around. "His wife?"

Obviously the young clerk had been busy since his drunken bacchanal a few months ago.

"*Da,*" the sentry replied amiably. "Who would

have thought it, that the Countess Karanova would wed our own acting chief clerk.''

Josh went still. Completely, rigidly still. Every muscle in his body seemed to take on a layer of ice.

Oblivious to his listener's reaction to his news, the guard scratched his beard. "They were wed four...no, five nights ago."

Josh had no idea how long he might have stood there, as unmoving as a granite outcropping, if the Russian hadn't sent him a knowing, man-to-man grin.

"You are surprised, no? So were we all, until it became clear why they married so quickly." His shoulders lifted in a philosophical shrug. "Ah, well, it is good for a woman who carries a child to have a husband, even this so young clerk."

Josh's frozen immobility melted in a hot rush. A thousand emotions poured through him. Disbelief. Fury. Jealousy. And overriding all, a searing, single-minded possessiveness that ripped away every layer of civilization and exposed the savage male beneath. Flinging his mount's reins at the astonished sentry, he spun on one heel and charged across the compound.

The warehouse door slammed back on its hinges. Josh crossed the unlit vestibule in two swift strides and took the narrow wooden stairs to the upper story three at a time. His fist crashed against the door at the top of the stairs.

The thunderous pounding jerked Tatiana from a sound sleep. She lurched upright in the bed, clutching the feather-filled counterpane to her chest. On the other side of the great bed, her husband fumbled on the bedside table for his spectacles.

More great, hammering blows slammed against the wooden panel.

"Who is there?" Mikhail called in Russian.

"Open the damned door!"

Tatiana's jaw dropped. The bellow carried the fury of an enraged bull. She recognized the one who shouted it instantly.

She sat motionless with shock while Mikhail threw aside the coverlet. His nightshirt flapping about his calves, he hurried toward the door. Tatiana found her voice just in time.

"Wait!"

He jumped at her shrill screech and spun around. Spectacles askew, nightcap tilted to one side of his head, he goggled at her.

"Do not open that door!" she cried frantically. "Do not!"

Her order proved unnecessary. The sound of a resounding thud filled the room. Before her horrified eyes, the wooden latch splintered, the door flew open, and Josiah shouldered his way into the room.

He stopped just inside, his chest heaving and murder in his face. Mikhail took an involuntary step back, his whole body jerking.

Josiah ignored him. His lips curled in a feral smile as he spotted Tatiana in the depths of the huge bed.

"How...how dare you enter uninvited like this?" she sputtered.

He started toward her, his eyes hard and glinting.

"Oh, I dare. I dare a hell of a lot more than just entering uninvited."

Instinctively Tatiana shrank back against the ornately carved headboard. Never had she seen him like this. Never had he looked so dangerous.

"Wh...what do you want?" she stammered, clutching the counterpane higher on her chest.

"You," he snarled.

At his reply, Tatiana's world seemed to tilt crazily and three things happened all at once.

Josiah yanked the coverlet from her grasp.

She shrieked a protest.

And Mikhail launched himself across the room.

With the agility of a mountain cat, the American spun to meet the attack. Effortlessly he caught the clerk by the throat and raised him to his toes.

"Stop!" Tatiana flung herself out of bed and pounded on his shoulders with both fists. "Stop, Josiah! Do not hurt him!"

In response, he gave the choking clerk a furious shake. Without stopping to think, Tatiana ducked under his arm and dove for his knife. Cursing, the American flung his captive halfway across the room and caught her wrist.

"I warned you once about pulling a knife on me, lady. If that blade clears leather, you'll regret it."

For an instant they stood motionless, eyes locked, breath coming hot and fast. Then his gaze dropped to her breasts. Full and ripe under her thin linen nightdress, they gave mute testimony to her body's changes.

"So it's true. You're carrying a child."

It was a flat statement, not a question. She had no idea how he'd learned about the babe, nor did she care.

"Yes, it is true."

"Is it mine?"

Her head went back. For the space of a single heartbeat, Tatiana considered lying. She wanted to throw her months of worry in his face. Tell him that she'd slept with half the garrison, any one of whom could have fathered her babe. Shout that she'd married Mikhail because he, at least, was man enough to stay and sleep beside her.

"It is mine," she spit. "That is all that matters."

A thundering silence descended, broken seconds later by Mikhail's thin, high voice.

"If you don't unhand my wife, I will blow away your head."

Her stomach lurching, Tatiana looked beyond Josiah to her husband. Mikhail stood with both hands wrapped around the butt of the pistol he kept in a felt-lined box on the dresser.

The American didn't turn. Didn't even glance over his shoulder at the clerk. His gold-flecked eyes held only Tatiana's.

"This woman is not your wife," he stated flatly. "She's mine."

Tatiana's jaw went slack. Mikhail goggled at them both.

Josiah's lips curled back in a smile. "I paid the headman of the Hupa tribe the equivalent of six woodpecker scalps and a white deerskin for her. She came with me willingly. By the laws of this land, that makes her mine."

"Count...Countess!" Mikhail stuttered. "Is this true?"

"Yes, yes, it is true. But..."

Still holding her eyes with his, Josh ruthlessly cut off her protest. "You came with me willingly, and you bedded with me willingly. Now you carry my child. I'm claiming you both, here and now."

The pistol wavered in Mikhail's hands. His pale eyes sought Tatiana's.

"Mikhail," she began desperately. "I..."

She fumbled for the words to explain what could not be explained. Her distress stiffened the youth's spine. With a loud click, he pulled the hammer back to full cock.

"Take your hands off my wife."

This time, Josh didn't dare ignore the threat. He turned, keeping his body between the muzzle and Tatiana. His glance flicked from the pistol to Mikhail's white, determined face.

Although it went against every raw urge within him, Josh admitted the painful truth.

"Listen to me, you young fool. The only reason I didn't snap your neck a few moments ago was because you stepped in to care for my woman when I wasn't here to do it myself. For that, I..."

Tatiana gave a sound that rose to somewhere between an outraged screech and a squawk. She yanked her wrist free, her eyes glittering with fury.

"Do not dare to speak thus of me! I am not your woman. I am nothing to you."

"The hell you're not. I told you I'd come back."

"You said you would come back within six weeks! Three months have passed, and more!"

"I told you in my letter that I'd been delayed."

"Letter! I had no letter!"

Josh's anger rose at her revelation. "Damn that puling first secretary!"

"First secretary! Who is this, this first secretary? No, do not tell me! I do not care to know!" Throwing back her head, she unleashed her fury. "Nor do I care why it was that you traveled south, when you told me your way went north? Or why I must learn from a stranger that you sailed away from California? I care only," she ranted, "why did you not drown on your so *stupid* journey?"

The unmistakable hurt beneath her rage pierced Josh's own anger as nothing else could have. He had a lot to answer for, he knew. More than she realized. Right now, though, his need to claim her overrode all else.

"I couldn't drown, Tatiana Grigoria," he replied with a heroic effort at calm. "I had a promise to keep to you."

Her hands went to her hips. "Shall I tell you what you may do with your promises, Josiah Jones? You may skin them, and fry them, and stuff them down your throat. And then you may…"

She spit out a Russian phrase he was glad he didn't understand.

With no other recourse at hand, Josh did what he'd intended to do from the moment he saw the walls of Fort Ross rising in the moonlight. Reaching out, he tumbled her into his arms.

"Hear me out, Tatiana. Please."

She squirmed indignantly and dug her nails into his forearms, but she didn't push away. The realization shot through Josh with the same potent kick as the press of her full breasts against his chest. Aching, he speared a hand through the hair at the back of her head and held her still.

"I carried the feel and the scent of you with me every hour I was away."

"I care not!"

"I've dreamed of you like this."

"I care not, I tell you!"

"Your hair loose. Your mouth ripe. Your body hard against mine."

"Pah! You do not dream of me. You dream of your beautiful Katerina."

"Maybe once I did," he admitted more slowly. "But now I can't seem to bring her to mind."

Her indignant wiggles stilled. Startled, she searched his face. "What do you say?"

"I'm saying that I want you, Tatiana. Only you."

While the low, gruff words sent a thrill darting straight to her belly, Tatiana had finally learned the lesson of her weak heart.

"Animals want," she snapped. "Peasants want. Crude, oafish woodsmen want."

"All right." His jaw worked. "Maybe it's something more than want."

"Oh, so? And what, precisely, is this something?"

He gave a small shake of his head, as though this sentiment he professed to feel for her afforded him little gratification.

"It's like a fire, deep in the gut. A need to touch you. To know you're safe. To hear your voice, even when it's screeching at me like a scalded cat."

The reluctant admission hardly qualified as a passionate, poetic declaration of devotion. Tatiana could only stare up at him, her emotions still raw and lacerated.

"Are you sure of this?"

"I'm sure."

"*Most* sure?"

"Most sure."

"But...? But what are we to do?"

"First, we do this."

His mouth covered hers with the hunger that had been his constant companion since he'd ridden away from Fort Ross.

For a mindless instant, Tatiana gloried in the feel of his mouth and his hands and the muscled thighs bracketing hers. With everything in her, she wanted to fall back onto the bed and...

The bed!

Her marriage bed!

Gasping, she pushed him away. "Holy Father above, I cannot!"

She turned to the young man who stood frozen in place, the pistol still gripped in both hands. He looked stricken, as though a glorious dream had turned to ashes before his eyes. Remorse and shame flooded every corner of Tatiana's being.

"Mikhail, I am sorry. I am so sorry."

He turned agonized eyes to her, then to Josiah. Whatever he read in the American's face caused his shoulders to slump. Carefully he laid the pistol on the massive dresser.

"I, too, Countess."

Thoroughly wretched, Tatiana turned her back on Josiah and her heart. Her bare feet skimmed the wooden floorboards as she crossed to stand before the youth.

"You are my husband, Mikhail Pulkin. I said my vows to you, and I shall honor them. I...I forgot myself for a moment, for which I most abjectly beg your forgiveness. I shall not forget myself again. Ever. I swear it, by all I hold holy."

He didn't speak for several moments, and Tatiana had no words to ease the pain she saw in his face.

"Is that what you wish?" he asked at last, his voice low and raw. "Is that truly what you wish?"

"It's what is right."

Josiah scooped the counterpane off the floor and tossed it over her shoulders.

"It seems to me you're both forgetting those woodpecker scalps. Come on, Countess. We're going to settle this now."

"Now?" Tatiana squeaked. "But I cannot! I have not the shoes, nor the..."

"Now!"

Bundling her up in his arms, he headed for the stairs.

Mikhail followed, his nightshirt flapping around his calves.

They stepped through the front door into the compound to find a full entourage descending on the warehouse.

The anxious sentry led the way, followed by Alexander Rotchev in nightcap and elaborately frogged dressing gown. Princess Helena paced at her husband's heels, her hair hanging in a fat braid over one shoulder and her face fierce. Other residents in various states of undress poured from the fort's buildings.

Josh strode to meet the vanguard, his mortified burden hissing imprecations at him with each step.

"You shall put me down, Josiah. Most immediately!"

"Not likely, sweetheart."

"When this is done, I swear I shall skewer you with that knife of yours."

"When this is done, you'll have your hands too full to wrap them around a knife."

"Pah!"

"Countess Karanova!" His face blank with astonishment, Baron Rotchev hurried forward. "Are you all right?"

"No. Yes. I know not!"

"But what occurs here?"

"Ask this rude and unmannered American."

The baron was no fool. His gaze swung from Tatiana to Josh to Mikhail. In his kind way, he searched for the words to inform the American that he had returned to Fort Ross too late.

Princess Helena had shared too much of her friend's pain to feel the least inclination toward kindness. Stepping forward, she pinned Josh with a cold, imperious stare.

"You will release Mikhail's wife immediately."

"I'm afraid you have it wrong, Princess Helena,"

he replied. "Tatiana is my wife, not Pulkin's. She was bought and paid for in the way of this land. I am reclaiming my property."

A storm of Russian broke out all around him. The princess, the countess, the baron, and half the population of the fort seemed to have an opinion on the matter. Even Johann Sutter joined in.

"So, Lieutenant! I see now why you have the greatest of interest in the future of Fort Ross!"

Rotchev swung around, his face a study in surprise. "Johann! I did not see you. When did you arrive?"

The Swiss strolled forward. "I come with Lieutenant Jones. We have business to discuss, my friend. Important business. But first I think you must settle this matter of the bride."

"Yes," Princess Helena echoed. "We shall settle this matter of the bride. But we shall do so privately, if you please. Come!"

Josh followed in Helena's wake, a thoroughly discomfited Tatiana in his arms. Rotchev, Sutter and Mikhail streamed after them.

His jaw tightened as they approached the manager's house. He had a good idea that the next hour was going to test his mettle far more than any high mountain blizzard.

Josh had underestimated the matter by a considerable degree. Depositing his burden on the settee, he waited while the lanterns were lit and the fire fed. Then he gave an expurgated account of his detached status in the army of the United States, his orders from President Van Buren and his journey to Mexico.

He and Ambassador Kent had agreed that the details of any deal struck with Captain Sutter would remain an absolute secret until ratified by President Van Buren. All Josh could or would confirm was the American interest in purchasing Fort Ross and, if Russia would not deal with the Americans, their support for Sutter's bid.

Stunned, the nightcapped Rotchev turned to the Swiss. "You wish to buy this property?"

"*Ja*, I do!"

"But where will you get the monies? All you own, you have invested in the lands you now hold."

"I vill find what is necessary. Perhaps you vill accept some payment in trade, yes?"

"I can't accept anything without authority from the tsar...and without approaching first the British and French, as I have been instructed. I am to leave next week for Vancouver."

"Before you go we vill talk more, yes?"

"We will talk."

Josh stepped forward. "As will we, sir."

"Yes, yes, we will talk."

Tatiana clutched the counterpane around her with both hands, her throat closing as she grasped the implications of what she had just heard.

For months she'd stubbornly clung to two separate hopes. That the man who now stood before her would return, and that the tsar would relent when proof of her father's successful experiment reached him.

The first hope she'd given up two weeks ago. The second she still refused to abandon. Now the man who only moments ago had said he'd come to claim her had betrayed her hopes and cut her to her core.

"So," she whispered, her throat aching. "You came to Fort Ross not as my escort, but as a spy."

He didn't try to deny it. "I couldn't tell you. I wanted to, many times, but I was under orders."

"Orders," she echoed hollowly. "And when you knelt beside me in the orchard, helping to make the cuts in the trees, were you under orders then?"

"Tatiana..."

"When you lay with me, were you but following orders then?"

"Damn it, what happened between us had nothing to do with any trees or forts or orders. You know that as well as I do."

"I know nothing, it seems." She surged to her feet, her knuckles white where she clutched the coverlet. "No, that is not true. I know that I hate you for this. *Most* passionately."

She tried to sweep past him, but he moved to block her way.

"How you feel at this moment doesn't change facts. I bought you from Cho-gam. You came to me willingly. My seed grows within your belly. You're mine, Tatiana, you and the babe."

Her lips pulled back. Hurt and betrayal darkened her eyes to near black. If she'd had his knife in her hand at that moment, Josh knew she would have gutted him without a second's hesitation.

"I shall be damned to a thousand hells before I acknowledge your so grand and noble claim."

"Is that so?"

"That is so."

"And I'm damned if I'm letting you return to Russia to put yourself at the mercy of a man who stripped you of all you hold dear and forced you to watch your husband's execution. Think about that before you deny my claim. Think who can best protect you and your child. Me, or a clerk dependent on the tsar's whim for his very life."

Chapter Sixteen

A few hours after sunrise, Tatiana entered the chapel for the second time in less than a week to exchange vows of marriage.

This time, no incense filled the air with fragrant clouds. The curly bearded shepherd didn't chant the sacred verses, nor did her groom sweat nervously and tug at his neckcloth.

This groom stood tall and straight in a uniform she'd never seen before. It belonged to a brother officer, he'd informed her tersely when she'd emerged from Helena's room, washed, brushed and dressed in an embroidered muslin day gown hastily retrieved from her quarters.

The dark blue uniform jacket stretched tight across her soon-to-be husband's chest and shoulders. Ropes of gold braid draped the frogged and buttoned front. More braid decorated the collar and epaulets, and a red sash banded his waist. Clean shaven and square jawed, he looked so different from the Josiah Jones she knew that Tatiana's sense of unreality deepened with every passing moment.

Did she really stand beside this stranger in front of solemn, unsmiling witnesses? Was that her voice pledging—yet again!—to hold to a husband and honor their marriage contract? Sweet Mother of God, would she really lie beside him this night in the bed she'd so recently shared with Mikhail?

She closed her eyes, swept by so many tumultuous emotions she knew not which to cling to. The rest of the brief ceremony passed in a haze, as did the wedding breakfast that followed.

For all that the feast had been prepared on such short notice, it left no one feeling hunger. Ale flowed freely. Crusty fish pies, pungent cheeses, platters mounded with sugared pastries and huge baskets of bread weighted the trestle tables. Alexander had even ordered the head cook to open a cask of precious sturgeon bellies and extract their roe from the preserving brine. He'd been saving the delicacy for a special occasion, he informed the assembled throng with a touch of dryness. This was as special as any he could recall.

The residents of Fort Ross took the countess's change of husbands with the stoic acceptance of most Russians to the fate prescribed by God and the tsar, or in this case, the tsar's representative, Baron Rotchev. No one questioned Alexander's ruling that Tatiana's marriage to Mikhail Pulkin was invalid due to the American's prior claim to her person. Now they appeared as willing to celebrate her third set of nuptials as they had her second.

To Tatiana's consternation, more than one woman came up during the noisy breakfast to whisper congratulations on her good fortune. This husband had already proved his virility, one said with a sideways glance at the groom, and looked most able to prove it many times over.

Even Helena eventually thawed. The truth be told, the princess had accepted the wisdom of this marriage long before Tatiana had. She knew well her uncle's heavy hand, and had no more desire to let her friend feel its cruel weight again than did the American.

Any day, Helena expected a reply to the missive she'd sent notifying Nikolas of Tatiana's return from the dead those long months ago. She had no idea what his reaction would be to the startling news, or to Tatiana's heroic efforts to fulfill her father's promise to increase the harvests at the fort. The princess hoped Nikolas would forgive the countess and restore her titles and wealth. She feared greatly that he would not. The American, Helena had concluded, was Tatiana's only hope.

Seated on the groom's right, she studied his profile from beneath her lashes. In his uniform, he looked as rigid and unyielding as any of her uncle's hand-chosen Imperial Guards. And as ruthless. Could they bridge the chasm that now separated them, Tatiana and this so fierce American? Not only the distance caused by their harsh words of yesterday, but that spawned by their different beliefs and cultures? For her friend's sake, she could only hope so.

From her own experience with Alexander, the night to come would aid greatly in bridging that chasm. Assuming, of course, that Tatiana intended to bed with her latest husband. If she did, she wouldn't wish to do so in the same bed she'd shared with Mikhail.

Helena nibbled on a flaky pastry. Nothing in all her years at court had trained her for quite this situation. How did one delicately suggest to a groom where he and his bride should spend their wedding night? Setting aside the roll of sugared dough, she decided to tackle the issue head-on.

"Tatiana will not wish to occupy the quarters above stairs tonight. You are welcome to stay in our home this night, and for as many nights as you desire."

"I appreciate your generosity, Princess Helena, but I must decline."

"Should you not inquire as to the countess's preferences in the matter?"

His jaw jutted above the tight gold collar. "I will provide for my wife."

"Will you?" Helena's jaw set at a similar angle. "Tatiana has suffered much these past months. As long as she is within the walls of Fort Ross, I give you to understand that she will not suffer more."

"Nor will she suffer outside these walls, if I have anything to say in the matter."

The steely promise in his voice did much to ease Helena's ire. This was not a man to turn from danger, nor to run recklessly into it, as did Tatiana's irresponsible first husband.

"And outside the walls is where I intend to take her now," he added in a tight, controlled voice.

Josh had had enough. Of the noisy, curious crowd. Of the overpowering smell of fish eggs slathered on white bread. Of the silent, unsmiling woman at his side. He and Tatiana had to settle matters between them before he left Fort Ross once again to complete his mission in the Oregon Territory.

Rising, he addressed the surprised princess.

"Will you excuse us?"

"I..." She looked beyond him to Tatiana. "Yes, of course."

Executing a small bow, Josh turned to his wife. She glanced up at him, her face a mask of polite civility. That was how she intended to conduct herself in this marriage, she'd informed him when they'd signed the contracts a few hours ago. Politely. Civilly. She asked only the same of him.

Josh figured he had an entirely different definition of civility than she did.

"Gather what you need for a few days," he instructed quietly. "I'll meet you outside in thirty minutes."

She didn't stir. "Where do we go?"

"Someplace where we can talk."

She regarded him for several moments, then nodded. "I shall meet you outside."

With a grunt of relief, Josh shucked Rutherford's dress uniform and pulled on his buckskin leggings. A loose white linen shirt and his familiar flat-crowned hat would be all the clothing he needed during these warm summer days and nights. Slinging his possibles bag over one shoulder and his powder horn over the other, he grabbed his Hawken and went to raid the kitchens.

He was waiting with two heavily laden mounts when his bride appeared. She'd changed her filmy muslin gown for a more serviceable one of blue linen. Without a word, she handed him a small carpetbag. Josh tied it behind his saddle and aided Tatiana into hers.

"Where do we go?" she asked again as he moved to his own mount.

"To a deserted cabin some miles south of here, on the edge of the bluffs. I spotted it when I traveled south."

"Ah, yes. When you went to Sutter's Fort, to plot these so wonderful schemes of yours."

Josh rammed his rifle into its fringed holder. "We'll talk of them later." Swinging into the saddle, he led the way through the gates.

After the tumult of the past night, the short journey should have provided a welcome stretch of calm. With the rainy season well past, the sun shimmered in a clear and cloudless sky. Fields that hadn't fallen under the plow wore a mantle of colorful wildflowers. Their light fragrance carried on the breeze gusting from the cliffs. Some miles south of the fort, the checkerboard pattern of plowed fields and riotous flowers gave way to low, rolling hills covered with native grasses. Cattle and sheep ranged the open lands, tended only by the occasional shepherd and his dog.

Just past noon, the travelers arrived at the north bank of the Russian River. Dismounting, they walked their mounts onto a flat-bottomed ferry operated by a smiling Pomo. It took both the boatman and Josh working hand over fist to pull the raft across the fast-flowing river to the small landing on the opposite bank.

A well-tended farmstead occupied the land on the south side of the river. Rail fences surrounded the wood and adobe structures that served as ranch house, granary, threshing and winnowing floors, and a large barracks for the farm laborers. Always alert for new arrivals, the manager of the ranch and his red-cheeked, aproned wife came out to greet the travelers.

The news that the Countess Karanova had taken yet another husband less than a week after they'd feasted and drunk toasts at her last wedding stunned the Russians. After Tatiana's clipped explanation, they stammered out their best wishes and invited the travelers to share their noon meal. Since the wedding feast still sat heavy in their bellies, both Josh and Tatiana declined everything but cool, refreshing ale and a slice or two of bread.

The news that the countess and her husband intended to spend the next few days in the ramshackle shepherd's hut at the edge of the bluffs astonished their hosts even more. Exchanging a bewildered glance with his wife, Ivan Petrov tried to dissuade Josh.

"It is but a shack," he protested. "Four walls and a roof, with only dirt for a floor. You cannot sleep on the earth."

"I've bedded down on the ground many times before. So has my wife."

The word sounded strange to Josh's ears. To Tatiana's, as well, if the swift look she threw him was any indication. Rising abruptly, she took a hurried leave of their hosts and strode outside.

When the shepherd's hut came into view some time

later, Josh experienced a momentary qualm. Protected by only a stunted cypress tree, the weathered, rough-planked building leaned into the wind at the edge of a bluff. Gulls swooped and dived above it, while the surf washed onto a narrow strip of sand at the base of the cliffs.

"Maybe Petrov had the right of it," he told Tatiana, his brow creased. "This place looked far sturdier in the shadows of dusk, the last time I passed by."

A stiff breeze tugged tendrils of Tatiana's hair free of the braids coiled at either ear and whipped them against her cheek. Putting up a hand to protect herself from their sting, she surveyed the isolated scene.

"It will do."

It would more than do.

The windswept grandeur seeped into Tatiana's soul like a soothing balm. Fort Ross seemed far distant from this lonely meeting of the sea and sky. Russia another world entirely. What better place to sort through the tangled ties that bound her to the man who'd betrayed both?

By unspoken agreement, she and Josiah fell into the routine they'd established during their weeks together on the trek. While he descended to the narrow beach to gather driftwood for a fire, Tatiana unpacked the gear strapped behind the saddles. Tugging the heavy buffalo robe with her, she pushed open the door to the hut and cautiously stepped inside.

A flicker of white on black drew her startled gaze to a pile of debris in one corner. A bushy tail shot straight up, and Tatiana backed out of the hut far faster than she'd walked in. Leaving the small shack to its present occupants, she made camp under a twisted cypress tree some distance away.

She had the horses hobbled, the tin coffee pot unpacked, and the buffalo robe rolled out when Josiah returned with an armload of wood.

"The hut is home to those odorous creatures with the white stripe," she explained.

"Skunks?" He dumped the wood and dug in his bag for his flint. "I'll get a fire started, then smoke them out."

"No, no, it is not necessary."

"I didn't intend for you to sleep in the open."

She tilted her head, her eyes carefully shuttered as they met his. "Where did you intend for me to sleep, Josiah?"

"Beside me on that robe...if you so choose."

"And if I do not so choose?"

He hunkered down to strike a spark with the flint. "I told you our first night together that I don't do the fandango with any woman who doesn't wish me for a partner. That includes my wife."

The painful constriction that had wrapped itself around Tatiana's lungs for the past hours eased a fraction. In her anger and hurt, she'd let herself forget this man's strange code. He had not taken what she'd offered willingly in exchange for his escort through the mountains. He would not take what she did not offer now.

It struck her anew how little she understood him. Why should that surprise her? From the moment they'd met, she thought bitterly, he'd withheld from her what he did not wish her to know. Now she knew nothing except that he had loved a woman named Katerina. That he served in his country's army in some unspecified capacity. That his seed had taken root within her.

And that he had betrayed her.

"Why did you not tell me why you escorted me to Fort Ross?"

"I couldn't."

"Why?"

He bent to blow the spark he'd struck into a glowing ember. A thin spiral of white smoke curled upward. The ember flickered into a tiny flame. Slowly Josiah fed the fire bits of dried grasses and driftwood.

"The president himself issued my orders, which call for strict secrecy."

"These orders were to spy on our settlement?"

"No. If you recall, I didn't decide to come south until you told me that your tsar was thinking of abandoning Fort Ross."

Her hands balled into fists. "Did it not matter to you that my life, my father's life, depended on changing his mind?"

"It came to matter to me. A great deal."

"Ah, yes."

Despite her best efforts, she couldn't keep the scorn from her voice.

"You cared so much. That is why you knelt beside me in the orchard and helped to place my father's cuttings in the tree trunks. That was why you made love with me in Helena's front parlor, then rode off to make these secret deals of yours."

Resting his arm across his knee, he met her accusing

look. "I won't apologize for doing my duty as I saw it, Tatiana. My secret deals won't matter a whit if the tsar changes his mind because of your precious cuttings. If he does not, my country has as much interest in what happens to Fort Ross as any other."

Deep within her heart, Tatiana knew he spoke the truth. In the dark of night, his actions had seemed like the most despicable act of betrayal. In the more reasoning light of day, she understood that Nikolas alone would decide the fate of the Russian settlement. Still she wasn't ready to forgive Josiah.

"The tsar will change his mind! He must! I have nothing to bring to this...this marriage or give to my child if he does not."

The skin stretched taut across her husband's cheeks. "I didn't ask you to bring anything into the marriage. I'll provide for you and our children."

"Oh, so? Perhaps you will tell me how? Or is that also a secret?"

"I have some land in Kentucky. A few hundred acres. My brother and his wife are farming it now."

A few hundred acres? Tatiana bit her lip, thinking of her father's vast domains and the properties that had come to her through her mother. Even Aleksei's lands, considered poor by court standards, had stretched for hundreds of versts.

The size of his holdings aside, Tatiana could not see the man across from her as a farmer. He didn't possess the urge to put land to the till, as had her father, or the desire to watch his efforts bear fruit. He was a wanderer, a man most at home like this, under the open sky.

"Is that what you wish?" she asked stiffly. "To return to this farm in…in…"

"Kentucky." He fed more wood into the now leaping fire. "Not especially. I was thinking of selling the acreage to my brother. With that, and the back pay that's been collecting in my name all these years, we'll have plenty to live on."

"And where shall we live?" She swept the dilapidated structure at the edge of the bluff with a pointed glance. "In a shepherd's hut?"

Incredibly he grinned. "I think we can do a bit better than that."

Tatiana had yet to come to grips with her anger and sense of betrayal. She was still slightly stunned by the sudden dissolution of her marriage to the young clerk and her subsequent joining to this American. She knew not what the future held for either one of them, or for her babe.

Yet, for reasons she would ponder for the rest of her days, his easy grin somehow restored a measure of her balance. Perhaps it was the utter confidence in his gold-shot eyes. Or the promise of a future she had not contemplated to this point…a future that didn't depend on Nikolas, damn him, or her own desperate efforts to save herself.

For a few seductive moments, the urge to lean into this man's strength pulled at her. Could they make a home together, she and Josiah? Could she bring herself to trust him again?

Had she a choice?

"Tell me how we would live," she ordered, less stiffly this time. "And where."

He tossed a piece of driftwood onto the fire and settled himself cross-legged across from her.

"President Van Buren has been after me to come to Washington as his military aide. You'd like Washington, Tatiana." His grin deepened. "And for all their republican sentiments, the folks in Foggy Bottom will fall all over themselves at having an honest-to-goodness countess in their midst...especially one who could put a bad-tempered grizzly in its place with a single haughty look."

"I?" Her chin lifted. "Haughty?"

"Yep, that's the look. It will bring them to their knees." He shook his head. "It puts me in a quake every time."

"Pah! I've yet to see you in this quake, Josiah Jones."

How did he do it? Tatiana wondered. How did he ease her sore spirits with only a smile? How could he grin at her, just so, and make her want to forget these past months of despair?

"Tell me of this Washington," she demanded. "And of your president's court."

"He doesn't have a court. He has a cabinet of advisors."

"How strange. Why would this ruler of yours wish to put his advisors in a closet?"

Josh chuckled, remembering some of the scandals that had rocked the beleaguered president's cabinet.

No doubt Van Buren would love to lock away one or two of his more flamboyant appointees. Patiently he explained the American system of political appointments.

His amusement faded, however, with the telling. It came home to him...really came home to him...that he'd soon plunge back into the tangled political scene Catherine had first introduced him to. He hadn't thought much of Washington's posturing, peacocking politicians then. After all these years of open skies and winds roaring through rocky gorges, he suspected he'd appreciate their narrow view of the world even less.

Still, he'd gone beyond any choice in the matter. He'd acquired a wife who belonged in sophisticated circles, and would soon have a child who'd need a solid roof over its head. It was time, past time, he put his wandering days behind him.

To his considerable surprise, the prospect didn't daunt him quite as much as it would have a few months ago. Watching Tatiana set Washington back on its heels would keep him amused, at the very least, and sharing a house with her would keep him on his toes.

The question yet to be answered was whether Josh would share more than a house. Would she also take him into her bed? Could he wait for her to make that choice?

Despite his avowal that he wouldn't take an unwilling bed partner, Josh had come close to losing all restraint last night. He'd wanted to wring Mikhail's neck. Even more, he'd wanted to tumble Tatiana back onto the bed and stake his claim to her in a savage act of possession. He'd retained just enough of a civilized veneer to stop short of either act, but even now, the thought of his wife sharing a bed with the clerk had the power to twist his gut into tight, painful knots.

He had only himself to blame for that, he thought for the hundredth time. He'd left her in her time of travail, with only the clerk to turn to for comfort. No, he didn't blame her, but he was damned if any man but him was going to share a blanket with Tatiana from this night on.

If he shared a blanket with her, this night or any night.

From the cool, still-distant way his wife regarded him across the small blaze, that issue had yet to be resolved. Schooling himself to patience, Josh kept his voice calm and his talk easy.

After a while, they made a simple meal from the remains of their wedding breakfast. Slowly the sun sank into a sea tinted to liquid silver. The sky swirled with pinks and golds for a while, then darkened to a deep violet that reminded Josh all too forcefully of his wife's eyes. He counted the stars as they appeared, and waited for her to decide their sleeping arrangements.

As darkness wrapped around them and the fire burned low, Tatiana knew she had to answer the unspoken question that hovered between them.

She couldn't do it. Despite the slow lessening of her hurt and anger during these hours beside the fire, she still couldn't bring herself to forgive Josh for his betrayal. She'd thrown her lot in with his for the sake of their child, it was true. And she now looked on the future with something less than bleak despair. But she wasn't ready to abandon the desperate gamble that had brought her across a continent.

Swallowing the knot in her throat, she met his gaze with a steady one of her own.

"I will not join with you, Josiah. Not as a wife joins with a husband. I cannot, until the fate of Fort Ross is decided."

He regarded her thoughtfully. "That could take a while."

"So it could."

"I won't say I'm happy about this."

Tatiana wasn't particularly happy about it, either. In her one brief, and altogether awkward, attempt to be a wife to Mikhail, she'd discovered that neither she nor the young clerk could take any pleasure from each other. He'd been too much in awe of her, and she too determined to bring their union to its natural consummation. The mortified youth had spilled himself before he'd even removed his nightshirt. After that, he couldn't look her in the eyes, much less rise, and Tatiana couldn't bring herself to coax him to a ready state.

It would come, she'd assured the agonized clerk. When the time was right, it would come. And so she'd slept beside him and forced all thoughts of the breathless, dizzying passion Josiah had given her out of her mind.

Perhaps...perhaps that passion would come again.

When the time was right. When the matter of Fort Ross's fate was determined. For now, though, Tatiana had decided they would wait.

Always, always she would regret that decision.

Had she chosen otherwise, she might have found a woman's joy with Josiah once more before the tsar's emissary came riding out of the mists and plunged a sword into him.

Chapter Seventeen

Everything happened so quickly, like a crack of deadly lightning streaking across a dark summer sky.

For two days, Tatiana and her husband had walked and talked and eased the stiffness between them. For two nights, they'd slept across the fire from each other. Suddenly, early on the morning of the third day, the sound of pounding hooves shattered the stillness.

Tatiana was sitting on the tattered buffalo robe, cradling a tin cup of coffee in both hands while she watched Josiah search the beach below for firewood. His tall, broad-shouldered figure had just disappeared in the fingers of mist when she caught a distant rumble. Within seconds, the rumble grew to an ominous thunder.

They came at a full gallop, the riders, and were upon her before she could do more than snatch up the percussion pistol Josiah had left with her and scramble to her feet. She had the pistol at half cock and her mouth open to scream a warning to her husband just as Alexander Rotchev rode out of the mists, accompanied by three men in uniform. Relief coursing through her veins, Tatiana lowered the pistol.

Her relief exploded into instant alarm when she saw the expression on Alexander's face...and the officer who rode beside him!

Colonel Dimitri Garanski, commander of the Imperial Guards!

The blood drained from Tatiana's cheeks. An icy quiver raced down her spine. For a moment, she feared she would faint.

The last time she'd faced the hawk-eyed man in the bearskin shako draped with gold ropes and tassels had been at Aleksei's execution. On the orders of the tsar, Garanski had gripped Tatiana's arms in a cruel, unyielding hold and forced her to watch her husband's horrible death.

As Aleksei's commander, Garanski himself had come under suspicion because of his subordinate's traitorous actions. He'd been cleared of all charges, but the mere fact that his honor had been questioned had added to his furious determination that the Countess Karanova suffer greatly for her husband's perfidy.

Tatiana stumbled back, the horror of that day brought back in full force by the flat, unnerving expression in Garanski's black eyes. Her throat raw with fear, she turned to Alexander.

"What do you do here? You and this man?"

Helena's husband dismounted and passed his reins to one of the grenadiers who'd accompanied their colonel. Coming forward, the baron took the pistol from Tatiana's shaking hand and laid it aside.

"The ship we have long awaited arrived yesterday

on the afternoon tide," he told her gravely. "We rode out at once to find you."

Her hand went to her mouth.

Clearly unhappy with the turn of events, the baron continued. "The tsar sent you a personal message, Tatiana, and Colonel Garanski to deliver it."

The officer stepped forward and clicked his heels. Bowing at the waist to the merest degree required by her rank, he performed the task that had brought him across an ocean.

"Nikolas, Tsar of all Russias, sends his greetings to the Countess Karanova. He wishes her to know he has ordered special prayers said in thanksgiving for her deliverance from the sea."

For a wild moment, Tatiana considered telling Garanski just what she thought of the Tsar of all Russias and his thrice-damned prayers. Had she been able to form the words, she might have done just that.

"The tsar was greatly saddened to hear that so much of your father's work was lost, but he wishes you to know that he admires your valiant attempt to salvage what you could from the sea. Your father's lands and titles shall come to you in honor of his memory, and of your bravery."

Tatiana knew from the expression on Garanski's face that there was more to come. She felt no relief at the long-awaited promise of restitution, only dread at the unnamed price she would pay for it.

The colonel's lips twisted in a travesty of a smile. "It was only out of respect for your father that the tsar agreed to this impossible scheme in the first place. With his death and so much of the shipment lost, he has no desire for you to continue in this futile effort. He orders your immediate return to St. Petersburg, and the sale of Fort Ross to the highest bidder.''

"No!"

The thin smile disappeared instantly. "Yes, Countess. Do not think to defy him, as your husband did. This time, I warn you, he shall show no mercy."

"You don't understand! The cuttings have sprouted. The trees have blossomed. Nikolas must wait for the harvest. He must!"

The colonel didn't deign respond to that piece of foolishness. All present knew that Nikolas *must* do nothing he did not wish to.

"I shall not return to Russia." Despite her best efforts, Tatiana couldn't keep the tremors from her voice. "I have decided to remain in this land, with my husband."

"That is not your choice to make. I have my orders."

"A pox on your orders," she cried. "A pox on all men and their vile orders. I shall not return to Russia, I tell you."

His jaw working, Alexander stepped into the breach. "I have explained to Colonel Garanski that your husband is an American."

The gold tassels on the officer's shako swung as he shook his head. "And I have explained to the baron that the matter of an unsanctioned, unblessed marriage to a foreigner does not concern me. You are a Russian by birth and by blood, Countess. You stand on Russian soil. You must obey the orders of your tsar."

"No, I tell you, I shall not!"

"Yes, you shall." His black eyes glittered. "I'll not allow you to put a knotted rope around my neck, as well as yours."

"No," she spit. "You'll just stand by and watch while it is done. That seems to be a particular fondness of yours, does it not?"

Whipping out a hand, he wrapped his fingers around her upper arm. "We sail on the morning tide."

"Colonel Garanski!" Alexander's sharp protest cut through Tatiana's near panic. "You will release the countess, and do not dare to touch her again. She is my responsibility until this matter is resolved."

"I have my orders," the officer repeated coldly.

The baron drew himself up to his full height, which was several inches shorter than that of the man he confronted. His voice rang with absolute authority.

"I represent the tsar in this land. Release this woman, on the instant, or I shall personally take your head from your shoulders."

The two grenadiers who'd accompanied their officer exchanged frightened glances at this unexpected confrontation. They were too new to this land to fully appreciate the baron's powers here, Tatiana knew, and too fearful of their colonel to disobey his orders. If it came to a contest between Alexander and Garanski, the soldiers would back one of their own.

Fear for Alexander's safety added to her desperation. She would never forgive herself if she brought harm to Helena's husband.

"Please," she begged in an attempt to defuse the volatile situation. "Let me call my husband. Let us talk about—"

His eyes flashing contemptuously, Alexander cut
her off. "You have overstepped your authority, Colonel. Release the countess. At once!"

For several seconds, they stood in a frozen tableau.
The three main participants breathed hard and fast.
The two grenadiers nervously shifted their bayoneted
muskets from their shoulders to their hands.

Suddenly a drawling voice broke the stillness.

"I don't know who you are or what the hell's going
on here, but I'm giving you exactly five seconds to
get your hands off my wife."

The men spun around. Tatiana winced as Garanski's
fingers gouged deep into her arm. She barely heard the
clatter of steel as his sword whipped from its scabbard,
or the rattle of muskets quickly leveled. Her only
thought was for the man who stood a few yards away,
his rifle in his hands.

"Four," Josiah counted laconically.

The colonel's lip curled as he raked the newcomer
from head to toe. "Is this the American you have
taken to your bed, Countess? This peasant?"

"Three."

"Josiah!" Tatiana gasped, tugging at her arm. "Do
not shoot. Do not!"

If he discharged the rifle he held pointed at Garanski's chest, the grenadiers would cut him down
where he stood. Not even Alexander could save him,
should he wish to.

"Two."

It was Tatiana's worst nightmare all over again! She
would see another husband die before her eyes. Only

this one, she would mourn. Holy Father above, this one she would mourn to the end of her days.

She would not watch in silent, agonized horror once again. She *could* not!

"No!" she cried, throwing herself bodily at Garanski. "No!"

"Tatiana! Damn it...!"

With quicksilver reflexes, Josh reversed his hold on the Hawken. He couldn't risk a shot with his wife clawing at the bastard's face like a mountain cat, but he could sure as hell swing a deadly club. In less than the blink of an eye, he brought the stock smashing down on the colonel's head.

Another man would have crumpled instantly. Without the thick, bearskin shako to soften the blow, this one might have toppled, as well. Instead, he staggered back a couple of paces, dragging Tatiana with him. Josh leaped forward and swung the long rifle again. Only this time, he spun in a complete circle.

The grenadier lunging at him from behind took the full force of the swing in his neck. His neck bones snapped like kindling. He dropped to his knees, his bayonet sinking into the earth, while Josh was still spinning.

Garanski threw Tatiana aside and brought his sword up just in time to meet the American's attack. Tempered steel struck sparks off the metal rifle barrel. Both men grunted at the shattering impact. A Russian oath matched an English curse as they leaped apart.

Choking on her fear, Tatiana tried to push herself to her feet. Her knees caught on her skirts and she pitched forward. When she hit the ground, a sharp pain lanced into her belly. To her everlasting shame, she cried out.

She didn't know whether it was that cry or the way she wrapped her arms across her stomach that proved the fatal distraction. Alexander spun in her direction. For the barest fraction of a second, Josiah's head turned.

The colonel's sword flashed.

The second grenadier lunged.

Josiah parried the soldier's thrust with a twist to the right and a brutal fist to the side of the man's head, but he couldn't avoid the colonel's long, deadly blade. The sword buried itself in his shoulder.

As Garanski pulled the length of tempered steel free, his snarling opponent reversed his rifle once again and jammed the barrel into his belly. It exploded in a deafening roar. The colonel flew backward, bloody sword in hand, spilling entrails from the gaping hole in his midsection.

It was the gore that proved Josiah's undoing. He spun to meet the second guardsman's attack. His moccasin-covered foot slipped on the bloody remains and went out from under him.

Tatiana watched in terror as the soldier's bayonet plunged downward at his sprawled victim. Josiah's legs scissored in a vicious kick at the same instant another explosion ripped through the morning.

A look of utter surprise gripped the grenadier's face. His bayonet faltered in midsweep. Slowly, so slowly, he toppled forward.

Josh twisted sideways to avoid the falling body and sprang to his feet. His chest heaving, he spared only a quick glance at the smoking pistol in Rotchev's hand.

"Thanks," he grunted, his eyes on Tatiana.

He reached her side in two swift strides and went down on one knee. He didn't touch her. Didn't try to uncurl her drawn-up body. Didn't ease the tight hold of her arms across her belly.

"Are you all right?"

"I...I think so."

"The babe?"

Swallowing, she loosened her hold on her stomach. "I don't know. There was a most...a most sharp pain when I fell. It's gone now."

She pushed herself up with one hand, her frightened gaze on the blood staining his white shirt at the shoulder and sleeve. "We must tend to you!"

"I've been stuck worse. Let's get you up and see how you fare first."

His face like granite, Josiah slipped his good arm under hers to ease her upright. Tatiana drew in a long, shuddering breath and gained her feet. She stood immobile, her eyes closed, praying to every saint she knew.

Finally she opened her eyes and tried a tentative step. No wrenching pain answered her. No gush of liquid. She bit her lip and tried another step.

"I'm all right," she repeated, more firmly this time. "Now we will see to you."

Some hours later, a solemn party rode into the farmstead alongside the Russian River. Behind them trailed three horses laden with gruesome burdens.

Alexander Rotchev wasn't the kind of man to run from his actions, any more than Josh was. Between them, they'd decided that only the truth would serve.

The farm manager and his wife gaped at the account of the incident at the shepherd's hut. Shocked, they shook their heads over the fact that Colonel Garanski had overstepped his authority and dared to lay hands on the Countess Karanova. No one could wonder that her husband had responded violently to that provocation! Or that the two unfortunate grenadiers were killed in the ensuing melee.

Goodwife Petrova dragged her chest of medicines from under her bed. Clucking in dismay, she unwrapped the bloody, makeshift bandages Tatiana had tied over Josiah's shoulder.

"He is of the most fortunate!" she exclaimed after cleansing and probing the wound. "The blade went in sideways, missing bone and sinew. He shall ache, but not lose the use of his arm."

Swiftly Tatiana translated for the sweating, white-lipped patient.

"We shall stitch him," the farmwife said briskly, "and make for him the sling. Then we shall feed him red meats to replace the blood he has lost and much vodka, yes? To ease the pain."

Josh downed a good portion of both. Over Tatiana's protests, he also insisted on pressing on to the fort.

"It takes worse than this to lay me up," he told her bluntly. "Far worse."

For all his brave words, he couldn't quite hide a grimace as she helped him into a borrowed linen shirt.

"This is madness, Josiah!" his wife exclaimed. "You must rest, and regain your strength."

"I'll rest at Fort Ross."

"Why do you wish to push yourself so?"

"We are only a few hours away. We might as well finish the ride."

"Pah!"

She spun on her heel and headed for the door, clearly disgusted with his stubbornness. Josh followed at a more deliberate pace.

He couldn't rest, any more than he could explain to Tatiana the tension that tore at him like the talons of a fierce, ravaging vulture. He hardly understood it himself. A part he could ascribe to the fire of battle still pumping through his blood. A part to the shaft of fear that went through him when he saw Tatiana curled in a tight ball on the ground.

Most, he knew, stemmed from the gut-wrenching realization that had come to him in the instant she'd turned her white, frightened face up to his. He didn't just *want* his wife. He didn't assert his claim on her because of the babe. He held her in his heart in a way he'd never held Catherine.

Tatiana was like the mountains he'd come to love. Strong. Clean. Dangerous as a late spring blizzard at times, and so beautiful he couldn't recall any features but hers. Couldn't ache for any touch but hers. Couldn't love any woman but her.

And now he might lose her.

For two days, they'd talked and tried to ease their differences at the shepherd's hut. For two nights, they'd slept apart.

Tatiana had said she couldn't be a wife to him while Fort Ross's fate was yet undecided. Now that fate no longer hung in the balance.

The bastard hanging head down over his horse had brought startling news. The tsar had restored a good portion of Tatiana's lands to her. He'd ordered her home and decreed that Fort Ross was to be sold.

Rotchev must leave immediately to consult with the British at Vancouver. Josh had to complete his damned mission.

And Tatiana....

What would she choose to do?

What could he allow her to do?

If she decided to return to her native land, could he let her go? The question haunted Josh all the way back to Fort Ross.

The fort's walls came into view just as the sun dipped toward the sea. Josh's jaw, already tight with the pain in his shoulder, clenched even more when he spied the three-masted schooner riding at anchor in the small half-moon bay.

Given the heat of the season, the baron immediately set men to digging graves in the cemetery outside the fort. The three soldiers were laid to rest at dusk, with proper prayers said for their souls and sufficient quantities of vodka downed by the residents of the stockade to honor their memories.

Night had fallen by the time Princess Helena finally, firmly, shut the door to her parlor and faced the three weary survivors.

"Now one of you will tell me in truth what occurred!" she demanded.

Her husband rubbed a tired palm across his bald crown. "It was just as we said, Helena. Garanski grew overzealous in the execution of his duties. Josiah was forced to come to his wife's aid."

"And your husband was forced to come to mine," Josh added, crossing the room to hold out his good hand. "I didn't thank you properly, Baron. If ever I have a chance to repay the debt, I will."

"I know it." Alexander returned his firm grip. "If not here, perhaps in Russia."

"Perhaps."

The unspoken acknowledgment of Fort Ross's numbered days descended like a pall over the room. Sighing, Helena wrapped an arm around Tatiana's shoulders.

"I'm sorry, my friend. So very sorry. For you. For Alexander. For all of us who tried to make a home in this land. In my letter, I begged Nikolas to give your precious sprouts time to bear fruit. At least..." She gave Tatiana's shoulders a gentle squeeze. "At least he has spared your life and given you back some measure of what was taken from you and your father."

"So he has."

The flat, unemotional response had Helena chewing on her lower lip.

"What will you do now?"

A frown creasing her brow, Tatiana glanced across the room at Josiah. His tanned, weathered face gave her no clue to his thoughts.

"We must talk about that, my husband and I."

"And so you shall," Helena declared. "After you both have bathed and rested and we have tended to this wound which even now drips blood onto my carpet."

"I told him he should not ride," Tatiana said tiredly. "He does not listen."

Helena lifted a brow. "He shall listen to me. Come, you shall sleep here this night, and I shall prepare a draft for this stubborn American."

She swept Tatiana toward the hall that led to the back rooms, then cast a minatory glance over her shoulder.

"You will come with us. Now, if you please."

Josh didn't much care for being ordered about like one of the princess's children, but he was too anxious to get his wife alone to argue. He nodded to the baron.

"If you will excuse me?"

Alexander waved a hand in dismissal. "Go and drink Helena's draft. It's most efficacious, as any of us at Fort Ross can attest." He heaved a long, slow sigh. "I must write my report of today's events, so the captain can take it with him when he sails tomorrow morning."

Chapter Eighteen

Hampered by his injured shoulder, Josh left the copper hip bath tucked behind a lacquered screen for Tatiana's use.

While the servants bustled into the room with bucket after bucket of hot water, Helena instructed her daughters to remove their dolls from the massive sleigh bed, gather their nightdresses, and go curl up in Papa and Mama's bed. The two girls left with their arms loaded and many a sidelong glance at Josh.

"You shall bathe," Helena ordered Tatiana sternly, before turning her eye on Josh. "You, you shall wait while I prepare my draft."

After helping Josh remove his shirt and pouring a pitcher of lukewarm water into a porcelain washbowl painted with delicate pink roses, Tatiana disappeared behind the screen. One-handed, Josh sluiced himself down. He was scraping his palm across his whiskered cheeks, wondering how he'd manage a razor when the Princess Helena reappeared, mug in hand.

"You will swallow this all," she instructed Josiah,

plucking the razor from his grasp. "Most immediately."

He took the sickly sweet-smelling drink. "Are all Russian women so managing, or only those who hitch a title before their names?"

"Most of us like to take matters in hand, regardless of rank," she replied tartly. "You'd best keep that in mind."

Josh's gaze slid to the lacquered screen. "I will."

Helena followed his glance, then flapped an impatient hand. "Drink. Drink. Then I shall go and leave you and Tatiana to your rest."

Steeling himself, Josh tipped the mug to his lips. A combination of chocolate and tincture of opium mixed with alcohol slid down his throat. Even the sweet chocolate couldn't disguise the laudanum's bitter taste.

"I hope this brew works better than it tastes," he sputtered, choking.

"It does," his hostess replied. "Few of my household require a second dosing."

Josh didn't doubt it. He'd claim an instant cure, too, to avoid another treatment.

"You shall sleep well this night," Helena declared. "You and Tatiana."

That remained to be seen, Josh thought grimly as the door closed behind the princess. He surely hadn't slept much the past few nights, with Tatiana so close and so very distant.

Feeling shakier than he'd wanted to let on, he heeled off his moccasins and loosed the ties on his leggings. He tossed the pants atop a humpbacked chest and made for the bed. Gratefully he stretched out on sheets smelling of sunshine and lavender.

Within moments the fire in his shoulder dulled to a steady, throbbing ache. A welcome lethargy crept up his arms and legs. His senses roamed free, then gradually centered on the activity taking place behind the lacquered screen.

He could hear the quiet splashes. Smell the faint tang of violets that scented the bathwater. See the shadows his wife cast on the far wall with each bend and stretch.

When at last she stepped out of the copper hip bath, Josh's fingers curled on the soft linen sheet. The shadows on the wall shifted, softened, sharpened, forming a silhouette of long, curving legs, a gently rounded belly and lush breasts.

The sudden, urgent ache in Josh's loins pushed the ache in his shoulder completely out of his mind. Not even the laudanum could dull his fierce hunger.

Gritting his teeth, he closed his eyes.

Behind the shield of the screen, Tatiana pulled on the nightdress Helena had left for her. The soft sun-washed lawn settled over her like a filmy cloud. Fine lace edged the neck and the cuffs. Her fingers fumbling with the buttons at the neck, she tried to understand her foolish reluctance to leave the bathing alcove.

She was weary in both body and spirit, unutterably so, and Josiah lay sorely injured. They could not consummate their strange marriage this night, even if she wished to. Which she did, she admitted tiredly.

Why, then, did she dread to face him? Why did she

fight the urge to curl up against him and draw upon his strength, as she longed to do? And why, God help her, did she not wish to hear him speak again of the future he had planned for them, in this far-off Washington?

She knew the answer in her heart.

She'd felt it even before she'd seen him unleash his fearsome fury.

He was a wanderer. A man more suited to the wild, untamed land he roamed than to the walls of a city. He professed willingness to trade his beloved mountains for her safety and that of the babe, but would the trade truly bring the safety and security?

For a few terrifying moments this morning, Tatiana had feared that she would watch Josiah die at the hands of the grenadiers. She'd known then that if he died, she would mourn him always, *always,* as she'd never mourned Aleksei.

Now she wondered whether caging a man such as Josiah Jones might not kill him as surely, if more slowly. Much troubled, she stepped from behind the screen.

He lay asleep. The oil lamp on the dresser cast his face in soft light. Tatiana studied his profile from across the room. With his head nested in pillows edged with lace and a fine linen sheet drawn up to his chest, he still managed to appear as rugged as his mountains.

Could she tame him?

Should she?

Step by hesitant step, she approached the bed. Her fingers curled into fists to keep from reaching out, but the urge to touch him was too strong to deny.

As light as it was, the brush of her fingers across his cheek brought him instantly awake. With the speed and the instincts of a wild creature, he whipped up a hand to capture hers.

"I'm sorry," she breathed. "I didn't mean to disturb you."

His sun-bleached brows slashed downward as he fought the laudanum's pull. Slowly his bruising grip relaxed.

"You do that with or without meaning to, Tatiana Grigoria...Jones."

It was the first time she'd heard her named attached to his. The arrangement sounded awkward and strange to Tatiana. To Josiah, too, if the frown still creasing his brow was any measure.

He nodded to the empty space beside him. "Will you join me? I'd like to share a bed with my wife at least once before I leave."

She hesitated. "Still you must go north?"

"Yes."

"When?"

"Within the next few days. I've delayed too long as it is."

"And how long shall you be gone this time?"

"Two months, maybe more, maybe less."

Two months, more or less? Involuntarily Tatiana's hand went to her stomach. The babe she carried barely showed as yet. The only real signs of her pregnancy were her full, tender breasts and rounded belly. In two months, though, she would grow heavy. In two more after that, she would give birth.

He saw the protective gesture. Shaking his head to

throw off the effects of the sleeping draft, he pushed himself up on his good arm. The sheet drifted downward, leaving bare his chest and the bandages wrapped around his shoulder.

"Join me."

This time, it wasn't a request.

Still Tatiana hesitated.

"I won't leave you or the child unprotected, if that's what you fear," he told her bluntly. "Nor will I leave you at Fort Ross. I don't want to take the chance that the bastard you call tsar will send another ship for you."

"Where, then, shall you leave us?"

"I want you to go south, to the presidio at Monterey. You'll remain under the protection of the American vice-consul until I return."

"And then?"

"Then we'll sail for Washington."

She searched his eyes. "Is that what you wish, Josiah? What you truly wish?"

"What I wish," he replied, exasperated, "is for you to get in this bed. You're my wife, Tatiana. However it came about, you're my wife. Your place is beside me."

Inexplicably his disgruntled scowl decided the matter in her mind.

She'd seen this man in so many moods and manners. Slack jawed with astonishment at her unexpected intrusion into the Hupa sweat house. Grim as he pulled her with him through a blinding, iridescent wall of white. White lipped with fury when he burst into the bedroom she'd shared with Mikhail. Exploding with awesome fury when confronted by three heavily armed grenadiers.

Never had she seen him sulky.

Tatiana could not explain, even to herself, why the sight of him thus, wounded and weak and most petulant, should melt her heart. But it did. Holy Father above, it did!

From the moment she had met this man, she'd drawn on his strength. Now, for the first time, he came close to admitting that he needed to draw on hers. It was not, perhaps, a passionate declaration of love. Nor even an acknowledgment that they had differences yet to work out between them. But it soothed her troubled soul.

She needed him. He needed her. Little else mattered.

Smiling, she crossed to the dresser and blew out the oil lamp. Darkness descended, lightened after the first instants by the moon's glow shining through the crack in the curtains. Following the silvery path, she retraced her steps to the bed and crawled in beside her husband.

He gave a grunt of satisfaction and settled her against his good shoulder.

Josh woke the next morning to dazzling sunshine, a head still fuzzy from Helena's damned draft, and a sense of something missing. It took him less than a second to identify the loss.

Tatiana.

He swept the bedroom with a quick, searching glance. His gaze snagged on a splash of filmy white touched with lace. The nightdress lay folded neatly over the top of the screen.

After the long hours of deep, drugged sleep, Josh had regained a measure of his strength, but not the peace of mind that should have come after sharing a bed…finally!…with his wife. The tension that had clawed at him yesterday returned.

Where was she?

Josh suspected this tight, curling unease wouldn't leave him until he saw Tatiana on her way to Monterey and knew she was beyond the reach of this bastard, Nikolas.

He threw off the sheets and sat up, grimacing at the fire in his shoulder. It ached like the devil now, and would for some time, he suspected. He didn't look forward to the weeks of hard travel ahead.

Naked, he crossed the room to his clothes piled atop the humpbacked chest. Setting his jaw against the pain in his shoulder, he pulled on his leggings. The borrowed linen shirt proved more of a challenge. Sweat filmed his forehead by the time he got the blasted thing over his head and his good arm into the sleeve.

Swearing under his breath, he reached for the belt that lay across the chest. His string of colorful oaths broke off when he noticed that his knife was missing. He fingered the fringed sheath, frowning. His tension took another tight turn.

Damn it, where was Tatiana?

Tying on his belt with some difficulty, he shoved his feet into his moccasins and headed for the bedroom door.

Sunshine and silence filled the Rotchev house. The

front parlor was empty, as was the kitchen. Curtains fluttered at open windows. A basket of unwashed vegetables sat on a worn worktable alongside a plate covered with a napkin. A low flame burned beneath a brass samovar in the corner. Josh's senses recorded the scent of spicy meat pastries and well-steeped tea. The aromas set his stomach to rumbling but didn't deflect him from his one consuming concern.

Where was Tatiana?

He yanked open the back door and stepped out into the blinding sunlight. Throwing up his good arm to shield his eyes, he searched the compound. Except for two women kneading wet clothes beside a tub of water and the sentry leaning from a window in the southeast blockhouse, the fort stood empty.

His gut knotting, Josh strode to the women.

"Have you seen the Baron Rotchev?" he asked. "Or the Countess Karanova?"

The women answered in a cheerful jumble of Russian and a slap of wet clothes. Cutting across the compound, Josh put the same question to the bearded sentry.

The guard waved a hand toward the cove. "The ship, it sails."

"What?"

"The ship from Russia. It sails with the tide. They have gone…"

Josh didn't wait to hear more. Spinning on one heel, he raced for the east gate.

He halted just outside, his heart hammering. Below him, the sea sparkled with a thousand points of light. A crowd was gathered in the small cove that edged the sea. Every resident of Fort Ross was present, it appeared, except the washerwomen and the sentry. Josh spotted Helena's blond curls, and Mikhail Pulkin's thin, angular form. But he caught no sight of Tatiana among the crowd.

He started for the stairs leading to the cove. At that moment, the three-masted schooner raised sail. Ropes rattled. Timbers creaked. Barked orders in Russian carried across the cove. Josh gripped the wooden handrail as the sheets caught the wind and bellied. The schooner's prow dipped, rose and dipped again. Slowly, then with gathering speed, the prow cut through the blue waters.

A man's voice called what sounded like a farewell. The ship's captain answered with a wave and a shout.

With the intentness of a people far from home, the watchers on the shore remained silent as the schooner stood out to sea. Equally silent and intent, Josh descended the stairs.

He searched the crowd that streamed toward him a few moments later but couldn't see the face he sought. Nor did he find Rotchev. His jaw so tight it matched the ache in his shoulder, he approached Helena.

"Where is my wife?"

His abrupt tone didn't sit well with the princess. "Do you mean the Countess Karanova?" she snapped.

"I mean my wife."

Giving him a look that sent the others back a pace, she lifted a hand to hold back the hair whipping at her face.

"Do you not know?"

"I wouldn't be asking if I did," he snarled.

She eyed him with acute disfavor for a moment, then enlightenment dawned.

"Do you think she is on the ship?"

Josh didn't reply. He didn't have to. The princess could read the answer in his eyes. Taking pity on him, she shook her head.

"Tatiana will not go back to Russia, even for the lands my uncle has promised to restore to her." Helena's mouth twisted. "She does not trust his promises."

"So where is she?"

"In the orchard. She went there most early this morning. She did not even come to see the ship off, or to say farewell to Alexander, who decided to sail to Vancouver on this—"

She broke off as he spun around and stalked away. She called after him, indignation overlaid with a genuine concern lacing her voice.

"Josiah! Have a care to your shoulder! You must not take the stairs like that. Slow your pace, you fool. At once!"

Josh ignored her imperious command. Ignored the gaping spectators who scrambled out of his way. Ignored pain that lanced through his shoulder with each pounding step.

He found Tatiana halfway up the orchard slope. She was on her knees, wielding his knife with fierce concentration. Dirt streaked her face, and perspiration plastered her yellow dress to her back. Josh's relief and pain spiked at the sight.

"What in thunderation are you doing?" he demanded.

She didn't lift her head or bother to reply until she'd finished carving a shallow *X* in the trunk. Then she sat back on her heels and surveyed her handiwork with a look of intense satisfaction.

"I am marking the trees I shall take cuttings from when the winter comes. I don't intend to abandon my father's work to the British or the French. Nor," she added with a glare at Josh, "to the Americans."

He stared down at her, his heart twisting. The woman kneeling before him looked so fierce and determined, so damned much like the one who'd trekked through the mountains with him, that Josh could hardly force out an answer.

"We can't stay here until winter," he said at last. "Not if we want to beat the storms around the Cape. We'll have to sail south as soon as I return from Oregon Territory and join you in Monterey."

"I do not go to Monterey."

Josh stiffened. "We talked about this last night."

"No, you talked of it."

She held out a hand for him to help her to her feet. Josh pulled her up, eyeing her set expression warily. He'd gone head to head with this woman before, and lost every time. This time, he decided grimly, he'd hold firm.

"I won't leave you here," he stated flatly.

She dusted the dirt from her skirts. "I do not stay here. I go with you."

"What?"

"I have decided that I shall accompany you when you go north."

"You can't."

"Why can I not?"

"I'm traveling hard and fast, Tatiana."

A smile played at the corners of her mouth. "So you said to me once before. As I recall, I had no difficulty in keeping pace with you."

"The circumstances aren't the same and you know it."

The smile moved to her eyes, and something Josh had never thought he'd see again shone in their violet depths.

"So they are not."

"Tatiana..."

"I love you, Josiah Jones. I did not know it when we walked the mountains. Perhaps I did not feel it then. I feel it now, however. *Most* seriously."

Gritting his teeth, Josh resisted the urge to wrap his arm around her waist and pull her against him.

"Listen to me, Tatiana..."

"I did listen to you."

She didn't show Josh's restraint. Taking care to avoid his wounded shoulder, she brought her breast and hips and thighs to his.

"Last night, when you scowled and reminded me that I am your wife, I listened."

"Not closely enough, it appears."

"Most closely! You said my place is by your side, and so it is. As yours is by mine. Together we shall travel to the north, and someday...if not this winter, then the next, or the next after that...we shall return to Fort Ross. I shall take my cuttings and place them in a basket, and you shall carry them for me until we find a place to root them."

"We'll root them in Washington," Josh said stubbornly.

"Pah! I have no use for this so large city with the foggy bottom. *Nor,*" she added emphatically when his jaw squared, "for a husband who does not answer my words of love with similar phrases of his own."

She placed her palms against his cheeks, bringing the scent of lavender and earth to Josh.

"Say them, Josiah. Say the words I know are in your heart. A woman needs to hear them."

He tried to hold firm. Damn it, he had to hold firm.

"Say them."

His breath went out in a slow, resigned gust.

"I love you, Tatiana Grigoria Jones."

She waited, then pursed her lips in a disappointed pout. "That is all?"

"Oh, no. That's not all, but the rest will have to wait until tonight."

"When we are alone, you and me? Under the stars?"

Josh brushed a kiss across her lips. He fully intended to put down the roots she spoke of before their child came. He'd send a message to Van Buren before he left Fort Ross, detailing the arrangement with Sutter and inquiring about that attaché position.

But the tantalizing prospect of a few more months with only the sky for a roof and Tatiana in his arms called to him like the song of the wind.

"When we are alone," he replied with a crooked grin. "Under the stars."

Epilogue

Off the Northern California Coast
October 1847

Tatiana gripped the ship's rail with one hand and pointed with the other. "There, Helena! There it is!"

Her five-year-old daughter hopped from foot to foot in a fever of anticipation. The girl's velvet traveling cloak, dyed a deep violet to match her eyes, flapped in the breeze.

"Where, Mama?"

"There, on the bluff. Do you see the crosses atop the chapel?"

"Oh, yes! I see them!"

Her whole being alive with excitement, Tatiana turned to the three males standing in the lee of the forward cabin.

"Come at once, boys. And you, Josiah. You can see the fort!"

Her youngest, a towheaded imp of three, escaped his father's hand and scampered forward to join his mother. His brother, a soon-to-be-seven-year-old, possessed more of the dignity of the president in whose honor he'd been named. Martin took two running steps, collected himself, then moved at a more deliberate pace to the rail.

Smiling, Josiah joined his family. His strong arms wrapped around Tatiana's waist. Her heart thumping, she leaned back against his chest.

She could not believe they at last returned to Fort Ross! Seven years had passed since they'd left to travel to the Oregon Territory. Seven exciting, tumultuous, most passionate years.

In those years, governments had changed. Wars had been fought. Tatiana had discovered an unexpected liking for the city with the foggy bottom and the witty politicians. Her husband had been promoted several times and taken his ever-growing family to foreign lands exotic enough to satisfy even his wanderlust.

And in those years, the Russians had abandoned their settlement at Fort Ross.

The Russian flag had been lowered for the final time on the first of January, 1842. Alexander Rotchev, his family, and some one hundred colonists had sailed the same day for Sitka, never to return.

Tatiana had not been present to see it, of course, but Helena had sent her the details by letter.

Poor Alexander. Through Helena's missives, Tatiana had learned of the baron's long, frustrating negotiations for the sale of the fort. After many meetings with British and French officials, his every deal had fallen through because the Mexican government claimed title to the land around the settlement. Despite the deed that Alexander produced, signed by the Pomo

Indian headmen, the European governments would not commit to such an expensive venture unless they could obtain full title.

Nikolas, damn him, refused to allow the baron to negotiate with the untitled, uncouth peasants who comprised the elected government of the United States. Gleefully the Mexicans had awaited the Russians' departure, expecting the ripe prize of the fort and all its holdings to fall into their hands.

To the astonishment of all, Captain Johann Sutter had made a formal offer for the fort, which Alexander accepted in the tsar's name. To this day, no one knew how Sutter had come up with the funds for such a purchase.

According to Helena, the Swiss had stripped the fort of all that could be carried or carted or driven on the hoof to New Helvetia before the ink was even dry on the agreement. Sutter's Fort had soon rivaled the strongest of the Spanish presidios…which stood the Swiss in good stead during the recent war. With his wealth and his armaments, Sutter had helped the settlers in California throw off the yoke of Mexican rule.

Now the United States flag flew over the presidio at Monterey. And soon Tatiana would discover the results of her father's work.

Her whole body strained with the effort to see the trees that climbed the slope behind the fort. From this distance, all she could discern was a canopy of green.

"Mama!" Martin exclaimed, forgetting his dignity in his childish disappointment. "You said it was a *most* grand fort. It doesn't look grand from here."

Tatiana shifted her gaze from the orchard to the stockade. Gasping in shock, she gripped Josiah's forearms and stared at the remains of the Russian settlement.

After just seven years, the once sturdy outpost consisted of nothing but hollow shells. The gates were gone. The buildings had been stripped of all removable lumber. What remained of the roofs had tumbled in.

Only the Orthodox crosses remained atop the chapel towers to remind viewers that this was once an outpost of the Russian Empire.

Helena turned wide, adoring eyes on her father. "Was it really grand, Papa?"

"Yes, chicken. It was grand."

Up close, the emptiness and disrepair became even more apparent. Tatiana climbed stairs grown rickety, calling every other step for the children to have a care. Her hand in Josiah's, she walked through a compound overgrown with weeds.

Even the glass was gone from the windows, she saw with dismay. And the great, cast-iron bell that had called the residents to worship. Yet the deserted ruins still carried a ghostly and distinctly Russian air. She shivered, sure that if she listened closely enough, she would hear the lively strains of the *hayivka*.

Josiah caught her shiver. Taking her hand, he tucked it into the crook of his arm.

"Nothing remains the same, Tatiana."

"Yes, yes, I know."

She knew, but she couldn't resist a last, forlorn look over her shoulder as he escorted her through the gaping gate.

Her melancholy vanished the moment the orchards

came into view. She halted abruptly, dragging her husband to a stop with her.

"Holy Father above," she whispered. "Even I would not have believed it."

Lifting her heavy velvet skirts, she plunged under the canopy of boughs.

The children raced ahead of her, darting back and forth among the rows of trees with all the exuberance of healthy youngsters at last released from weeks aboard a narrow, confining ship.

Tatiana let them run. She felt like a child herself. She could have laughed and wept and danced for joy, all at the same time.

"But look, Josiah! But look!" She spun in a circle, hands outflung. "Every tree I marked with the *X* bows almost to the ground with the weight of its fruit. Never have I seen such a harvest!"

She plucked a succulent, yellow-striped apple from a low-hanging branch, polished it on her sleeve and bit into it. She munched delightedly, juices running down her chin.

"Good?" Josh drawled.

Laughing like a girl, she swiped her chin with the back of her hand and offered him the apple.

"Try it for yourself! I swear to you, you'll taste the sweetest, ripest, most succulent fruit ever put upon the earth."

Grinning, he pulled her into his arms. "I already have, my love. I already have."

* * * * *

Author Note

I can still remember the first time I saw Fort Ross. My husband and I were on a leisurely drive from San Francisco to Oregon and Washington, following the spectacular coast. We saw a sign for a historic Russian fort and, of course, had to investigate.

There it sat, just off State Highway 1, shrouded by mists. Al and I spent a wonderful couple of hours exploring the blockhouses and chapel and manager's residence, then walked along the windswept cliffs to an orchard that to this day bears a rich harvest.

Several years later, I started writing historical romances. I knew I had to set one in that haunting spot. We made another trip to the fort, where I did some serious research and fell in love with the place all over again.

You might be interested to know that I've portrayed the historical events as they occurred. The Russians established Fort Ross in 1812 as a base for sea otter hunting and a resupply post for their settlements in Alaska. The otter played out soon after the fort was built, and, sadly, agricultural efforts didn't bring the yield that was hoped for. Tsar Nikolas I ordered the fort sold. Alexander Rotchev and his beauteous Helena, for whom the mountain to the north was named, sailed home on the first of January, 1842. California, along with the pesky Texas, was ceded to the United States in the Treaty of Guadalupe Hidalgo in 1848. It became part of the union in 1850.

To this day, historians scratch their heads over Captain John Sutter's surprising purchase of Fort Ross. No one's quite sure how a man who'd overextended himself in his own enterprises could produce the necessary wherewithal for this extraordinary expansion.

Storyteller that I am, I had to come up with my own explanation. As Tatiana would say, it was *most* fantastical.

KEY TO MY HEART

Unlock the secrets of romance just in time for the most romantic day of the year— Valentine's Day!

Key to My Heart
features three of your favorite authors,

**Kasey Michaels,
Rebecca York
and Muriel Jensen,**

to bring you wonderful tales of romance and Valentine's Day dreams come true.

As an added bonus you can receive Harlequin's special Valentine's Day necklace. FREE with the purchase of every *Key to My Heart* collection.

Available in January, wherever Harlequin books are sold.

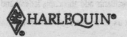 **HARLEQUIN®**

PHKEY349

Harlequin® Historical

"One of the top five historical trilogies
of the nineties." —*Affaire de Coeur*

Bestselling Harlequin Historical author

THERESA MICHAELS

presents the story of the second widow
in her heartwarming series

THE MERRY WIDOWS
Catherine

"Sensitivity, sensuality and a sense of humor are
hallmarks of Theresa Michaels' captivating storytelling."
—*Romantic Times*

Don't miss reading about Catherine in the second book in the
Merry Widows trilogy, coming to you in February 1998.

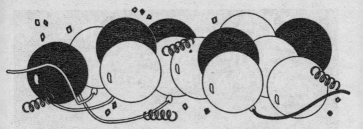

Ring in the New Year with

New Year's Resolution:
FAMILY

**This heartwarming collection of three
contemporary stories rings in the
New Year with babies, families and
the best of holiday romance.**

Add a dash of romance to your holiday celebrations
with this exciting new collection, featuring bestselling
authors **Barbara Bretton**, **Anne McAllister** and
Leandra Logan.

Available in December,
wherever Harlequin books are sold.

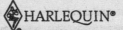 HARLEQUIN®